Never Trust Old Men in Hats

A. K. Richards

1. They've Come to Take Him Away

B enny put on his best smile. At eighty-three, it wasn't quite so charming as it once had been. "Come on, Hannah. Only a couple hours. That's all I'm asking for here."

"Department of Safety guidelines determine how many hours retiree wards are allotted each month." She clutched a bulky Department of Safety (DoS) datapad over a belly that strained against the waist of her slacks. The datapad didn't come close to hiding the woman's paunch and Benny wondered if she realized it. It was a question he'd never ask her. Not if he ever wanted extra hours.

The door of the government-issued microhome to the left of Benny's opened. Four hundred pounds of his best friend, Mastiff Barkey, filled the doorway. As the enormous man lumbered out, the porch protested in a chorus of creaks and pops.

Mastiff knocked his porkpie hat crooked and set it straight. "You can help us both out, Hannah. And I'm sure my friend Benny was going to express my need too."

Benny tugged his beige boonie hat to block the sun rising over the row of microhomes across Bile Street. "I was getting there until you stuck your fat ass in the middle of it. While you're at it, why don't you get a hat that fits? That Dixie cup's two sizes too small. Or be done with it and get a beanie with a propeller like you obviously want. Or a fez, maybe. I bet you'd rock a fez."

"You leave my hat alone and get back to begging."

Benny's scoff froze in the air and dissipated. "I'm not begging. Seeing that we're some of Ms. Hannah's best wards, I'm sure she'll be happy to help us out."

Hannah dipped her chin and raised an eyebrow. "You are not even close to being one of my best wards, Mr. Benny. And Mastiff definitely isn't."

"You hurt me, woman," Mastiff said.

"If it's that important, you two should be more careful with your time. Retiree gaming restrictions are primarily based on health concerns." Hannah pursed her lips at Mastiff. "And some people need to be more concerned about their health scores than their server scores."

"Look who's talking," Mastiff muttered.

The smile melted from Hannah's face. "What was that?"

Benny looked away from Mastiff. That dumbass was going to ruin it for both of them. Some best friend. As Hannah repeated her question to Mastiff in the gentle, beguiling tone that usually preceded officially prescribed punitive action, Benny noticed the assistant administrator approach.

"Hey, Jodie," he called.

Hannah's face tensed before turning to her assistant. Benny mouthed, "Dumbass," to Mastiff, who grinned and pantomimed backhanding Benny. Gripping his cane, Benny mouthed, "Bend over."

The Bile Street retirement ward administrators wore their usual bland, government-mandated suits and slacks. While Hannah's face alternated between polite professionalism and pursed lips, Jodie's smile was one of constant, sardonic disapproval.

"You're late," Hannah said.

"Begging for game time again, Benny?" Jodie asked. She looked unconcerned about her boss's disapproval.

"I'm trying," Benny said. He hiked his thumb at Mastiff and rolled his eyes. "But, you know old Mr. Helpy over here."

"You're late," Hannah said again.

Jodie finally met Hannah's gaze. "The roads are icy."

"I got here for Mr. Jimmy's pickup."

"You're a super-duper employee, Hannah. Someday I want to grow up and be like you." Jodie smiled, revealing crooked, yellow teeth.

Benny looked back at Jimmy Flint's microhome across the street. "Where they taking him? Hospice?"

Hannah stared at Jodie for a second before turning to Benny. "Yes. You didn't think I was here to listen to you yammer on about game time, did you?"

Benny grinned and shrugged. "I know how important it is to you to keep your favorite wards happy, is all. You take fine care of us. Right, Mastiff?"

Mastiff's chins and jowls bounced as he nodded vigorously. Benny thought that might be the most his friend had exercised all month. For all of Hannah's talk about the DoS being concerned about people's health, Benny knew it had more to do with telecom contracts. Jodie had shown him the documents.

A DoS ambulance rolled to a slow stop in front of Jimmy's microhome. Bile Street and the adjacent sidewalks were covered with a sparkling sheen of ice left over from last night's freezing rain and temperatures. Red lines of graffiti ran along the bottom edges of the ambulance. Two medics exited the cab, slapping their hands together as they made their way up the ramp to Jimmy's door. The door opened as they approached and the medics walked inside.

Benny knew they'd come for him someday, maybe one day soon. Few left the DoS retirement program. If someone had the ability to leave, they'd never have come in the first place. Although he could move in with his daughter, Benny didn't want to be a burden. Because that's what old people were, a burden. So his son said.

Clouds of breath gathered above the heads of the watchers as they waited. Benny saw a few more people on their porches now. Bile Street was not a place where things went unnoticed—at least not by the residents. The Department of Safety wasn't always so observant or concerned.

Jimmy's door opened several minutes later. First a medic emerged; then Jimmy, strapped into a wheelchair being pushed by the second medic. Finally came Jimmy's son, who must have been in his seventies. Benny wondered if the son might one day inherit his father's government-provided microhome.

The lead medic braced himself between the railing of the icy ramp and the wall. He grabbed the arm of the wheelchair and used his purchase to keep it from sliding. The medic pushing the chair held the handle with one hand and the railing with the other. Benny grimaced when the lead medic lost his grip and they all slid down the ramp the last two feet. It was a miracle the chair hadn't tipped and the medics hadn't fallen.

"Shouldn't someone have de-iced that ramp, or something?" Mastiff asked. "You know, put salt on it, maybe?"

Hannah lifted her datapad and unlocked the screen. "I put in the work request yesterday and Maintenance said they'd have a crew over an hour ago."

"Maybe he won't die on the way to hospice," Jodie said. She ignored Hannah's level stare.

Benny chuckled and looked back to watch the medics guide the chair over the frosty lawn. Staying off the icy walkway seemed like a good idea, but Benny would have moved the ambulance a little closer too. He shrugged and gripped his cane as Jimmy and the medics approached the sidewalk.

Jimmy's face was wrinkled like old paper sticking out of the thick, red house robe he wore. The man wasn't the oldest on the block, but Benny was surprised it'd taken them this long to come collect him. While Jimmy was well known for vociferously sharing his discomforts, Benny knew they'd been getting worse. He knew because Jimmy had stopped complaining. Jimmy's face had expressed his painful decline in a way mere words couldn't.

As the medics struggled to push the wheelchair while keeping their balance, Jimmy sat obliviously. Even when they nearly dumped the chair over the curb, Jimmy didn't seem to notice. The only signs Benny could see that Jimmy was still alive were the thin curls of breath that rose from his nostrils.

Jimmy's son rushed from the porch, his arms gesticulating as he slid down the ramp and almost fell face-first onto the frozen lawn.

Benny motioned to Jimmy's son with his cane. "That boy's spry for his age."

"Youth is wasted on the young," Mastiff said. "And you sure as hell wasted a lot of it, I'd say."

Benny drew a breath to reply, but cringed as Jimmy's son slipped on the sidewalk and slid into the wheelchair. The medics fought again to keep Jimmy upright. The medics both glared at Jimmy's son after getting their footing.

Benny let out his breath in a long, swirling cloud and eased his grip on his cane. "Oh, God above."

"Jimmy were right all those years," Mastiff said. "His boy gonna be the death of him yet."

The feet of the medic pushing the chair flew out from beneath him and he had to let go of the handle to keep from tipping over. The man's face flashed red and he leaned in close to Jimmy. "Stop fucking with the brake."

Jimmy's son slipped on the ice and teetered for a second before regaining his balance. "Don't you yell at my dad like that!"

"Oh, Jesu," Mastiff said, bringing his palms together and raising them to the sky. "He's gonna break more than a hip."

"There will be no broken bones this morning, Mr. Mastiff," Hannah said. "The DoS has the best medics around. They'll take excellent care of Mr. Jimmy."

Jodie rolled her eyes and swung her fist up and down in a pumping pantomime of masturbation. Mastiff guffawed; the bouncing of his belly brought more creaking from the porch.

Hannah turned to her assistant with a mirthless smile. "Is there something you wanted to add, Ms. Jodie?"

"Of course not, Hannah." She held out a supinated hand to the medics, who were now pushing a catatonic Jimmy down the sidewalk towards the ambulance. "I'm watching DoS excellence at work."

Benny and Mastiff exchanged mischievous grins. Though Hannah did a pretty good job, watching Jodie give the woman a hard time was one of Benny's guilty pleasures. And he suspected everyone on Bile Street enjoyed it too. That Hannah hadn't already fired Jodie for her constant insubordination spoke either to her skills as an assistant or the power of the federal employees union.

Jodie's face was ugly enough to make her age indeterminate, but Benny guessed she was over sixty. The drab clothes she wore didn't fully conceal her shapely body. In his youth Benny would have said she was a "butter face": everything was hot *but her face*. Since he'd now thought of her as a butter face, he couldn't blame his puerile thinking on young Benny alone.

Hannah's reply was interrupted by the drama in the street.

"Stop it!" screamed one of the medics.

"You stop screaming at my dad," Jimmy's son yelled.

"Then tell him to stop setting the brakes on the chair." A sheen of sweat glistened on the medic's forehead despite the chill.

Jimmy's son put his hands on his hips. "He is not."

The second medic thrust both hands towards the wheelchair. "I watched him do it!"

Jimmy didn't respond to the accusation or the cacophony raging around him. But Benny had been neighbors with the older man for over two years and gamed with him on the servers that entire time. Normally something of a blabbermouth, Jimmy only got quiet when he was planning something. It didn't matter if it was the collectible card game *Star Masters* or online.

Benny groaned. The old fool was getting ready to do something stupid. No fool like an old fool, as the saying went. "I think Jimmy's going to lose it."

Mastiff beamed and rubbed his hands together. "Ooh, I smell a wager. You on, Benny?"

"There is no gambling in the retirement wards," Hannah said.

"Man, I don't want to bet on that," Benny said.

"How about you, Jodie?"

Jodie smiled, revealing crooked, yellow teeth. "Fiver that he goes batshit."

Hannah pursed her lips. "There is no gambling in the retirement wards. You shouldn't be encouraging this, Jodie."

Mastiff pointed his finger at Jodie like a pistol. "There's a girl. You on." Mastiff danced a little victory jig that elicited a symphony of creaks from the protesting porch.

Benny looked at Hannah and shrugged. The ongoing struggle in the street moved to the ambulance. The Department of Safety had been failing in many of its mandated services. Although the DoS was the largest employer in what was now only a shadow of the United States Benny remembered, he figured the road crew wouldn't be along to salt the neighborhood streets until tomorrow at the earliest. If the massive department had done its job, the medics wouldn't have slid Jimmy's wheelchair into the side of the ambulance.

Clusters of aged retirees, huddled in robes and blankets, gathered on their porches to watch. Benny saw other Bile Street residents peering from their windows. Every hand held a mobile voip pointed at the scene and recording. Any minute now he was expecting to see old lady Landerson's drones flying overhead. Nothing went unrecorded in 2052 after all. Not even on Bile Street.

The first medic crouched face-to-face with Jimmy. "Sir, please don't make us strap you to a gurney. Ours is very cold and not in the best shape. Don't make us jerk you out of that chair. You gonna behave?"

Jimmy stared on as before. The medics stared back for a long moment, then exchanged glances. The second medic, currently behind the wheelchair, shrugged and motioned up the ramp to the back of the ambulance with a nod of his head. The lead medic walked beside the ramp, while the other pushed the chair up.

Mastiff put his hands to his cheeks. "Oh, Jesu, here it comes. Don't do it, Jimmy!"

The medics stopped halfway up the ramp. "Don't you do it, sir," said the medic next to the ramp.

"He's gonna do it." Jodie tittered and clapped her hands with excitement. Hannah glared at Jodie and shook her head.

Jimmy continued to stare into the distance from under his wool flatcap. The medic behind the wheelchair gave a quick nod and they started up the ramp again.

One inch later, Jimmy's catatonia exploded into a flailing conniption. "Never!" Jimmy screamed. He bucked and rocked and swung at the medics with one hand, and tugged at the restraints with the other.

The medic next to the ramp slipped on the ice as he tried to keep Jimmy from tipping the wheelchair over the far side of the ramp. When the medic lost his grip, Jimmy rocked side to side hard enough that the wheels of his chair bounced on the ramp.

Benny grunted. "I didn't realize how much piss the old guy had left in him."

"Stop it!" screamed Jimmy's son and both medics in unison.

"That's it, you old bastard. You're getting strapped to the gurney." The medic next to the ramp grabbed the wheelchair and jerked it back towards him.

With a triumphant shriek, Jimmy leaned out and grabbed the medic and pulled, adding enough momentum to the rocking wheelchair to topple it. Benny, Mastiff, Hannah, and Jodie gasped collectively as Jimmy's head bounced on the frozen asphalt. The wheelchair and both medics came tumbling after.

"Oh, shit," Benny whispered.

Jimmy's son raced towards the jumble and slipped, landing hard on his backside. "Dad!"

The wheelchair lay on its side, and Jimmy twisted himself up onto his elbows. His mad grin was made ghoulish by the crimson streaming from his nose onto his teeth. Blood also ran from his forehead over his twisted and shattered glasses. Despite his battered and bloody face, Jimmy looked around with glee. "How'd ya like that, bastards!"

When he lifted his fist to shake it at the nearest medic, Jimmy's other hand slipped and his chin slammed onto the street, sending his dentures spinning across the ice. They came to a stop, grinning at Benny.

Hannah glared at Jodie. "I guess you won your fiver. Happy?"

"I only wanted Jimmy to give them a hard time," Jodie said. "I wasn't counting on the medics being such dumbasses. Besides, I only won if Mastiff pays up."

Mastiff put a hand over his heart. "You a cold, cold woman. You know I'm good for it."

Groans and curses came from the retirees up and down the street. A few started shuffling towards the ambulance. One medic used the side of the ambulance to pull himself up on shaky feet. When he saw the approaching people, he waved them off. "Stay off the street. It's slippery."

The other medic extricated himself from the tangle. He grimaced as he clutched his elbow and glared down at Jimmy. "You old sonofa—"

A small, orange drone buzzed down from above and hovered near the medic's face. Red and green safety lights blinked cheerfully from the booms that supported the whirring propellers. A creaky, satisfied voice came from a small speaker next to the drone's camera dome. "I got all that on video. I'm streaming it now."

"Yeah?" the medic asked with a sneer.

"Yeah," the drone operator answered.

The medic snatched the drone out of the air with both hands, almost slipping again. "Then stream this!" He hurled the drone to the street, and it came apart in a shower of tiny plastic pieces and shards of glass. A single propeller spun in crazy figure eights, its shaft bent by the impact. The medic stomped on the camera dome and kicked it under the ambulance.

"We're going to hear about that bit of excellence," Jodie said.

"There's a type of help that's help indeed," sang Benny, "and a type of help that you just don't need."

"Amen, bro," Mastiff said.

Hannah pursed her lips but said nothing.

Benny watched as the medics pulled a gurney from the ambulance and strapped Jimmy to it. They worked hurriedly, jerking the restraints tightly around Jimmy and trying to shoo Jimmy's son away. The medic with the hurt elbow looked as if he wanted to tighten a strap around Jimmy's neck.

Jimmy looked terrible staring blankly into the distance. As the medics began cursory first aid on Jimmy's forehead and nose, Benny hoped the old fool hadn't hurt himself badly. At least he could see the small puff of breath from Jimmy's mouth drifting upwards.

"They camera-shy now," Mastiff said. "Too late though. That shit's up on the SafetyNet."

Jimmy's son stood nearby, crying and offering words of encouragement. If Jimmy heard those words, he showed no sign. The medics finished their work, slid the ramp inside the ambulance, and shoved the gurney in the back with a clatter. One medic crawled up inside the back and the other got behind the driver's wheel. Moments later, the lights flashed and the siren wailed as the ambulance crawled back down Bile Street in the direction from which it had come. The grounded drone crunched beneath one of the ambulance's rear tires.

Benny stared after the retreating ambulance. As he tried to work through everything that had happened, he noticed his hands were trembling. There'd been worse scenes on the force, but that was a lifetime ago. He clutched his cane until his swollen knuckles ached. Why had Jimmy done all that? What was the point? Hell if he knew. But as Benny turned his attention to the bright red blood on the street, he realized now was the best time to ask Hannah for extra hours. She was usually good for a pity play.

As he drew a breath to ask, more drama exploded from another neighbor's house.

2. Blood on Bile Street

Mack's microhome was next to Benny's on the opposite side from Mastiff's. Everyone gathered around Benny's porch turned as Mack's door opened. It wasn't Mack that came out, but his son Ricky.

Ricky looked suspiciously at the small crowd staring at him. Then he noticed the other people in the neighborhood, who were now all staring his way. "What's going on, Benny?"

"The medics just took Jimmy Flint," Benny said, grimacing. "It didn't go well." He pointed to the bloody street with his cane.

"Geez. Did my dad train those guys?"

"Looked like it to me," Mastiff said.

"Shut the damned door," Mack yelled from inside.

Ricky looked reluctant as he let the door close. "My dad's bedside manner is ... lacking. I shudder to think of the Big Mackas a medic."

Mastiff laughed. "Own it all the way, boy. Your dad is an asshole."

"No argument there." Ricky frowned back at the door and pulled it open again. "Hurry up, Krysta. And don't mess up Pappi's bathroom washing your hands. Because you always wash your hands, right?"

Hannah cut her eyes at Mastiff. "That is not the kind of language someone deserving extra play time should be using, Mr. Mastiff."

Benny cut his eyes at Mastiff, too, jabbing his cane at his rotund neighbor.

Mastiff waved one hand dismissively at Benny. "It might be best then. Benny a glitch king anyway. No fun playing with Cracker the Hacker."

"You think anyone who can install their own downloads is a hacker," Benny said. "You suck worse than the kids out there."

"That's what cheaters always say. You ain't as bad as ol' Mack though. He cheat like a sailor in port!"

Benny grinned. "He might cheat a little."

"Dad always cheats," Ricky said. "Even when he's not hacking or side coding, he's still being a cheese-dick."

"An exploit-abusing, camping, glitch bitch, cheese-dick," Jodie said. When Hannah pursed her lips, Jodie shrugged. "What? It's true. It's also true that Mastiff sucks."

"Krysta!" Ricky called. "Will you hurry, honey?"

Hannah turned from Jodie and smiled at Ricky. "It's nice you bring your granddaughter to visit Mack."

"Her mom needed a break. I'm taking Krysta to an appointment this morning, so I thought I'd swing by for a bit. We wouldn't normally come by this early, especially with the roads the way they are."

The door behind Ricky swung open and hit him. Five-year-old Krysta ran through the door, crying hysterically. Tears and snot streamed down her face as she ran by, clutching her backside with both hands. She ran past when Ricky reached down for her and headed to his car parked on the street. Benny flinched, expecting her to slip, but was relieved when she hopped into the back seat and buckled up safely. Krysta sat with her arms crossed, glowering through the window.

Ricky's brow furrowed. "What's wrong, Krysta?"

"She was playing in the bathroom and wouldn't come out," Mack said as he shuffled through the door and closed it behind him. A ragged, red ball cap with a faded bulldog logo sat far back on his head. Mack's back was hunched to the point that he had to look up to see what was in front of him. The cap's bill blocked his vision if it sat too far forward. It wasn't the only reason Benny pitied the old bastard.

"I was not!" Krysta screamed from the car.

"Don't sass Pappi," Mack said, slapping his hands together. "Or you'll get another."

Ricky sighed. "Dad, I've asked you not to spank her."

"The Department of Safety does not allow the use of corporal punishment on its facilities," Hannah said.

Mack waved his hand at her. "This whole damn place is corporal punishment. Besides, she might have found my booze and I'm sure drunk kids are against the rules too." He exaggerated his already thick Jersey accent as he spoke.

"The Department of Safety doesn't—" Hannah began.

"Yeah, yeah. I know. The DoS doesn't allow much of anything. I'm just fuckin' with you, sister."

Hannah's eyes grew wide and her pursed lips puckered.

"Geez, Dad." Ricky shook his head and offered Hannah an apologetic shrug.

"Oh, for Christ's fuckin' sake," Mack said. "I mean sister, like girl. That goes all the way back to the Bible and shit. You know, hear me brothers and sisters, and all that. Ever read it? Black chicks didn't come up with sister." Mack looked again at the stony faces and shook his head. "What-the-fuck-ever."

Ricky shook his head and stepped face-to-face with Mack. Mack craned his neck to see around his son, but Ricky gently placed his hands on Mack's cheeks, forcing him to look.

"Dad, I need you to listen, please. I don't like it when you spank Krysta. Please don't do it again."

"I spanked you and you turned out great."

Ricky pulled his head back. "Great? Since when have you thought I was great?"

Mack squeezed Ricky's shoulder. "Always. You know that, come on."

"I mean it, Dad. Don't spank her again. I don't want her to have to go through what I went through."

Mack looked away for a moment before sighing. "Fine."

"I won't bring her around anymore."

"Jesus on a giraffe," Mack muttered. "All right already. But she's going to grow up to be a shit."

Ricky's hands slipped from his father's cheeks and he stepped back. "No, she won't."

"What-the-fuck-ever." Mack looked up and down the street and turned to Benny. "What're all the gawkers looking at?"

"Now, they're looking at a grumpy old butthole," Benny said. "But they were watching Jimmy getting taken away."

"Jimmy?" Mack turned to Hannah. "That was today, huh?"

"Yes, Mr. Francisco," Hannah answered curtly. "That was today."

"Please, it's Mack. You know that."

Hannah raised one brow and stared back.

Mack looked to Jodie. "Did he freak out?"

Jodie laughed. "Oh, yeah. And I won five bucks. Maybe."

"I told you I was good for it, woman," Mastiff said.

Benny rolled his cane from hand to hand. The cold was making his hip ache and he groaned. "It wasn't pretty. You can still see the blood in the street. Well, you probably can't."

"Damn," Mack said. "I knew he would show those assholes." He saw Krysta glaring at him. When the girl saw him looking, she turned away. Mack muttered something and looked at his feet.

A sudden silence fell over the group and Benny could hear the creaking of the door to the microhome on the other side of Mack's.

Terrence was a tall, handsome man, and he stretched his arms as if to embrace the cold sunlight and the whole world beneath it. His biceps and pectoral muscles bulged and danced. A wide-brimmed straw hat sat above his twinkling eyes. Though he was close to Benny's age, Terrence looked to be in his forties.

"Good morning, all," he said.

Hannah offered a coquettish smile, while Jodie smirked and eyed him up and down. "Good morning, Terrence," they said in unison.

Benny shook his head. He accepted the jealousy he felt as what it was. That Terrence, called Trance by his friends, maintained his physique through dedicated efforts was also not lost on Benny. But part of Benny, who could barely walk without his cane, screamed at the unfairness of it. He'd do almost anything to have Trance's body instead of his own. He'd probably even kill Mack.

"Morning," Benny said.

"Good to see you finally awake, Trance," Mack said. "Up too late meditating again? I'd have thought you'd be up already sipping at the morning dew."

"I was hoping to miss out on the tragedy of them taking Jimmy," Trance said. He peered at the street where the ambulance had been and grimaced. "I cautioned him about doing anything harmful, even to himself. But everyone was posting the video to the Bile Street group, so I saw it anyway. It's a shame he didn't listen."

"Well," Jodie chimed in, "to be fair, he did cause them a fair amount of trouble."

"Fuckin' A." Mack laughed. "I missed it. I'll have to go watch. I was thinking he might check in to the Hotel Catatonia and stay there. Good for him."

"It is a shame, Mr. Terrence," Hannah said. "But they'll get him taken care of. No worries."

"You know they dumping him off to the death house, right?" Mastiff asked.

"Sector hospice house, Mr. Mastiff," Hannah said.

"You can call it the International fucking House of Pancakes," Mack said, "it's still a death house. Or at least a death sentence." He spread his arms wide to encompass the neighborhood. "But at least we don't have to pay for our fine treatment. The DoS will kindly pay for it with the money they stole from us our whole lives."

Jodie shot a fist in the air. "Preach on."

Mack gave Jodie a conspicuous wink and slapped his hands together. "You know it."

Ricky sighed. "Dad, can you watch your mouth please? Krysta's right over there."

"It's a medical facility, Mr. Francisco," Hannah said.

"Please, lady. Call me Mack. Or at least Frank. Francisco sounds so faggoty." Mack shook his head. "I always hated that name."

Hannah made a noise that reminded Benny of the clucking of an angry hen. "Mr. Francisco!"

Jodie made jazz-hands to the sky in mock outrage.

Ricky sighed. "Dad..."

"What?"

Ricky stared at his dad with wide-eyed expectation. When he got no reply, Ricky motioned to himself with his hands.

"I know you're a fruit. Good thing you found that out after having kids or I'd never have had the pleasure of being a grandpa." Mack glanced at Hannah, then Benny. "What does that have to do with my name being all faggy?"

"Do you really not get it, Dad?" Ricky asked.

"What I get is that I can't control what people choose to get offended by, son. What if a bunch of folks decided red ball caps offended them? Do I need to throw mine away to protect them? Oh, shit. I know some people call it pop instead of soda. Better watch what I say before the DoS diversity squad kicks in my door and protects me to death. Holy fucking hopped-up Christ."

Ricky stared at his decidedly unrepentant father for a long moment before shaking his head. He lifted the red hat and kissed his father's bald scalp. "I love you, Dad, but I've got to get Krysta to her appointment."

Mack embraced Ricky. "I love you too, boy. And Krysta." Mack leaned around his son and shouted to the car. "I love you, Krysta."

Krysta stuck her lip out farther somehow and looked away again. Ricky fished the driver fob from his pocket and was turning to go when Mack reached out and grabbed his shoulder.

"You know I don't hate you for being a fag, right?" Mack looked up into his son's face. "What?"

Ricky gave a resigned chuckle. "Yeah, I know, Dad. I'll see you."

The gathered onlookers started dispersing as Ricky walked to his car and verified Krysta was buckled properly. The girl sobbed and glared out the window when the door shut. She seemed to be staring at everyone near her pappi, and when she mouthed the words "I hate you" as the car pulled away, Benny thought she might have been talking to all of them too.

The silence that descended over Bile Street was short-lived as the whine of a drone's propellers filled the air. It stopped and hovered a foot over the smashed remains in the street, like a parent staring down at an injured child. A stream of curses issued from the drone's speaker, but Benny couldn't make them out over the hum of the propellers.

The drone, a match for the wreck below it, rose a foot and spun around. The camera swept past Benny and then turned back, focusing on Hannah. It shot forward. Hannah screamed and hid behind Jodie.

"You keep that away from me, Ms. Landerson," Hannah shrieked.

Jodie looked over her shoulder and rolled her eyes at Hannah. "Didn't you see how easy it is to smash one of those things on the ground?" Jodie yelled at the top of her lungs. She turned back to the drone and slowly reached for it with both hands.

The drone tilted away from Jodie and stopped short. "Don't you dare!" squawked Ms. Landerson's voice through the tinny speaker.

"What are you going to do about my other drone, Hannah? Huh? I've got it on film what those assholes did. They smashed it on purpose."

"Your drone was interfering with a DoS medical response," Hannah said.

"More like a medical assault!" Ms. Landerson said. "They smashed it to try to destroy the video of what they did to poor Jimmy. You owe me a new drone and I want to know when you're going to take care of that."

"File a loss report on the DoS SafetyNet page—" Hannah started.

"Not good enough!" the drone's voice screeched. "Not good enough. You file it or you pay for it."

"You know that's not how it works," Jodie said. "We can't. You're the injured party. You or an assigned representative—"

"I'm assigning you as my representative," Ms. Landerson said. The drone swayed back and forth in the air.

Hannah stepped out from behind Jodie and pointed her datapad at the drone. "We work for the department and can't represent you. I can put you in touch with the ward's Advocate Department."

"Bullshit. I knew it. More lies, more excuses." The drone leaned forward and Hannah jumped back behind Jodie.

"Look," Jodie said flatly, "we're not allowed. The SafetyNet pages won't even let us access those forms."

"Lies!" The drone dipped closer.

While Hannah shrieked and ran towards Trance, Jodie lunged forward and snatched the drone out of the air. She shook it and shoved her face into the camera.

"Let go," cried Ms. Landerson. "Hands off, you old slut!"

"You need to fill out the forms," Jodie said, her voice calm. "Your choice now is whether you want to file for one drone that's smashed to bits, or two."

The drone wobbled in Jodie's grip and the whine of the small propellers changed pitch as it tried to escape. "I see you've decided to go for a twofer." Jodie raised the drone over her head.

"Wait-wait-wait!" the drone cried. "Fine. Let it go."

Jodie smiled and shoved the drone into the air. "I knew you'd see reason."

The drone hovered above the street, pointing its camera at them. Benny could imagine old lady Landerson flipping her gnarled middle fingers at her screen. A second later the drone rose, tilted, and disappeared over the rooftops.

"You a cold, cold woman," Mastiff said.

Jodie laughed and turned to see Hannah hiding behind Trance. "Hey, you gotta share."

Hannah straightened and stepped away from Trance. "What on earth are you talking about, Ms. Jodie?"

"Duh, gee. I don't know, boss," Jodie said in a low-pitched drawl.

Hannah huffed and strode back to where she'd been standing before the drone drama. Jodie offered a lurid wink to Trance, who smiled and nodded.

Trance stepped gingerly to the center of his tiny, immaculate lawn and descended into a graceful, cross-legged sitting pose.

"Careful," Benny said with a grin. "He's starting his yogi voodoo. He'll grab you by the chakra if you get too close."

Jodie thrust out a hip. "Oh, do tell."

Hannah spun and stomped her foot. "That is enough, Ms. Jodie!"

Jodie leaned in and motioned to Trance with her brows. "But look at that."

Benny thought Hannah might hold out, but after a long moment of glaring at Jodie she turned. Trance was moving his hands in large, slow circles that caused his muscles to ripple. With his eyes still closed and keeping his butt on the ground, he spread his legs into side splits. A moment later, he brought his hands into a prayer position in front of him.

"How do he do that?" Mastiff asked, shaking his head. They watched Trance stretch and contort for a while. Jodie sighed.

"Real amazing," Mack said. "I bet his balls are freezing. Of course, it probably helps not to be four hundred pounds overweight, right, buddy?"

"It probably helps not to be a Notre Dame bell-tower-living Quasimodo motherfucker too," snapped Mastiff.

"You try driving a long-hauler for thirty-plus years. It's hell on the spine."

"Anyone can learn yoga," Trance said in a distant, placid voice. "It's a salve for all manner of ailments of the mind and body."

"My body has an ailment—" Jodie started.

"Enough of that inappropriate talk, Jodie," Hannah said. "Mr. Trance probably doesn't appreciate it."

"Well," Trance said, "I never said that."

Jodie smirked at Hannah.

Hannah narrowed her eyes and glanced sidelong at Trance. "Irregardless, that kind of harassment won't be tolerated on Bile Street."

"All the other kinds of harassment are A-OK though," Mack said. "Irregardless ain't a word, by the way."

Benny sensed his chance slipping away. "It's been a hell of a morning with everything that happened. Would you approve a little extra game time, Ms. Hannah?"

"He's a twinker," Mack said. "You should ban him instead."

Benny glared at Mack and shook his cane. Then he put on his most sincere hangdog face for Hannah. It wasn't too much of a show either; he wanted that extra game time.

Hannah looked at the puddle of Jimmy's blood in the street, then at each of the men. Benny noticed that even Trance stopped moving and had cocked his ear to listen.

She let out a long sigh that gathered in a frosty cloud around her face. "Yes, Mr. Benny. That'll be fine. I'll authorize it when I get back to the office. But don't expect it to be a regular occurrence."

Benny forced himself not to smile and gave a solemn nod. It was what Hannah usually said.

3. The Travails of Friendship

It was after 2am when Benny surrendered to his insomnia. He pushed his blanket aside and struggled to sit up, causing his hip and back to protest with the snapping, crackling, and popping of use, age, and injury. The darkness made his body's complaints sound even louder.

When Benny tried to stretch, every other part of his body joined the joint-cracking chorus. It seemed no part of him was having any of that stretching. Benny cursed Trance for the man's commitment to health and body, before reaching for his cane.

The cane always felt good in his hand, even when his hand was stiff with arthritis. It was a gift from his daughter Dakota and was made of a sturdy, laminated hickory. A pattern of light- and dark-wood staining twisted down the shaft. The handle was worn smooth from years of use and worrying. It fit his hand perfectly, but Benny didn't know if this had shaped the handle to perfection, or if his hand had taken the shape of the handle.

Benny rocked forward until he was almost folded over the cane's handle, and pushed. A soft groan escaped his lips as fiery pain shot up from his hip. There were no juicy bratwursts or hot dogs in the Department of Safety fridge. Nor was there anything else his spotty memory could recall that would make his arduous shuffle into the kitchen worthwhile. He'd known that before starting, but he didn't really have much else to do. Checking the fridge was a habit, nothing more. He knew that, but he didn't feel like hopping on the servers either.

The DoS delivered his meals three times a day. Nothing in there would be a surprise. He opened the door and the tiny light illuminated the leftovers he knew were already waiting for him. At least the meals were coming on time again, even if the delivery people couldn't always be bothered to put the food in the fridge if no one was home. It was too bad the DoS had let the auto-drone maintenance contract expire. Those little robots never missed a trick. And they never reminded Benny how old he was.

Benny shut the fridge. One of the advantages of the retirement ward microhomes, which looked bigger in the pamphlets, was that no section was too far from any other section. It was a short, but wasted trip.

The display screen looked impressive only until the minuscule size of the wall on which it hung became apparent. It was like most DoS benefits: presented in a way that made it look far grander than it really was. Benny didn't care. Even before the SafetyNet was instituted to protect the citizens from offensive, subversive, or otherwise triggering media, he'd hated what his father had called the boob-tube. His father would roll over in his grave at what was on the screen these days—especially boobs.

And Benny still hated the sewage spewed by DoS programming. He wasn't desperate enough to watch it even to help him go to sleep. He'd once asked Hannah why the screens were there when everyone had voips or VR goggles.

"Habit," she'd said. "Some people of your generation can't sleep without a TV on in the background."

Benny knew it was true. His mother had been the same way. Benny could remember when KVTV still played the national anthem after the last broadcast, the screen with colored bars, and then finally the static would wake his father, usually with a blanket of blue cussing. He missed his mom and dad, even now. Benny figured he'd miss them until the day he joined them.

It wasn't missing his parents or the TV keeping him awake. Though he'd played on Hannah's sympathy, it had actually been a hell of a morning. He saw his chipped teacup on the counter and considered brewing some tea, but he knew his stomach wasn't up for anything.

Blue light from Mastiff's window flickered on the rim of Benny's glasses. Mastiff loved to watch the video feeds, no matter how asinine. Not the professional SafetyNet propaganda twaddle, he watched the amateur stuff, which Benny had to admit was usually better than the vapid VR whores on the government stations. Even though each digital personality was manipulated to appear and speak in ways pleasing to Benny based on eight decades of viewing data, they creeped him out.

Benny pushed the button to open the window. Chill air rushed in and caused him to gasp. It was almost too invigorating on his weathered, papery skin. He reached out and tapped on Mastiff's window with his cane.

After a moment, a shadow grew to fill the entirety of the window, obscuring the blue glow from within. The blinds folded upwards and the window followed to reveal Mastiff's obsidian face. Sparkles of the blue lighting danced in his sweaty pores.

"Morning, Benny." Mastiff's bright smile shone in the darkness. "Hip hurting?"

"Some. But I don't think that's what's keeping me awake."

"Jimmy?"

Benny nodded. "Yeah. Every time I close my damned eyes, I see his bloody face." He looked towards the street where it had all happened, wondering if the stray Jimmy took care of had come and licked up the blood. "That grinning, bloody face. I mean, I half-expected he'd do something crazy. He always said he would, but shit."

"Lord Jesu, yes," Mastiff said, his gaze on the street too. "That was one crazy old white dude."

"And that's part of what I think's bugging me. Do you think he really was?"

Mastiff cocked his head quizzically. "An old white dude? Course he an old white dude. Just like you an old white dude."

"No, dumbass. Crazy. Do you think he was really crazy or was he only trying to cause trouble?"

Mastiff grumbled deep in his chest as he considered. "Everyone always jokes this shithole be enough to drive someone crazy. But after seeing that shit this morning... maybe it ain't a joke. It sure weren't funny."

A sudden, frigid gust howled between the houses and stole Benny's breath for a moment. "See, that's what I mean. I can deal with someone getting fed up and wanting to give The Man a big FU. But Jimmy, he looked so broken. Truly, truly done in. I don't want to end up like that."

"What?" Mastiff said in a voice a full octave above his usual boom. "Fuck The Man? You *were* The Man, Officer Benny."

"Jesus, Mastiff. That was like fifty years ago. I can't even remember it."

"Don't you take the Lord's name in vain. And everyone know you can take the man outta the pig suit, but you can't take the pig outta the man."

Benny glared at the looming shadow that had insulted him, and snorted. Pain stabbed deep into his hip again, a visceral reminder of the chase that crippled him and ended his career in law enforcement. That was one memory he wished he could forget. There were other memories that hurt worse than his hip.

"Look, man," Mastiff said with a rueful smile. "You know we cool. But even before the DoS, the cops treated me and my people like shit, to put it mildly."

"And who are your people, Mastiff?" Benny asked. "Were your people the ones burning Wichita to the ground? Were your people the ones gunning down my friends while they ate lunch?"

"Oh, Lord Jesu, I know you done didn't just go there." Mastiff's shadow expanded past the frame of the window as he leaned farther out. Benny shrank back involuntarily. "No and no. My people were the ones getting gunned down by cops for going to work while black. And if they made it there, they got gunned down trying to get home. And when my people decided we'd had enough of that shit, my people got gunned down for protesting, motherfucker." Mastiff jabbed a sausage-like finger at Benny and nearly fell out of the window.

"Setting people's homes on fire and trying to run over cops? That's not protesting, that's attempted murder."

"Like I said, you can't take the pig outta the man!"

"You're so full of shit. If you'd have actually been there, you'd know it was a bunch of thugs bussed in to stir the shit up."

Mastiff bristled. "Why? 'Cause they were angry and black? 'Cause the rest of the blacks were good ol' house niggers that did what massa' tol' 'em?"

Benny sneered and flopped his hand against his chest several times. "No, retard. Because they smashed the place up and hurt people that lived there. They weren't there for justice." He poked the head of his cane at Mastiff's nose. "People who, by the way, weren't cops and hadn't done a thing to anyone."

"I'm gonna shove that up your butthole if you don't get it out of my face."

"He might like that," came a voice from the sidewalk. "Not that there's anything wrong with that."

The breathless old men snapped their heads in the direction of the voice. Trance stood at the front of the grassy path between the microhomes. His placid smile was visible in the dim, buzzing light of one of the working streetlights nearby. Benny and Mastiff retreated into their windows like two old turtles who had decided they were too tired to tussle.

"Hey, Trance," they said in unison.

"Oh, decades ago and the Wichita riots still cause so much pain." Trance shook his head. "Both of your scars run so deep, but why open them again and again?"

Benny looked away. Mastiff stared at Trance as if the hippy was a simpleton. Trance returned Mastiff's glare with his usual, at-peace-with-the-universe smile. After a moment, Mastiff's face softened and he looked at the ground outside his window.

"Well," Trance said, "as long as you two are OK."

"Sorry if we woke you," Benny said.

"You were shouting," Trance said. "But I'm not able to sleep any-way. Even my meditation is uneasy. Peace." Trance walked towards his house and out of sight. Benny and Mastiff stared after him until they heard the distant opening and closing of Trance's door.

Benny broke the long silence. "I wouldn't have liked it."

"What?"

"I wouldn't have liked it."

"I heard you," Mastiff said. "Wouldn't have liked what?"

Benny held up his cane and smiled. "Getting this shoved up my butthole."

"Man, you ain't gotta worry about this place making you crazy. You already there."

They broke out in laughter that was carried into the night on the frigid breeze.

"Well, I think I'm ready to try sleeping again. So, thanks for that if nothing else." Benny motioned towards Mastiff's house with a smirk. "You should try going to bed too. That shit will rot your brain. We cool?"

Mastiff held out a fist and Benny bumped it. "Yeah, we cool, man. I'm surrounded by crazy old white dudes. Good night."

"Night." Benny turned to go inside.

Mastiff's head cocked to the side. "Hey, Benny?"

"Yeah?"

"All that you said about your friends and stuff. I thought you said you were a cop in Oklahoma City?"

"I was." Benny grimaced and rubbed his hip. "That's where I got this. But that was after I left Wichita. I keep telling you I was only a cop for ten years. Just long enough for a medical pension, which, of course, I signed over to the DoS for the privilege of this majestic dwelling."

"So you were actually a Wichita cop during those riots?"

"Yeah, lucky me. Not that my time with the OKCPD treated me much better."

"That was some bad shit," Mastiff muttered. He gave Benny a small wave and struggled back in through his window, shutting it against the gusting wind.

Benny did the same and shuffled to his bed. He clutched his blankets to him to drive out the night's chill that had settled in his bones while he spoke. The hint of blue from next door told him Mastiff had not taken his advice. Once his body had warmed up, Benny fell right to sleep and didn't dream of a blood-drenched Jimmy Flint.

4. A Little Feud Among Friends

B enny looked on in silence with the usual mix of bemusement and envy as Trance did his morning exercise. The old yogi slipped from one position—he called them *asanas*—to another beneath the bright but chilly January sun. When not stretching, Trance closed his eyes to meditate. Whenever this happened, Benny stared at Trance's head to see if he could distract the yogi with some secret and undiscovered form of ESP or something. If anyone had any special mental powers around here, Benny figured it would be Trance, not him. Though it seemed both were lacking in the mental powers department, it was still amusing to try.

Long wisps of breath rolled from Trance's nostrils and faded away. Benny thought he detected a trace of hesitation, maybe from a subtle ache or tension, when Trance breathed deeply or stretched long. It was a contrast to his friend's usual aura of wellness. Trance might describe it in spiritual terms. Such things were low vibrations.

Benny didn't know about vibrations and spiritual maladies. But he took pride in his powers of observation. There were small catches in Trance's breath here, masked grimaces there. And Benny thought it was more than age catching up with the preternaturally ageless yogi. Benny was surrounded by bent, wrinkled, and rheumy neighbors—not to mention his own adventures in seniority. He was familiar with the ravages of time and the frailties that accompanied them. It was only a hunch that there was something going on with Trance, but Benny trusted his hunches.

Mack's head poked from his door, looked left and right, then retreated from view like a prairie dog looking for danger. A moment later, Mack emerged covered with thick flannel and with brilliant orange earmuffs set over his dilapidated bulldog cap. Shuffling to the railing of the small porch, Mack squinted through his thick glasses. He glanced at Trance, then tottered to Benny's porch.

"It's as cold as my dead Aunt Alice's ass," Mack said.

Benny nodded, but made no reply. He was absently rolling his cane from hand to hand, watching Trance through the thin clouds of his own breath. Mack shuffled next to Benny and watched too. After a moment, Mack slapped and rubbed his arms.

"It's not that cold," Benny said.

Mack stomped his feet. "Speak for yourself. I bet Trance's nuts are frozen in place."

"You always think his nuts are frozen. In fact, I'm starting to think you're obsessed with his nuts." Benny turned to Mack. "Besides, I thought you were from New York or something."

"Oh, you're a fucking riot." Mack pinched the thumb and forefinger of each hand together and poked them at Benny to punctuate his irritation. He reminded Benny of an angry, hunch-backed orchestra conductor. "Newark. Not New York. New-erk."

"Oh, right." Benny chuckled.

Mack jabbed his conductor's pinch at Benny one more time. "Prick."

Benny flipped Mack a half-hearted bird and turned back to watching Trance.

Mack slapped his arms again and followed Benny's gaze. "You see it, too, don't you?"

Benny nodded.

"He spends more time praying than yoga-cising these days," Mack whispered. "I wouldn't have noticed it on your slowpoke ass, but the old swami ain't moving like he used to."

Benny poked his cane at Mack. "You shuffle over here like the Crypt Keeper and you're going to call me slowpoke?" Benny scoffed. "I don't think anyone would be able to tell if you got frozen in place."

"What-the-fuck-ever." Mack lowered his voice again. "But you know what I mean, right?"

A long sigh escaped Benny's mouth and drifted away. "Yeah. I see it."

They watched together in silence. Trance finally roused himself into a long lunge pose. A grimace crossed his face and was gone. It was so slight Benny didn't think he'd have normally noticed. Embarrassment heated Benny's face; he was afraid that Trance had only moved because he'd overheard them.

"He said anything to you?" Benny asked.

"Naw." Mack shrugged and shuffled his feet. "But I ain't asked him, and he ain't offering. He just smiles and asks if there's anything he can do for me. Then he starts on the whole be-a-utiful universe, unicorns, and life energy jive."

"I'd almost prefer if he just lost it. You know, went off and ripped you a new one. Then I might ask." Mack slapped Benny on the back.

"Maybe if you asked him, he'd lose it."

"Good point. Why don't you go ask him and see what happens?"

"Being rude and obnoxious is your forte, not mine."

"Another good point," Mack said. "But don't sell yourself short, prick." Mack laughed at his short prick joke. "Well, I guess time even catches up with holier-than-thou swamis."

"I think it's more than that."

The smile melted from Mack's face. "Yeah."

They stared at Trance until Benny felt uncomfortable. "So for a complete subject change. Have you seen Ugly Dog since Jimmy left?"

"Naw, but I think I heard him the other night." Mack shrugged. "Probably just a fucking raccoon though. Those damn trash pandas are all over the place. Ugly is probably dead somewheres."

Trance rose to his feet, reached for the sun, and exhaled a contented-sounding breath. "Ugly is fine." He turned and strode towards them.

Benny's stomach clenched. How much had Trance heard? The man was in touch with the universe and all that and not that far away. Benny mentally kicked himself for blabbering away while Trance was so close. It might have been Mack's bellowing gob he'd heard, but Benny felt the guilt anyway.

"Oh, good," Benny said. "I didn't know if he'd hang around."

"I've been leaving out leftovers," Trance said, grimacing. "I'm surprised the poor beast will even touch them. He won't let me touch him though. He actually tried to bite me the other day, so be careful."

"Who'd even want to touch that nasty fucker anyway?" Mack shuddered. "Next time you want to give some food away, give it to me, for Christ's sake. I love those burger-like things."

Trance shook his head. "I love you too much to do anything so horrid."

"You keep your veggie-queer ways to yourself, Trancy-pants." Mack waved his hand at Trance. "There's no real meat in those things anyway."

"That's what they say," Trance said, affecting a teacher's tone. "Do you know what's in them?"

"No."

"Neither does anyone else. Not outside of Proctor-Bayer, a.k.a. Monsanto bastards. And your dutiful friends in Congress..." Trance paused and took three deep breaths. "Sorry. As I was saying, Congress decided they don't have to label it at all. Whatever it is, they at least can't label it as being healthy or meat-free. If they could, they would."

"Trance," Mack said, "I don't give a fuck."

"It could be ground up pig fetus, for all we know," Trance said. "Or worse."

"Great. I love pig fetus. I got my first real taste for it in biology class in high school. Full of vitamins, I hear."

Mastiff's door slammed and all three men turned towards the noise. The porch creaked as Mastiff lumbered out. "It sure is hard to get a good sleep around here with all you crackers yapping on like old grannies."

"Sorry, Mastiff," Trance said.

"Ain't you. These assholes been gossiping about you for a while." Mastiff stared at Benny as he spoke. "Some people are backstabbing motherfuckers, ain't they?"

Benny winced. Trance acted as if he'd not heard the accusation. Mastiff fixed Benny a moment longer with his baleful glare, stomped down the stairs, and strolled down Bile Street without looking back.

Trance moved closer and hefted his elbow over Benny's rail. "He seems upset with you."

"I'll say," Mack said. "You shit on his Monsanto burger?"

Benny's brow furrowed. "I don't know. He's been giving me the cold shoulder for almost two weeks now. Completely ignores me. And he won't tell me what's wrong. I've asked him over and over. I even sent him messages in-game. He actually left a server as soon as I logged in."

Mack rubbed his gloved hands together gleefully, nodding towards Mastiff's house. "You know, I've seen Jo-Jo over at Tubby's place three nights lately."

"I saw Jodie there once." Benny shrugged. "So?"

Mack and Trance exchanged knowing glances. Mack tittered and covered his face. He made screeching coughing sounds as he fought to keep from laughing. When Benny frowned, Mack gave up the fight, slapping his knee as he broke out in raspy guffaws.

"What?" Benny asked. Mack's laughter became a hacking fit. Benny turned to Trance. "What?"

Trance offered a distant smile and walked away.

"What?" Benny yelled, pounding the boards between his feet with the tip of his cane. Mack looked up, tried to speak, but was caught in another spasm of coughing. Benny gripped his cane in both hands and planted it firmly on the porch while he waited.

"Oh, jumping Jesus Jehoshaphat." Mack paused to let out a final giggle. "Jo-Jo's never come over to your place?"

"Of course she has," Benny said. "She and Hannah both come by for inspections and paperwork and all that. I don't see how that has anything to do with what Mastiff's all bent about."

"So she's never given you... extra special internet access?"

Benny sniffed. He didn't like being mocked; especially by that asshat Mack. "I can barely stand that crap on the SafetyNet as it is. Why don't you get to the damned point."

"Not on SafetyNet." Mack cupped his hand and moved it as if it was going around a corner. "Around SafetyNet."

"You mean the Archive?" Benny asked.

Mack held up his hands and jerked his head back and forth. "Shhh! Not so fucking loud. Yes, the Archive. The DarkNet too. Jo-Jo has system-level privileges and might know a thing or two about hacking. I mean real hacking," he said proudly, "not the cheesy shit Fatty is always on about. She can come by and set up a bypass for firewalls for a bit if you need a little unauthorized viewing."

Benny shook his head. "I don't get it. I don't watch porn. And if I did, there's a ton of govporn on SafetyNet."

"And you were a fucking cop? If Jo-Jo's been over there, Mastiff must be surfing around and saw something that pissed him off. She might even know what it's about, but she ain't nosey so I wouldn't count on it."

"So I'm supposed to invite her over so she can do some illegal hacking?"

Mack's exasperated sigh promptly froze and drifted away. "No, dipshit. Click on the sector net hub and you'll see her listed as an admin. Shoot her a message that you want a little help connecting to the web. She'll pop in that night or the next, set you up with about an hour of, uh, free time, and bingo! All done."

Benny stared at Mack. "Just like that?"

"Well..." Mack drew out the word in childish glee. "She usually works out some sort of arrangement. But that's between you two."

Benny wanted to slap the leering gleam from Mack's face. It hinted at some degradation his so-called friend would enjoy at Benny's expense. He couldn't fathom what a destitute and crippled octogenarian had to offer. By signing on to be a retirement ward of the state, he'd forked over all pensions, money, and valuables in exchange for lifelong care.

Care, as it turned out, was a vague legal notion not once defined in the voluminous legislation the program was built on.

Mack smirked as he waited for Benny. While Benny stared, waiting for some further clarification, Mack slapped his hands together several times. The thick gloves made dull poofs as they came together. "Well, my pecker's about to freeze to your porch. I'm going back inside. Drop me an invite if you want your ass blown off pretending you can run *War Masters*. Or Scrabble. I'm happy to kick your ass online or off."

Benny shook his cane at Mack. "You're a cheatware-using glitch bitch. And you make up bullshit words in Scrabble."

Mack waved his hands dismissively. "What-the-fuck-ever. You know where I'm at."

Benny watched his peevish neighbor shuffle back next door. The chill had never bothered Benny. It brought with it a stillness he enjoyed. Not merely by keeping yapping assholes away, but making even the air seem calm, somber. Sitting and rolling his cane from hand to hand in the frosty silence calmed him and helped him think. He loved gaming, had spent decades doing it. But there was something about sitting on a quiet porch and being still in a still world.

Maybe Trance's meditation had some merit. But his balls did look as if they would get cold. Benny's wrinkled old balls couldn't take that kind of abuse.

His mind returned to Jodie's "special arrangements." Nothing he could think of made sense—some were outright ridiculous. Mack could be hard to read through his prurient idiocy and he reveled in that confusion.

With a final shake of his head, Benny decided he wasn't going to try to get Jodie to break the law, especially on Mack's word alone. The whole idea was stupid.

A creak from next door caught Benny's attention. Mastiff waddled up the ramp to his door, not sparing Benny a single glance. As Benny watched his friend's bulk squeeze through the door, he reconsidered Jodie's services.

5. News Too Terrible

F reezing rain tinkled endlessly on Benny's window, showing no regard for his nerves or aching joints. It was a day full of aggravations. The rain. The loud clattering of the dice. The even louder cackling from Mack each time he added his points to the score pad.

Benny couldn't decide if Mack was more of an asshat when he won or when he lost. When Mack tossed the dice and laughed with glee, Benny rolled his eyes. It amazed Benny that such a loser knew so many victory jigs.

"Oh, Benny-Benny-Benny. Benny my man." Mack shook his head and spoke in the voice of an old-time Mafioso from the classics vids. "Yeah, ya see? It don't matter what the game is. You can't outrun the Big Mack Truuuuuuck!"

Benny rolled his eyes the other way and suffered through his friend's gyrations in silence. When Mack started moaning and dry-humping the small table, Benny grunted and turned his back. Facing this way, he could see the faint TV glow from Mastiff's house dancing in each of the icy splatters on the window.

"Aww, now don't get mad," Mack said. "You going to help pick up or mope like a chick because I kicked your ass again?"

Benny favored Mack with a flat stare over his glasses. "After humping my table, I'm thinking you should take it with you too. I'm not sure I can eat on it anymore."

"Mope like a chick it is, I see," Mack said, scooping up dice. "Would you like some frumunda cheese to go with that whine?"

"Frumunda cheese?"

When Mack's face split into a gleeful and puerile victory smile, Benny put his hand to his forehead. He'd walked right into one of

Mack's stupid jokes and would have to suffer through to the punch-line.

Mack reached down into his crotch and brought his hand forward as if handing something over. "From-unda my balls!" Mack guffawed and folded the game board up.

Benny did not help him pack up. What had once been Valentine's Day, before being declared misandry by the government and stricken from official calendars, was approaching and Mastiff hadn't deigned to acknowledge Benny once since his tirade two weeks ago.

"You still pining over that asshole?" Mack asked.

Benny looked at Mack and back to the window. "I guess so. He still hasn't replied to any of my emails, voips, cat-calls, or curses. And he's still avoiding me on the servers and won't answer his door.

"A few nights ago, I started pounding on his window until I was afraid it'd bust. I even screamed at him through the glass."

"Well, no one can say you didn't try. Did he answer at all? No fuck off or middle fingers or anything?"

"No. He turns off his screen and all the lights and sits there in the dark until I go away." Benny huffed. "I haven't bothered since. I only wish I knew what was up his ass." He sipped tea from his favorite cup. It had a picture of the cover of one of his favorite books, *With Our Dying Breath*. The look of despair on the astronaut's face matched how he felt. "Has he told you anything?"

Mack dropped the last of the dice into the game box and grabbed the lid. "Naw. The only people he talks to are Trance and Jo-Jo, but he hasn't even been talking to them much lately. And I'm thankful that he don't talk to me at all."

"Maybe I need to be more nosey."

"Maybe you do." Mack slid the cover over the box and grinned when it made a loud, flatulent squeal. "Then you wouldn't have to keep pestering me about his shit."

Benny blew the rising steam from his jittering cup before sipping again. It soothed his raw throat and warmed his belly. The two men sat in companionable silence listening to the rain on the window. Benny fidgeted with his cane while Mack drummed his gnarled fingers on the box, pausing once to dig a pinky into his ear canal.

Benny didn't usually mind Mack's odious behaviour—to a certain point. Sometimes, it was even amusing to play the perpetually unamused straight man to Mack's inappropriate humor. Other times, Benny refused to laugh in an attempt to knock Mack down a notch, to make sure Mack knew that he wasn't as funny as he thought he was. But now he was glad to have a friend with him. It was comforting, though possibly only because Mack wasn't running his yapper.

Benny was roused from his lazy thoughts some time later by a soft knocking on the door. He rocked forward onto his cane with a grunt and limped to answer it. "Think it's Mastiff?"

"Is the place tipping over?"

Benny chuckled despite himself and swung the door open. Hannah and Jodie were standing on the porch, looking downcast. Water was pooling around their feet and two dripping umbrellas leaned against the outside railing. Hannah wore a strained smile; Jodie wouldn't make eye contact.

"Hello, Mr. Benny," Hannah said. "May we come in?"

Benny's breath caught in his throat. He tried to swallow but his throat was suddenly too raw and thick. Bile burned at the back of his mouth. "Of course," he whispered as he stood aside, trying to give the women as much room as he could in his tiny domicile.

"Oh," Hannah said in a tone of mild disapproval. "Hello, Mr. Francisco."

"Please, lady. It's Mack."

Hannah turned to Jodie. "Would you please escort Mr. Francisco home? It's wet and slippery out there."

Jodie often looked petulant when Hannah gave her some menial or make-work task. This time she looked relieved. "Absolutely."

Benny stood leaning on his cane as Jodie helped an unusually reticent Mack into his coat and towards the door. Mack reached out as he passed and squeezed Benny's hand. Jodie tucked the game box beneath her slicker and ushered Mack along. She glanced up at Benny long enough to offer a sad smile. A final, chilly gust swept through the microhome as Jodie closed the door behind her. Hannah slipped her coat off and hung it on the back of the door.

Benny looked at Hannah for a long moment. Her eyes seemed younger now as her face shone honestly without her bureaucrat's mask. "Lay it on me."

"Please sit down, Mr. Benny."

"I can take it."

Hannah considered him for a moment before speaking. "The Department of Safety... Honey, please sit down. Please."

Benny didn't move.

"Please," she whispered.

When she dabbed the corners of her glistening eyes, Benny shuffled to his chair and collapsed into it. It was all he could do to look at her as she continued. But he forced himself to even as his heart seemed to liquefy in his chest.

"Benny, I'm so sorry," Hannah started. Benny watched as she seemed to choke on the rest of the words. Then her expression hardened back into the familiar, professional politeness of a DoS administrator. "I regret to inform you that your daughter and grandson..."

The words that fell from her mouth after that fused into a meaningless, droning malediction.

Losing his family had been one of Benny's recurring fears as a young husband and father. Whenever someone was home late or slow to answer the phone, his sphincter puckered. He was apt to conjure up ridiculous and terrifying scenarios as explanations. As his children grew and moved on, worries about their mortality had left with them, replaced with concerns about their success and happiness.

Now, decades and decades later, it turned out his fears hadn't been unfounded, only deferred.

"Mr. Benny? Can you hear me?"

The insistence in Hannah's voice stirred him from the darkness. He looked up for a second and nodded dumbly. A legal pamphlet emblazoned with a shiny Department of Safety seal rested on his lap, though he couldn't say how it had got there. His hands feebly clawed at it until Hannah leaned over and opened it for him.

Inside was the official notice and summary of the accident. It spared Benny the gruesome details. The words swam around the page, unwilling to stay in place long enough to be coherent, but he got the gist.

Icy conditions. Oncoming truck crossed into their lane. Possible alcohol involved. Declaration of death: Dakota Penko, 49 years. Declaration of death: Zane Penko, 11 years.

On the back were contact numbers for the people arranging the funeral. The paper slipped from his numb fingers. Hannah picked it up and set it on the table and waited silently. The administrator's mask softened once again for a moment and she gently stroked Benny's crepey cheek.

Benny started at the touch and stared up at her. He clutched her hand as if it were the only thing keeping him from falling over a cliff. His voice was a cracked whisper. "By now, I thought I'd go first. You know? Oh baby girl..."

"My granny always used to say she didn't believe in God because no god worth worshipping would let children die before their mommas." She knelt next to Benny and smiled ruefully. "She didn't care much about daddies since they were always walking out anyway. It was about the mommas for her. But I know you were a good daddy, Mr. Benny. I'm so sorry for your loss."

Benny didn't know how long Hannah knelt beside him, letting him squeeze her hand. If he was hurting her, which he doubted, she gave no indication. He tried to say thanks, but no words were ready to come yet, so he nodded.

"You're entitled to a number of survivor's benefits. I've emailed you the link to the SafetyNet pages that explain them. Please voip me if you have any questions about the travel voucher or counseling services." Hannah stood and looked down at Benny for another minute before sliding her hand from his grip. She stroked his cheek one more time and turned to go.

Benny swallowed hard until the words would come. "Could you hand me the box in the top of my closet, please?"

Hannah smiled. "Certainly." She pulled open the wardrobe and withdrew a small, richly colored, mahogany chest. She traced her finger along its edge before placing it in Benny's lap. "This is beautiful."

Benny unlatched the box and opened it. "And that, please."

Hannah's smile faded as she handed him the death notice. Benny could barely grab the hateful paper but managed to slide it into the box without dropping it on the floor again. "Thanks," he mumbled and stared into the box.

Hannah waited for another minute, then shrugged her raincoat back on. A gust of freezing wind howled through the door as Hannah struggled to shut it behind her. Benny's hat twirled on its hook once in the wind and fell to the floor in the puddle beneath where Hannah's coat had hung. Hannah grabbed her umbrella from the porch and slammed the door against the force of the wind.

Benny stared after her, staring but not seeing. He was gazing back back through his years, desperately seeking memories obscured by time and atrophy. Images of birthdays and recitals came into focus, then dissipated in blurry clouds. There was adolescent Dakota, demanding to be called Maria because some girl at school had said her real name was lame. He refused.

Now tears ran down her face because he'd screamed at her after she missed a curfew, which sent him into a panic. Benny cradled his daughter and dried her tears after Gary fucking Cabbert broke her heart, the little shit. Her beaming, gleaming smile when she pulled up the webpage that was going to publish her poem.

Sunset had been shrouded by the gloomy weather, but Benny's eyes were swollen shut. He wouldn't have been able to watch it anyway. There were vague notions of knocks on his door, and people coming and going. At some point, Benny became aware of his surroundings again. Two aluminum meal tins sat on the table.

The top of the mahogany chest in his lap was still damp from his tears in a spot where the protective lacquer had been worn away by his longing fingers. Benny opened the lid and peered through bleary eyes at the contents.

Memories flitted inside the box like ghosts trapped in a mausoleum. So many had escaped his recall completely and even shackling them to the menagerie within was no surety against his dying memory. Despair filled him at the thought of how much of his life's record was forever lost to him. Even if he'd taken the popular advice from gurus, philosophers, and life coaches to live each day as if it were his last, how much of it would he now remember?

He picked up the DoS pamphlet and set it aside, pinching it by the corner as if it were someone else's used tissue. Dakota's snot had ended up on him many times, including a sneeze that left his face dripping and him gagging. They were on the way to the breakfast bar in Shoney's and he'd lifted her so she could see. He told her to turn her head and cover her mouth. While she got the first part right, Dakota didn't quite get to the covering part. Benny was sure some had flown into his mouth.

It cheered him to know that some ghosts would still visit unbidden. As far as he knew, none of that snot was in the box.

His gnarled fingers brushed aside the mementos of his son Eli, seeking only those of his daughter. They rummaged until Benny felt a cool, familiar, metal disk and lifted it from the box. Attached to the medal was a faded and threadbare ribbon that snagged and jumbled the other items in the box as Benny pulled it free.

There was no indication of the year, location, or event name on the medal. Those details were long lost with no hope of rescue. Dakota's mother told him years ago that it didn't even belong to the girl. He'd nearly slammed the box lid on the bitch's fingers, already furious that she was poking around inside in the first place.

He didn't care what the hag had to say though. Even if she was right, it was Dakota he remembered when he rubbed the medal. It was his Dakota who'd worked her ass off and won—this was no participation trophy. The hugs and kisses and adoration Dakota had showered on him after the competition filled his heart to bursting. She jumped into his arms with her team jacket and bouncing ponytail.

Those scenes were clear in his mind, the medal be damned. Dakota died never knowing how much he hated taking her to those practices. He'd only done it to make her mother shut the fuck up.

"A regular father of the year, ain't you?" the bitch loved to say. Said it at least daily.

The resentment he felt towards his daughter and the subsequent drowning guilt were only amplified by Dakota's earnest appreciation for what he'd done for her. He still felt the shame of those thoughts, hated himself for them, as he traced a calloused thumb around the little girl's outline on the face of the medal. The medal slipped from his fingers and landed in the box with a soft thunk.

Next he pulled out a tiny, yellowed plastic container. Benny held it close to his ear and shook it. The rattle let him know his children's baby teeth were still inside. At least two had been Dakota's, though he couldn't have picked them out. It seemed some of the teeth might belong to his grandchildren, probably including Zane. The notion to open the container passed when Benny pictured the teeth flying out of the container as he struggled to open it. He put it back in the chest.

There was a worn envelope with curled, frayed edges that looked ready to split at the merest touch. Benny carefully upended it, spilling a small pile of photographs and an ancient thumb drive into the chest.

His vision was too blurry with tears to see the pictures, so he picked the top one up and held it up to his nose. It was a newly born Zane lying on Dakota, his delicate eyes still squeezed shut. Benny had fussed at her for getting pregnant so old, and then fussed more at her insistence to deliver him at home.

Everything had turned out beautifully, but he remembered how sullen Dakota became whenever he chastised her. He'd sullied his daughter's miracle because she'd done things her way, not his.

"Sorry again, pretty girl," he whispered wetly. "So, so sorry."

With his hands trembling as they were, there was no way he could get the pictures back in their envelope. So he grabbed the death notification and let it fall into the box. It covered all of Benny's memories like a shroud. A quavering moan escaped his lips and he barely managed to close and latch the lid.

Benny's bones felt as heavy as lead and his back was so painfully stiff that he nearly fell trying to set the box on the table. The stumbling shuffle to the toilet produced three meager drops and he wondered if he'd cried all his piss away. He glanced at the tiny, wooden crypt that held the remains of his beautiful daughter and grandson, before collapsing onto his bed. The darkness that swallowed him was a blessing and Benny didn't care if he ever woke up again.

6. Mastiff Speaks

It was the growl in Benny's belly as much as the relentless knocking that finally roused him from sleep.

"Mr. Benny? Mr. Benny?" Hannah called through the door. "Are you all right? I'm going to open the door if you don't answer."

Benny was about to object that he was still in his skivvies, but instead wondered at the crumpled clothes he wore. Had he been up drinking? It was years since he'd done that. Benny sat up and rubbed his eyes.

He saw the mahogany chest on the table and the previous night came crashing down on him again. Benny's chest constricted, squeezing a moan from him. The desire to get out of bed fled like a man's dying breath.

There were the sounds of a beep and a click, then Hannah and Jodi were there by his bed. He looked up at them and grunted. "I'm fine."

Relief washed over Hannah's face. She and Jodie eyed the place, their gazes pausing on the unopened meals on the table.

"Good morning," Hannah said with measured sympathy. Benny noticed the contrived tone, but he didn't hold it against her. She ran a geriatric pre-morgue and death was part of her job.

Jodie shuffled her feet, but was able to look at him this morning. "Sorry for your loss."

"Thanks."

"I know you've just woken up, Mr. Benny, so you probably haven't checked any of your messages." Hannah held up her datapad and pulled a small white card from the case. "The funeral is in two days and you've been authorized for a hardship travel chit."

"Ms. Jodie here," Hannah continued with an air of disapproval, "took it upon herself to request a chaperone assignee for you as well and it was approved."

"My usual dedication to customer service. Initiative and all that, you know." Jodie smiled, looked at Benny, then turned away.

"In any case, Mr. Benny, you have room for a guest and one DoS-provided assistant." Hannah glared at Jodie. "If desired."

Benny continued to stare up at her.

Hannah cast her eyes down at her pad and slid her fingers across the screen. "According to the DoS travel app, there are two trains and a single car rental itinerary that will get you there in time. Unless you have made other arrangements..."

Benny shook his head. "I was going to voip my son and see if he could help with a bus ticket or something. Travel's so damn expensive. And the whole point of this place is for me not to be a burden, right?" Tears welled in his eyes. "Thanks, Hannah. I didn't know if I'd be able to see my babies off."

"Don't thank us," Hannah said. "Thank the DoS."

She sounded like a public service announcer to Benny. There was no way she realized how insincere it made her sound. Despite being a stickler for every Department of Safety memo and suggestion, Hannah was a good girl and ran things as well as possible given what a train wreck the DoS and its programs had become.

"Feel free to thank me if you want," Jodie said.

Hannah cleared her throat. "Let me know who—if any-one—you plan on inviting and when you're leaving."

"Did I ever mention that I have family in Oklahoma City, Han-nah?" Jodie said. "I haven't seen them in so long. And Benny just pointed out how expensive it is to travel these days."

Hannah gasped and wagged her finger under Jodie's nose. "You should be ashamed of yourself! This man just lost his daughter and all you can think of is getting a free ride?"

"Look, I'd help... and, you know..." Jodie trailed off, glancing between Benny and Hannah. Color ran up her cheeks and she averted her eyes from them both. "Sorry."

Hannah swung open the door and jabbed her finger towards the doorway. Jodie muttered another apology and walked outside. Hannah spoke to Benny in a whisper. "I'm livid, Mr. Benny. And embarrassed. I'm so sorry. Let me know." Hannah walked outside and closed the door behind her.

No sooner had the door shut than there was a knock at it. Benny shuffled over and opened it. Mack poked his head through.

"Who you taking?"

"Mr. Francisco!" Hannah said from the porch. "Leave the poor man be."

"Bah." Mack waved his hand as if shooing a fly. He pushed in through the door and closed it with a kick from his heel. "And don't mind Jo-Jo—she didn't mean nothing."

"You were eavesdropping?"

Mack shrugged and took his usual seat at Benny's table.

"Jesus, Mack," Benny said. "It's all happening so fast. I have no idea who I'm taking or when. But thanks for caring." He walked to the kitchenette and started some tea. As he did so, an alarm began beeping from the small medical station on the counter.

Benny shut off the alarm and placed his hand on the small, white disk with a red heart in the center. It beeped in time with the LEDs that blinked along the edges as the station recorded Benny's vitals and transmitted them to some digital archive. After thirty seconds, the device gave the descending tri-tone chirp that signalled the procedure was over.

"Now you can rest easy," Mack said, "knowing that DoS has another file full of numbers no one will ever look at. I bet you even still read the emails it sends you."

"Sometimes," Benny said. "Should you go do yours?"

"I'll get to it. But I turned off my notifications a long time ago. If their algorithm finds something, I'm sure they'll send a meat wagon to haul me away."

Benny shook his head and watched the tea dispenser fill his cup with warm water. DoS regulated how hot a ward's drinks could be. The water was never quite hot enough for a proper cup of tea. But it was better than nothing.

"Anyway," Benny said. "At least they pulled through with something. Finally. No way I'd have found a ride to the funeral."

"About that," Mack said in the tone of someone about to share a great truth. "It may offend, but you know who'd really like a fucking trip to anywhere that ain't here?" Mack hiked both his thumbs towards his chest. "This guy!"

Benny set his cup down on the table and stared at Mack. The man always took pride in being crass. Benny knew this, but he could feel the heat building in his ear lobes. He squeezed his cane until two of his knuckles popped. "You realize we're talking about a trip to my babies' funerals, right?"

Mack looked hurt. "Of course I do, man. It really sucks, and I'm sorry for your loss. I don't know what I'd do if anything happened to Ricky, or Abby, or Krysta. But I won't get in your way, promise. I gotta get away from this fucking place. I've got a serious case of the Bile Street blues.

"I used to drive all over the goddamned continent and these hamster cages are killing me. I never should have signed that paper." Mack shrugged. "Anyway, I do have a sympathetic ear. Having someone to talk to about it on the way might be what you need."

Benny his eyebrows. "Sympathetic ear? You mean a pathetic ear. You're as deaf and loud as a wood chipper."

Mack reeled back in his chair and clutched both hands over his heart. "All right, hard-ass." After a dramatic pause, he reached out and patted Benny's arm. "I can't do much obviously, but really, if I can help, just give me a tap."

The table scooted a few inches as Mack pushed to his feet. Benny cleared his throat and stared over his glasses, first at Mack, then at the puddle of tea that had sloshed out of the cup.

Mack busily adjusted his own glasses and squinted at the table. "What?" Mack gave Benny a quizzical glance and shuffled out the front door without another word.

Benny watched his friend go and shook his head when the door closed. The door had been busy this morning. With a loud snort, Benny picked up a nearby towel and cleaned up the puddle. He had taken to keeping towels handy at all times. The number of accidents and spills had increased proportionally with age.

A loud, rolling gurgle in Benny's belly reminded him that not all of the morning's necessities had been taken care of. He pulled a food tin from the fridge and set it on the table. Nothing looked particularly appealing when he lifted the aluminum top. He settled for picking at the least soggy biscuit.

Gentle knocking stirred Benny from his brooding thoughts. He glared at the door, but found he didn't have the energy to stay irritated. Every emotion this morning was quickly devoured by the shocked numbness that covered him like a blanket. "Come in."

Trance cracked the door. "Hey, Benny. I can come back if you want."

Benny waved him in and Trance closed the door before stepping near one of the windows.

"I'm very sorry for your loss, brother. I've had friends and family return to the Source, but I've never been blessed with children. I can't even imagine your pain."

"Thanks, Trance."

"Mack told me last night something had happened. He said Hannah had arranged a travel chit for you. That's something to be grateful for at least."

Benny frowned. "Are you trying to get a ride too?"

Trance held up his hands. "Oh, no. Mack only mentioned it a few minutes ago, and was very convinced that you had already decided to take him." Trance made his way to the chair opposite Benny's and grimaced when he sat.

Benny did his best to look as if he'd not seen that grimace. "Mack does have some odd ideas. I can't blame him for wanting to go though, or Jodie, really. The only thing OKC might have going for it is that it isn't Bile Street. But that's something."

"Have you made any headway with Mastiff?"

"I don't really have time to deal with that asshole now, Trance."

"Exactly. A long train ride might be what you need to talk things out. Whatever has him angry is eating away at both of your guys' peace. You've said that you aren't close to your family—"

"Except Dakota," Benny said, wiping at his suddenly burning eyes.

"Except Dakota," Trance continued, his voice brimming with sympathy. "It might be a good idea to have a friend come along."

"That's what Mack said."

Trance chuckled. "You know what they say about broken clocks."

"What about you?" Benny asked. "You're all about feelings and psychoanalysis."

"Our spiritual health is important. Holding onto anger and bitterness isn't healthy." Trance looked into the distance as if considering something. "As for me, it wouldn't be a good idea. Mack is probably a bad idea too," he added, grinning.

Benny returned the grin. "Even if I wanted to, Mastiff won't talk to me at all. Believe me, I've tried everything."

"Would it be OK if I asked him for you? He might not even know about your loss."

Benny studied Trance for a moment, then stood to get more tea. He didn't like the idea of turning to anyone for help, but nothing he'd tried had moved Mastiff to answer. Why he even still cared what that asshole next door thought was a mystery, but he did. Maybe he should let Trance tell Mastiff; it might show that stubborn jackass.

The strength left Benny and his cane slipped in his grip, forcing him to catch the counter to keep from falling. The stumble left him looking through the window facing Mastiff's house. He heard Trance pushing up from the table, but waved a hand back at him without looking. Benny righted himself and finished brewing his tea.

Benny took a long pull from the chipped cup. "Would you?"

"Absolutely, brother."

"When?"

Trance smiled and got to his feet. "No time like the present. Especially since you don't have much time to get ready."

When Trance opened the door, Mack nearly fell through it and might have fallen if not for Trance catching him.

Mack shoved a finger in Trance's face. "You did it, didn't you? You used your yogi mind tricks and at-one-with-the-universe bullshit to convince him to take you instead, didn't you? I saw you sneaking over here and I knew it!"

"No," Trance answered. He shot Benny a bemused, knowing smile. "I've convinced him to take Mastiff."

The look of betrayal on Mack's face was almost comical. "No way."

"It's true," Benny said.

"What the fuck for? He's been nothing but a dick to you." Incredulity thickened his New Jersey accent. "He won't even talk to you and you're taking him?"

"It will be a good chance to remedy that, won't it?" said Trance.

"What-the-fuck-ever," Mack muttered.

Trance stepped around Mack and walked next door to knock on Mastiff's door. "Mastiff? It's Trance."

Benny stood on his porch and could follow the minute groans and creaks of the microhome as Mastiff made his way to the door.

The door opened. "What's up, Trance?"

"Did you hear about Benny?" Trance asked.

"No," Mastiff answered quickly. "Is he OK?"

The sound of genuine concern in Mastiff's voice brought a single sob to Benny's lips. Mack shot Benny a look of utter disbelief.

"His daughter and grandson were killed in a car wreck," Trance said.

"Lord Jesu, no," Mastiff moaned. Grief twisted his heavy brow and jowls. He looked as if he was about to say something more, but followed Trance's furtive glance to Benny's porch. Benny saw a shimmer in Mastiff's eyes.

"He has a travel chit for a guest and was hoping you'd go with him to his daughter's funeral," Trance said.

Benny's breath caught in his throat as he watched all sympathy drain from Mastiff's face. It was as if a giant invisible hand was pinching Mastiff's face, pulling his brow down and causing his jaw to jut forward. The transformation was so stark, so sudden, that Trance took a half-step backwards when Mastiff turned back to face him.

"You tell Benny that since he was too good for my daughter's funeral, that I don't really want to go to his."

"I'm sorry, Mastiff," Trance said. "I didn't know."

"I never heard anything about it," Benny called.

Mastiff pointed a sausage finger at Benny. "May your lying tongue fall out, because you surely did. Oh yes you did, motherfucker. Most surely you did."

Mack jerked his cap from his head and hurled it to the porch. "You fucking nigger!" he screamed, thrusting his own finger back at

Mastiff. "The man lost his daughter and you can't stop being a prick for ten fucking seconds?"

Mastiff leaned forward, glaring at Mack. Mack glared back and upped the ante by two middle fingers. Benny and Trance exchanged confused glances. Mastiff shook his head and lumbered back to his door. He paused and turned back before crossing the threshold.

"Fuck all you crackas." He glared again at Mack. "And double fuck you, goddamned spic." With that, Mastiff went inside and slammed the door.

Benny did the same.

7. A Cane and a Train

"**D**rop it already, Mack," Benny said. Rubbing his eyes, he added, "I'm too tired for this. It's way past my bedtime."

Mack ignored him. "Come on, Jo-Jo. You gotta know what's up Mastiff's lily-black ass." Mack leaned back in his seat as the compartment started to rock gently.

Lamp posts and caution signs slid past the window with increasing frequency. The distant lights of greater Chicago peered in through the window and followed the travelers from the station.

Bedtime was a word that held little meaning for Benny these days. But he couldn't stifle the yawns that came out of him one after another. The prospect of being able to drop off to sleep cheered Benny. It was probably all the hustle and bustle and Jodie pushing the two of them like sled dogs all day. Not that it mattered; Benny was looking forward to a nice, deep sleep.

Unfortunately, Mack's piehole didn't sound tired at all.

The train jostled to a stop next to a blinding, red crossing light that cast the three bleary-eyed travelers in a demonic hue.

Jodie offered a leering smile that exposed her stained, misshapen teeth. The red glare made them look blood-soaked and monstrous. The sight made Benny feel queasy. "Sorry, darling. I don't know a thing. I mean, aside from the fact that you're an asshole."

"Ha. Ha," Mack said flatly.

"When I hook someone up, I leave. You know that."

"You been over there plenty lately," Mack said. "And you're trying to tell me he ain't told you nothing? You haven't even taken an eensy-tinsy sneaky-peek?"

Jodie narrowed her eyes at Mack. "No. What you guys access is strictly your concern and none of mine. And even if I did catch you watching elephants humping quadriplegic midgets, Mack, I'd never tell."

"I have never—" Mack started until Jodie laughed at him. He turned to Benny. "She's in rare fucking form tonight, right? A regular laugh riot."

Benny tried turning his head away from the red light, but it was too bright to escape no matter which way he looked. "Yeah, she's funny and very ethical."

"Look," said Jodie, "when I make a contract, I stick to it. I keep my end of the bargain and I don't force people to do anything." The train rattled and the glaring red light disappeared. "I make the offer—people can talk or walk, no questions asked, no butts hurt."

"You use your DoS access to bypass the SafetyNet firewalls," Benny said. "I'm sure there's something in your contract about not doing that."

"Fuck the DoS," Jodie said.

"Those paychecks, though?" Benny had no love for the DoS. But since the other two weren't going to let him pass the night sleeping, he might as well give in to his fatigue-induced grumpiness.

Jodie leaned towards Benny and squinted one eye. "By definition, every contract the DoS is involved in is made under duress. You should understand that. Or maybe you don't, since you're living on Bile Street.

"And since the DoS destroyed our economy, it's about the only place to work these days. I do everything they pay me to do and I do it well. They certainly get more out of me than what they pay for."

Benny pointed his cane at her. "You *are* part of 'they.'"

Jodie glared at Benny. "They keep you locked up and on the SafetyNet, Benny. Why? Because it's easier to hide how bad they've fucked things up if they deny people any news except the DoS-approved corporate BS."

She fell back into her seat, but was back at Benny a second later, her finger jammed in his face. "Know why it's so expensive to fly? Because they took over the airlines in the name of 'safety' and fucked that sideways too. For the people, my ass. They killed the people who fought for their rights and called them terrorists, like always. And the rest of the sheeple just took it up the ass, like always."

Benny thumped the tip of his cane on the compartment floor and leaned forward. "Those people *were* terrorists, regardless of how much the DoS screwed up."

"And how do you propose to fix the DoS, dear Benny?" Jodie asked, a mocking smirk on her face.

"You change it from the inside, obviously. You vote, get involved."

Jodie let out a derisive snort. "You can't vote your way out of a tyranny. Look at what the founders did. They asked to be treated fairly, and the crown said no. Then our founders, the ones who set up the system you're appealing to for change, rolled up their sleeves and started slitting throats."

For once, Mack was the voice of reason instead of the instigator. "Jesus, guys. Benny, don't get her started. She got us on this trip."

"She got herself a trip." Benny paused to give Mack a suspicious look. "And so did you."

"What-the-fuck-ever." Mack waved off the accusation. "All I know is that it wasn't that bitch Hannah who did all the work for your travel shit.

"And Jo-Jo, leave him alone, OK? He's going to go see his dead kids. Cut him a fuckin' break from the revolution, huh?"

Benny and Jodie glared at each other through sleep-bleary eyes, then turned away to stare into the distance in opposite directions.

The train was at cruising speed and the distant city light had finally been outrun. Lights from remote farms and homesteads winked after them for a time, until only darkness peered in at them from the window.

Benny let himself be lulled by the gentle rocking of the train's compartment. It had been a long day for all of them and the warmth of the cramped car finally put Benny to sleep.

A tap to his arm woke him with a start.

"Hey, Benny," Mack whispered. "You awake?"

"Godammit, Mack," Benny muttered through clenched dentures. He reached up and wiped at the string of drool working its way downhis chin. "No, I wasn't awake. Can't you shut up, like ever?"

"I'll be quiet when I'm dead."

Benny hefted his cane. "If that's what it takes..."

"What-the-fuck-ever. I'd break both your hips like that," Mack said with a snap of his fingers.

Jodie snorted, mumbled, and smacked her lips, before tossing her head and falling back to sleep. Her snaggletoothed maw drooped open widely. Benny grimaced.

"Is your son Eli gonna be there?" asked Mack.

"Yeah."

"You two get along?"

Benny rubbed his eyes. "Well enough, I guess. I wouldn't say we're very close, but that's on me. His mother and I were separated for a while, but when we finally divorced he was already at college. I moved away and we sort of grew apart. We still message and voip and sometimes send Christmas cards."

Mack nodded. "You ever worry that you messed him up by doing dumb dad shit?"

"I did lots of dumb shit," Benny said. "But he seems OK despite my best efforts. You forget to send Ricky a birthday text or something?"

"Well, as you know, my boy is a fag," Mack said, shaking his head. "And if you can't see it, there's something wrong with you."

"Everyone knows it because you keep announcing it every time he comes up." Benny stifled a yawn with his fist.

Mack turned to stare into the darkness through the window. "I wasn't... well, I wasn't always very nice. And I'm not talking about letting him cry it out as a baby or any of that Dr. Giore whiny, tough-love shit either. I was really a hard-ass, sometimes. An asshole, really."

"Everyone screws it up sometimes, dude. When I was on the night shift, I used to get way tired, and if Eli or Dakota wouldn't stop crying when I was sleeping, I'd get up and scream at them like a madman." Benny sighed and shook his head. "Real Father-of-the-Year kind of stuff.

"I even shook Dakota so hard once I thought I'd hurt her. Scared the shit out of me. I'm glad she was too young to remember. I still screamed at them plenty, but I never shook them after that."

"I know we all fuck up," Mack said. "But I was a real bastard, a real crazy fuck. And I've read those articles about what childhood trauma can do to kids when they grow up. All sorts of bad shit. I... always worried that I somehow made him a fag."

"You're going to get us arrested if you keep blurting out things like that."

Mack waved a hand in the air. "Jo-Jo won't turn us in."

"I'm not talking about Jodie." Benny looked at the door to the cabin nervously. "Someone's going to overhear your big mouth and taze us before you can say 'hate speech.'"

Mack flipped up his two middle fingers and swept them in every direction. "Fuck the DoS. Besides, I love my boy, no matter what."

"Won't matter when the boot's on your wrinkled, old turkey neck."

Mack blew out his breath and glanced at Benny, before turning back to the window. Benny's heart raced as he watched the door, expecting a safety officer to come in and haul them both away.

When no arrest was immediately forthcoming, Benny faced Mack. "There's nothing you can do about it now. All that matters is that you love him, you know?" Benny grinned wryly. "Besides, I think the official position on nature versus nurture on orientation issues depends on who gets selected as Health Czar."

"Look, I worry that I caused him a fucking mess he didn't need."

Benny rolled his cane from hand to hand. "All parents—including our own children—screwed their kids up somehow. Accept it and move on."

"Easier said than done, pal."

"True enough," Benny said. "But you two seem to get along. Or at least, he tolerates you better than the general public." He grinned and nudged Mack, but Mack didn't respond. "Does he hold it against you? I mean, does he throw it in your face?"

"I sure as fuck would."

"That's not what I asked."

Mack took a deep, rattling breath. "Naw, I guess not."

"Then I say have a real come-to-Jesus talk or let it go."

"Yeah, I guess so," Mack said in a resigned tone. It sounded as if he was trying to convince himself.

"And while I'm being all sagely..."

"Go on, oh fucking wise one."

"Maybe not call your son a fag."

Mack squinted at Benny. "I don't call him a fag. I might joke about his boyfriends and shit, but I don't call him a fag."

"That day they took Jimmy—" Benny started.

"Oh Jesus, not this shit again. I said my name was faggoty—I didn't call him anything."

"You called him a fruit," Benny said. "And you describe him as a fag often enough when you talk to me."

"So the fuck what? If he doesn't hear it, who the fuck cares?"

"Are you sure he doesn't hear it?"

"You ratting me out, Benny?"

"No."

Mack gave Benny a "there you go" shrug and turned his back.

"Trance says—"

"That hippy's full of shit."

"Trance says," Benny continued, "we speak things into existence. And I don't think he only means crystals and frequencies and all that. But I think he has a point. If you use those slurs, which do come with negative connotations, it can affect how you think about him. We're talking about your son."

Mack snorted. "I drink soda, not pop. I put sheets on my bed, not bedclothes. I eat heroes, not hoagies. And I chased lightning bugs, not fireflies, when I was a kid. They're only words, so if you have some sort of baggage with them, don't shove your shit on me. I don't hate lightning bugs and I don't hate fags. Fags are dudes who get it on with other dudes. I think it's kind of nasty, but if you hate fags, that's on you."

Benny glanced at the compartment doors again. "Look, I don't hate fag—homosexuals."

"Neither do I." Mack pinched his index fingers and thumbs together and jabbed them at Benny as he spoke. "So stop accusing me. And before you take the fucking elevator any higher in your ivory tower, I don't hate blacks neither. Mastiff was being a prick and I called him nigger to piss him off."

"It's still not cool."

"Calling someone a motherfucker ain't cool," Mack said. "But I don't see your twat getting all twisted about that. And it didn't seem

to light you all up when he called me a spic. I'm fucking fifth generation. I don't even speak Mexican."

"Don't change the subject," Benny said as he shook his cane at
Mack. "We're talking about you and your son."

"Get that fucking thing out of my face," Mack said. "Like you
haven't told your kids to fuck off."

"I've said plenty I regret. And I already said I screwed things up,
in case you weren't listening. But that doesn't mean we shouldn't try
to do better. That's all I'm saying."

"Will you two cocksuckers shut up?"

Benny and Mack turned to Jodie. She glared at them through
one red, swollen slit of an eye. It slowly closed again and her head
lolled to one side. The two old men looked at each other and chuckled.

Benny leaned back into his seat and let the tension loosen from
his shoulders. "Look, just have that come-to-Jesus talk and see how
Ricky feels about it."

"What the fuck does that even mean? Come-to-Jesus talk? You
want me to tell him about fags in the Bible?"

Benny shook his head. "No, it means to have an important talk,
like an intervention. Though it was a bit more literal when I was a
kid."

"Well, I don't give a shit what Ricky thinks."

"Obviously you do."

"What-the-fuck-ever."

A low growl came from the other side of the compartment and
both men turned to see Jodie glaring at them again, this time with
both eyes. After a short beary-eyed staring contest, all three turned
away and drifted to sleep without another word.

THE TRAIN JOSTLED BENNY awake just enough to be irritated at the dim, gray light creeping in through the window. He tried to turn away from the damned light, but pain screamed up at him from his throbbing hip. Benny gave in when the middle-aged conductor, who'd been standing there for who knows how long, made his announcement.

"Sorry to wake everyone, but it's time for transfer."

Benny smacked his lips, trying to get rid of the foul taste in his mouth. After a few aborted attempts at getting up, the conductor offered a hand which Benny gratefully took.

Mack muttered incoherent complaints while Jodie helped him to his feet with a bit more vigor than Benny thought necessary. She made sure Mack was steady before reaching into the overhead compartments and retrieved three DoS- approved travel bags; only one allowed per passenger.

The conductor swept the cabin to verify all personal belongings had been removed and pointed them to the nearest exit as he moved to the next cabin. Benny staggered into the flow of passengers and made his way down the boarding ramp, where another conductor swiped their travel chits over a datapad. She briefly explained how to get to the security screening area and then to their next train, which should be leaving in an hour.

"Should?" Benny asked, looking at the woman over his glasses.

The conductor nodded. "I've been doing this too long to give anything but a should." With that, she dismissed him to begin swiping other passengers' travel chits. Once the last passenger had been swiped, the train emitted an electric hum. The conductor boarded and Benny watched the train until it disappeared around a bend. He'd always loved trains as a child.

"Come on," Jodie said. "I've got to piss." She led them through the concourse until they found the restrooms. "Need any help, Benny?" she asked with a leer.

Benny stiffened. "I can manage, thanks." He walked into the restroom, trying to ignore Jodie's giggles.

Soon they were reassembled on the concourse. Jodie led them according to the conductor's instructions until the safety enforcement officer manning the checkpoint came into view. He was a dour-looking brute of a man who towered over the luggage scanner he leaned against. Nearby, a female officer stared at her screen. Her eyes seemed to disappear into a blank, white haze. Her pointed chin rested in the palm of one hand.

"Proceed through, please," the large man intoned with grave indifference as they approached. "Place your bags, coats, and any metal objects on the conveyor."

Jodie was the first to set her belongings on the conveyor belt, stopping to eye the officer up and down. "No frisking, honey?" She bit her lip and winked. Benny winced.

The officer's eyes widened in surprise. "Damn, grandma. Haven't you hit menopause yet? It sure looks like it hit you—hard." He smirked at his partner and Jodie flipped him off with both hands before storming through the scanning booth.

Benny felt a tap on his left shoulder and turned to see what Mack wanted. Only Mack wasn't there; he was shuffling by on the right to cut in front of Benny. Not that Benny cared about going first or last, but that damned Mack chapped his ass. Somehow, Mack could sound like a grumpy old bastard and a child at the same time with that chuckle.

When Mack approached the booth, he shot the officer a sympathetic look. He twirled his finger next to his temple, then motioned at Jodie. The officer didn't respond, so Mack shuffled into the scanner. There he raised his arms as high as he could, as instructed. Then he gyrated his hips in lewd circles, which he was not instructed to do.

"Please stand still, sir," said the female officer.

"Oh, sorry." Mack grinned and winked at Benny.

Benny shook his head, twirled his own finger around his temple, and motioned to Mack. Neither officer responded. When Mack was cleared, the big officer waved Benny through. Benny's hip had grown painfully stiff again and he hobbled along on his cane for the first few steps. Jodie and Mack stood on the other side, yawning. Benny would be glad to get to the next train.

His heart nearly stopped at the buzzing shriek from the booth as he entered. Clutching his hands to his chest, Benny saw the woman behind the monitor jerk awake. Officer Brute's eyes grew wide as he glanced at the screen. They exchanged quick, furtive whispers and both looked at Benny over the monitor.

"Sir," called the man as he stepped around the desk, hand on the butt of his pistol. "Please drop the weapon and back through the scanner."

Benny raised his hands. "Whoa-whoa-whoa! What weapon?"

"Drop the weapon! The cane. Drop it."

"It's just his cane, meathead," Jodie said.

The female officer was out of her seat in an instant, a hand on her pistol. "Don't interfere. Step back."

Jodie and Mack both raised their hands and stumbled backwards into a row of chairs against the wall.

Benny stooped slowly, in part to keep the obviously excitable officer calm, but mostly because he didn't trust his hip. He leaned the decorated cane against the inside of the booth.

"Now step back, sir," the officer said.

Benny glanced over his shoulder as he shuffled backwards. The few passengers behind him had cleared out of the possible line of fire. A few had their voips surreptitiously pointed at the scene. Filming a safety enforcement officer was almost as dangerous as attacking one.

Benny stared at the officer, hands up and praying to something up there that his hip would hold out. No telling what the man would do if it even looked like Benny was lurching towards him.

At length, the big officer relaxed his grip on the pistol. He stepped forward and picked up the cane. "What's your name, sir?"

"Benedict Martin, sir." Benny heard the tremor of fear in his voice and hated it.

"Is there a concealed blade in this stick, Mr. Martin?"

"No, sir." Something like amused surprise replaced his fear. "Not at all."

"The scanner shows otherwise. It shows a blade of metal from here"—the officer traced a finger from the handle to halfway down the cane—"to here."

"What?" Benny barked a short laugh and lowered his hands.

The safety officer's hand shot back to his pistol. "Hands up!"

Benny reached for the sky with renewed vigor and terror. Out of the corner of his eye, he saw Jodie and Mack were doing the same on the other side.

"Wait, wait, wait," Benny said, daring a hesitant smile. "I know what's going on. There's a steel insert in the cane for added support. A lot of wooden canes have them. Look it up on the SafetyNet. The last station let us on no problem."

The muscled man stared at Benny before returning to his inspection of the cane. "Sir, I can't help it if other stations didn't do their jobs. Now, where is the release?"

"There isn't one, sir," Benny said. "Please believe me. It doesn't open at all."

"If you don't show me, Mr. Martin, I will break it open."

"Hey, fuck-stick," Mack called, "it's only a cane. If it was a knife, he'd have stuck it through me by now."

The female safety officer's hand was back on her weapon. "Do not interfere again, sir."

Benny watched in horror as Mack leaned forward and took a deep breath. It was the breath he took when making ready to launch a tirade, one usually laden with obscenities and insults. Jodie gripped

Mack's shoulder and gently, but firmly, pulled him back. Mack glared at her and she gave him a single, curt shake of her head. Benny let out his breath as Mack stepped back into place without another word.

"It doesn't open," Benny said. "There's no latch or blade."

The officer's face went red as he continued to not find the secret button he was looking for. He glared at Benny—and Benny knew that face. It was that of the zealot. He'd seen it plenty on the force. The man, or boy really, might be a rookie or he might be out to prove something. Anyone who questioned the zealot, or offered insult or mockery, real or imagined, was going to pay.

"Tell me, or I'll have you charged with hindering public safety and uncooperative behavior towards a safety enforcement officer." Without waiting for Benny to answer, the officer began twisting and pulling any part of the cane he could get a grip on. He jammed fingers into every whorl and groove to prise them apart.

"There's nothing," Benny said. He pointed a trembling finger at Mack. "And he's right, I would have stabbed him already. It was a gift from my daughter. We're on our way to her funeral. Please..."

The officer rolled his neck and shoulders. "No? All right then." His muscles bulged and his face grimaced as he twisted on the cane with all his might. A sound like ripping paper escaped from deep in the wood.

Benny reached for the cane. "No!"

"Step back, sir!" the officer yelled, putting hishand on his pistol butt again. When Benny stepped back with hands held high, the officer resumed twisting the cane. A bead of sweat rolled from the man's brow and he was rewarded with the deep crack of splitting mahogany. Next, the officer took the cane across his knee and grunted. He stumbled backwards as the cane snapped in two, revealing a thin steel rod jutting from the shattered wood.

"You motherfucker," Mack said.

The safety officer examined the ruined cane, speaking with mild, but genuine-sounding, surprise. "I guess you were right. That was a pretty strong cane." He held out the remains to Benny.

Tears ran down Benny's face as he scooped up the cane into his shaking arms. "Why?" Benny whispered.

The guard looked over Benny's head to the line behind him. "Move along, Mr. Martin."

Jodie stormed forward, ignoring the hands that fell on their pistols. "I want to see a supervisor now and I want your user labels, assholes." Jodie held up her DoS datapad.

The officers exchanged worried glances, but they barely registered for Benny. He was staring at the splinters of the most wonderful gift he'd ever received. And Dakota could never give him another. Two middle-aged women behind Benny whispered words that sounded sympathetic. He couldn't hear them over the pounding in his ears.

"Move along," the muscled officer said. Neither officer was willing to make eye contact with Jodie or Benny.

"User label and supervisor, now!" Jodie demanded.

The female officer muttered under her breath and tapped out a quick message on her terminal. "Supervisor will be here in a moment."

Jodie thrust her datapad towards the big man. "User label."

His eyes narrowed, but still refused to meet hers. "You wait for the boss, lady."

Jodie shoved her DoS ID card under his nose. "You are required to present your user label upon request as per Department of Safety regulations."

A lanky man with tousledhair and disheveled clothes strolled through a nearby door. He zipped up his DoS blazer, almost hiding his rumpled appearance. "What's the deal?"

"Oh, sorry to wake you," Mack said. Jodie glared at him over her shoulder. "OK, OK, Jesus."

"The deal is," Jodie said, enunciating every word as if speaking to a child, "your goon destroyed my ward's personal property. Not only is it a medical necessity, it is a family heirloom."

"A cane? Medical equipment?"

"He needs it to walk, idiot." Jodie held up her ID to the supervisor. The man held up a datapad and Jodie swiped it over the screen. He scanned the display while Jodie continued, "He willfully destroyed it while repeatedly ignoring us telling him it wasn't a sword."

The supervisor looked up from his datapad with a bemused sneer. "You're a first-level assistant?"

Jodie sneered back. "So? You're supposed to provide your user label for scanning upon request."

"Step back," the supervisor said. When Jodie refused, he stepped around her and walked to the officers. "Give this man one of the canes or crutches from the confiscation closet. Preferably one without deadly, hidden weapons. And you two apologize."

The supervisor yawned and looked down at Jodie. "Your train is about to leave. I'm sure you wouldn't want to miss it and be stuck here while we sort things out, right?"

"You are a son of a bitch," Jodie muttered.

The supervisor spun on his heel and slipped back through the door from which he'd come.

The pair of officers offered their contrived and seemingly well-practiced apologies in unison for being over-zealous in their efforts to keep travelers safe. The big man then opened a nearby locker and rummaged through it, producing an aluminum cane that looked as if it had come straight from a medical center.

Benny was leaningheavily against the scanner now, openly weeping and clutching the ruined cane to his chest. Jodie snatched the metal cane from the officer's hands. Gentle hands from behind helped Benny forward until Jodie wrapped her arms around his shoulders. Mack hefted their bags onto a small cart and shuffled away from the checkpoint.

"Come on, honey, use this," Jodie said, handing Benny the new cane. She offered him an apologetic smile. "I'm sorry. Let's go."

Benny looked up at Jodie and she looked away. Then Jodie glared over his shoulder. Benny followed her gaze and saw the safety enforcement officers waving other passengers through with sleepy disinterest. The glare of the screen filled the female officer's vacuous eyes. They must have felt her glare, because they both looked at her.

"Let's go," Benny said.

As the three of them rounded the corner to find their train, Benny saw Jodie point back at the officers and clearly mouth, "I'm going to fuck you up."

8. Friends, Families, and Funerals

Benny stumbled as Jodie pulled him and Mack onto the sidewalk. "Slow down, woman," Benny said.

"You guys have my voip, right?"

Mack clutched at Benny's arm to steadyhimself. "Jesus, Jo-Jo, we already told you we do."

"You say a lot of shit, Mack." Jodie hopped back into the rental car and rolled the window down. "I'll be living it up, so don't you two go worrying about me. Give me a ping if you need anything. But you might want to see if you can get a ride from here. It might take me a while to answer."

Benny looked at her over his glasses. "Because you'll be living it up with your family, right? That family you were telling me about that lived here in Oklahoma City?"

Jodie looked away for a second, then smiled at him. The thick layer of makeup that caked her face almost hid the dark, jiggling bags under her eyes. "That's right. You have such a good memory for a man your age."

Jodie gave a gleeful whoop and raced away, leaving Benny and Mack staring at each other.

"That Jo-Jo," Mack said. He turned towards the stairs to the funeral home and shook his head. "I guess we better get started."

Rows of bright carnations, daffodils, and lilies lined the stone steps. Their aroma was a calming potpourri. A somber, granite block with black lettering declared the place to be Drifting Clouds Memorial Home. Beneath the name, other letters rearranged themselves at regular intervals to display the service times. The letters had the appearance of being carved into the granite. Whatever digital display or projector that created them was hidden. Benny and Mack watched until the sign displayed the service for which they were here.

Services for Dakota & Zane Penko—11am, Blue Suite.

Benny swallowed back a sob. There was no reason to hope there'd been a mistake. He'd always prided himself on accepting what he couldn't change and moving on. But each step forward, each reminder of what today was about, weighed on his heart. Benny had never been a diver, but he'd seen documentaries explaining how the pressure and darkness increased with depth. That's how Benny felt as he plodded up the steps, like a diver sinking into heavy darkness.

Beside him, Mack was pulling himself up step-by-step with the railing. Mack, like Benny, wore slacks and a jacket that had once passed for stylish. Fashion was something Benny left forandrogynous designers and teenagers in chat rooms. Normally, he took a curmudgeonly pride in being threadbare and suitably out-of-date. Looking at how he and Mack were dressed now though, Benny felt a streak of shame. Dakota and Zane deserved better.

Mack stopped after a few steps, already panting. "Jesus, you'd think they'd have some sort of escalators for us old folks."

"Or some of those drone chairs," Benny said. "You have one in-flight failure and everyone stops using them."

Mack nodded and began climbing again. "Hey, Benny. I wanted to ask you something."

"Oh good."

"Back at the station, you told that putz your name was Benedict. I thought Benny was short for Bernard."

"Once again, you thought wrong. My dad was a history buff and liked Benedict. He figured the stigma of Mr. Arnold's betrayal had faded enough to make it popular again."

"Benedict. Benedict." Mack repeated the word as if tasting it. "Been-a-dick? Been-dick? I think it suits. I see why you prefer Benny, Been-a-dick."

Benny glared at Mack and the other man's smile faded. "Can you just leave me the fuck alone, Mack? For today at least? I'm going to put my girl in the ground, in case you forgot."

Mack looked down at his feet and took the next step. "Yeah, right. Sorry, man."

Benny waved a hand at Mack and started climbing again. The replacement cane was very light, but it was as uncomfortable as it was inelegant. The flat handle pressed into the meat of his hand between the thumb and forefinger with every step. And the more reluctant he was to use the cane to support his weight, the worse his hip throbbed.

Halfway up, Benny put his hands on the small of his back and pushed his hips in small circles. He felt bad about jumping on Mack for teasing him about his name. It was Mack's nature, and Benny felt childish using his personal tragedy to shut his friend down. Deciding he needed to apologize, Benny turned to speak to Mack. Before he could get any words out, he noticed Mack was wearing his tattered, bulldog ball cap.

"Take that damned thing off."

"What?" Mack squinted at Benny and cupped a hand behind his ear. When Benny pointed at the hat, Mack shook his head.

"Take that ridiculous thing off," Benny said between loud pants. "Eh?"

Benny jabbed his finger at the tattered hat again. Mack shrugged and turned back to his climb.

Being short of breath, Benny paused to rest to get enough wind in him to yell at Mack. When he raised his cane to shake it, Benny lost his balance and nearly fell. Adrenaline shot through him. Falling at his age, especially on a set of stone steps, was dangerous. He was already near the end of his road and he didn't want to push his luck. At least he was near a funeral home with his family. Maybe they could add him to the bill and get it all done in one day.

As Benny was about to call to Mack, a voice shouted down from the top of the stairs.

"Dad! Why didn't you voip me that you were here?" Eli's face was creased in consternation as he made his way down to meet Benny.

"I know you've got a lot going on," Benny said. "I didn't want to pester you."

Eli's children, Blake and Trina, appeared at the top of the steps behind him. Blake had his mother's looks, but Trina definitely favored Eli. Though their features came from different sides of the genetic divide, they were both good-looking kids.

Trina raced down the steps. "Grandpa!"

Benny braced himself for impact against the railing and spread his arms. "It's great to see you, Tina."

Eli followed a few steps behind. "Dad, it's Trina."

Benny shook his head."Sorry, Trina."

Trina shot her father a disapproving glance. "I know who you're talking to, Grandpa." She squeezed Benny in a bear hug and stepped back to look him over.

"You're as pretty as your granny," Benny said, reaching out to pat her cheek. "Before she got so ugly, that is."

Trina gave him a playful slap on the hand. "Be nice, she's inside already."

"Is that no-good hubby of yours here?" Benny asked.

Trina shook her head. "No. He's at work in the plant in Peru and apparently aunts-in-law aren't considered immediate family."

Blake stepped forward and Benny wrapped him in a hug. "Good to see you, my boy."

Blake returned the hug and looked down at Benny with a sad smile. "Sorry about Dakota and Zane, Pappi. It's good to see you."

Benny tried to speak, but couldn't. He could only manage to pat Blake's shoulder a few times with a shaky hand. Eli reached out and took his father in his arms. A primal moan rose from Benny's throat and was echoed by Eli. The moans transformed into deep-throated sobbing as father and son clung to each other.

The strength drained away from Benny, leaving him clinging desperately to his son. The tear-blurred shapes of other people surrounded him, reaching and hugging and patting him, joining Benny in his father's lament. He couldn't make out their faces, and wasn't sure he'd remember them all even if he could. What mattered was that when he sang out his pain, they joined him.

At length the crowd dispersed, but they milled around on the steps, dabbing eyes and blowing noses. Benny pulled out his own threadbare hanky and did the same. Even after repeated rubbings and his vision clearing some, he couldn't recognize most of the people around him. Trina was nearby, dabbing her eyes delicately as women do to save their makeup. Eli and Blake each had an arm over Benny's shoulders.

After wiping his lenses on a clean corner of his handkerchief, Benny squinted around again to see who he could recognize. He hoped to avoid eye-contact with anyone whose name he couldn't remember but looked like they wanted to talk. There was Mack stooped over the railing on the opposite side of the steps, tucking a rag into his pocket. Benny slipped free from Eli and Blake, and walked to Mack.

"You OK, Benny?" Mack asked.

"Yeah." Benny scanned the crowd and saw the warmth and sympathy on the faces he couldn't remember. He nodded. "Yeah."

"You got a real nice family."

"Thanks," Benny said. "I'm pooped. Want some help up?"

Mack shook his head, then took a long look at the top of the steps. "Well, maybe. You know, I mean, if someone doesn't mind."

Benny turned to Eli. "This is my friend Mack from the ward. Would someone mind helping us up the steps?"

"FYI, Pappi," Blake said as he shook Mack's hand, "there's an elevator around the corner."

"Fucking figure," Mack said.

The smile slid off Blake's face. He motioned to some children sitting on the nearby steps. If the children heard, or were bothered by, Mack's profanity, they gave no sign.

"Shit, I'm sorry." Mack grimaced. "I'm sorry, guys. I just... look... I'll just stop now."

While Benny was enjoying his friend's discomfort, he was also warmed by the honest contrition in Mack's voice. He decided not to give him a hard time.

"Our ride dropped us off here and we only saw the steps. So we did what old men do." Benny held his arm out to Eli and smiled. "We shuffled along as best as we could, grumbling the whole way, naturally. All ten steps."

Benny enjoyed the warmth of his son's hand, the strength of his arm. Though nearly sixty, Eli was still spry. It felt as if that strength wasn't merely supporting Benny, but flowing into him too.

How big a mistake had he made by agreeing to being cloistered away? Even if it was supposedly for the sake of his family. In the echo chamber of isolation, it was easy to be swayed by gloom and the twisted reasoning of the martyr. Amid the warm hands and feelings of his family, it was harder to accept his suffering, or that it was hard for them. But wasn't suffering supposed to be noble?

A dark vision of returning to Bile Street intruded like a snake at a picnic. The very thought made his stomach clench. But he'd signed it all away, three times before three different DoS attorneys. There would be no take-backs or do-overs. Even if he managed to walk away, he'd never get his assets back. Benny was seeing through red-rimmed eyes exactly what had been taken—what he'd signed away—with the final stroke of that DoS stylus.

But would there have been this outpouring of tenderness and love if he'd been a daily burden to these people over the years he'd been at Bile Street? Would Dakota have resented him to her dying day? Maybe Eli and his ex had been right in telling him to sign. Benny wiped his eyes but said nothing as Eli escorted him up the steps.

When they reached the top, the doors to Drifting Clouds slid open. An androgynous-looking person in a crisp, black suit apologized profusely for someone not helping them to the elevator. The usher offered Benny and Mack wheelchairs, but they politely refused.

Soothing scents and crystalline music drifted through the main lobby. Benny's heart sank when Eli released his grip. He fought the urge to grab his son, his living child. The outburst below now embarrassed him as he thought about carrying on like an old nag. Had it been selfish to put his son through those histrionics?

Eli looked down at his father with grave eyes. "The viewing room is to the right; the caskets are closed. The room over there is also reserved for us. But you need to prepare yourself before you go in."

Benny squinted at the door, then at Eli. "What's in there?"

"Mom."

9. Farewell, Fair Valkyrie

B enny looked back and forth between the doors. He felt as if he was in one of those logic puzzles where he was supposed to deduce which door was telling the truth. The truth of this riddle was that both doors were losers. Instead of figuring out cryptic hints, he had to decide which heartbreak to face first.

The day had barely started and it was already a roller coaster. Waking with the realization of what was to come. Then realizing how long it had been since seeing his family. Mack, of course, had to be an asshat and tease him about his name. He hadn't cared about the taunting; Benny was too old for that. It was Mack's complete lack of regard for what Benny was going through.

Then came the high and low and high of that scene on the steps outside. He was already drained and he'd just stepped into the funeral home. Pain—deep and dark—waited for him behind each door.

Benny could escape the viewing room to recover from the horrible truth of the caskets. But once Rose sank her harpy's claws into him, she wouldn't let go. If he ran from her, if for no other reason than decorum's sake, she'd follow and attack again. She couldn't break his heart—they'd been enemies too long. Rose would piss him off and probably embarrass him, but he didn't give a shit about her. She was just some crazy, old bitch that he used to know. There were too many open wounds today and he didn't need her opening any more.

"The food's in there too, Dad," Eli said with a rueful grin. "If that helps."

Mack visibly cheered at the mention of food and began fluttering his bushy, old eyebrows towards the food door. Benny sat in a nearby chair. It was a classical Queen Anne with sloping arm rests and not so comfortable as to invite visitors to nap.

Benny looked at Mack. "You just ate."

"Continental breakfasts ain't what they used to be," Mack said.

Benny shook his head. "Eli, I need a minute. Can you take Mack to the grub, please? It really is better for everyone if his mouth is full. He can't talk as much that way."

Mack's wrinkled face parted in a smile and he gave Benny two thumbs-up. "Ain't that the truth."

"Sure." Eli smiled and led Mack through the door. The aroma of fried chicken wafted into the lobby and set Benny's mouth to water. But even that temptation didn't help his indecision.

Family and friends wandered by, chatting as they approached. Those guests that recognized Benny passed in uncomfortable silence or paused to offer a hasty handshake or pat on the shoulder. Trina knelt next to Benny's chair and took his hand.

"Dad sent me to see how you were doing."

Benny patted her knee. "I'm all right. Just thinking." He tried rolling the metal cane between his hands, but it didn't feel right. It was too cold, too metallic. Lifeless.

"Where's your other cane?" Trina asked. "That one Aunt Dakota gave you."

Benny glanced away as he lied. "I, uh, forgot it back in the hotel. Would you take me to the viewing room, Tina?"

"Sure." Trina helped Benny to his feet and put her arm through his. She opened the door and led him into the viewing parlor.

The air inside was thick with the aroma of coffee-breath and perfume. There were weeping eyes and the occasional trumpet of a blown nose. The murmur of conversation was subdued and congenial.

Sarah Anderline clucked after her toddler triplets, shooting her husband, Jeff, a dirty look. Jeff was completely oblivious to his wife and children as he and a cousin Benny thought was named Miguel discussed the season's performance of the Oakland Penguins. He recognized them but couldn't remember their relationship.

Benny chuckled and it was as if a gong sounded to quiet the room. All faces turned towards him as the room grew silent and still. The crowd parted to open a sinuous path leading to where two polished caskets lay on raised platforms.

As he reluctantly shuffled forward, Benny tried to acknowledge the kind words and sympathetic touches from those around him. It was hard, as his attention was focused on the caskets. He clutched Trina's hand harder.

Photos of Dakota and Zane stood on their respective caskets in digital frames around two feet tall. Benny recognized the pictures from his own album. Dakota always made sure to include him on photo posts and send files when they got professional family shots. These were good, smiling, wholesome pics. A perfect counterpoint to the smashed bodies in the boxes below.

A choked sob escaped Benny as he stepped next to his daughter's casket. The strength left him and he felt Trina's arms wrap tightly around him. A chair appeared from the crowd and Trina sat him down. Her warm hands rubbed wide circles on his back as he rested his head on the casket.

The wood felt cool on his cheek and was polished to a mirror finish. A large wreath stood between the caskets, adorned with photo cubes, printed pictures, and other small mementos. Hot tears rendered them unrecognizable blurs to Benny.

The silence in the room grew heavier as he sat leaning against Dakota's casket. Even the Anderline triplets had been captured and subdued by their parents.

Benny's voice caught in his throat as he spoke. "I'm sorry to be such a damn drama queen, Tina."

Trina hugged him around the shoulders. "Don't be. You're her daddy. Take all the time you need."

Benny wondered if Rose had been in here yet and if she'd carried on like he did. She was always one for the drama. If she'd been shown an ounce of compassion, Rose would have played it to the hilt. And she would have been shown compassion like he had. Not that the bitch deserved it.

Even though he earnestly hated Rose, it didn't feel right to think that way about her. Not today. Whatever else she was, Rose was Dakota's mother and Zane's granny. Thinking that way, it seemed she did deserve a display of courtesy and sympathy. Still, he wouldn't be able to give it to her. Fuck her. Silent civility would be the best he could manage.

Benny leaned forward on his cane and pushed to his feet. He kissed Dakota's picture, leaving tears and a string of snot. "Goodbye, darling. I miss you already, Valkyrie Bennysdottir," he whispered. "Ride that cold wind to Valhalla."

Next he shuffled over and gazed at Zane's picture, though he found no words for him. In truth, he hadn't known him as well as a good grandfather should have. Not that he was a good grandfather, but now he wished he had been. Benny patted the casket where he imagined his grandson's head would be. When he turned away, Eli, Trina, and Blake were standing nearby, weeping. Blake wiped Dakota's digital frame with a handkerchief and tucked the rumpled cloth into his pocket.

Benny met their gazes and blew his nose. "I'm hungry."

10. Mouth Closed, Please

Benny watched in disgust as Mack, sitting across the table, unceremoniously shoved gobs of fried everything into his face. It was almost enough to make Benny lose his appetite. Almost. If he'd had to watch himself stuffing his face, as he was now doing in a similar fashion, it might be too much.

The pile of plates next to Mack was proof that he'd had a head start over Benny. Though priding himself at not being picky, Benny sat in absolute bliss as the fried chicken meat melted in his mouth and the skin crunched deliciously between his teeth. Nothing he'd eaten in the ward tasted so grand.

Mack paused from his shoveling and finger licking long enough to say, "I hate this." He reached out like a predatory sea creature and snapped the last fry from his plate and devoured it.

Benny nodded towards Mack's stack of plates. "Those dead soldiers say otherwise. But you can stop whenever you want."

Mack shook his head and wiped his face with a grease-stained napkin that did little good. "No, no. This stuff is the sh... bomb. I hate it because it makes me think of how much the food on Bile Street sucks."

Benny answered with an agreeable grunt since his face was now stuffed with food again. It didn't seem reasonable to interrupt his chowing down for something so trivial as agreeing with Mack.

The familiar feeling of ants crawling over his neck and ears made Benny's stomach clench. His appetite left him and he wanted to drop the chicken strip on the plate, but he wasn't going to give her the satisfaction of knowing she'd ruined his meal. He looked around and quickly found Rose. She stared back at him without emotion.

"Your old lady?"

When Mack spoke, Benny realized he'd been staring. And a few other people were staring at him. He turned in time to see Mack re-arranging the mushy remains of a half-chewed biscuit in his mouth. "That's her. I'm surprised she hasn't been over to shriek at me."

"She was asking your boy where you was at earlier, but she didn't seem like she was looking for trouble."

Benny snorted. "She's not done playing the victim yet. Rose is always calmest right before the shit-storm."

It had been years since they'd seen each other. Despite the discomfort, Benny looked back at her. He knew better than to show fear.

Rose was dressed in a fine, green gown; pearls drooped down from her turkey-wattle neck. An ostentatious jewel sparkled from a ring on her middle finger. Despite the show of wealth—and Benny was sure that it was a show—Rose suffered the depredations of her eight decades as much as he did. Her rigid posture couldn't hide the stoop in her back, and herhair had grown thin enough to show the scalp beneath. Makeup caked her face, but still managed to look classy, though it failed in its ultimate goal of hiding anything. Rose was as sour-faced as always, maybe more so.

Rose finally broke eye contact, thanks to a passing relative who stopped to chat with her. Benny turned back to his plate, willing his appetite to reassert itself.

Mack let out a long, soft belch and blew it towards Benny. "Can't live with them, can't kill them."

Benny let the ancient bromide and the belch go without reply. "I wasn't the best husband, but she got me back plenty. You know, she's the real reason I ended up on Bile Street."

"What?" Mack sputtered, dropping a slobbery green bean from his mouth. He was now staring with jaw dropped at Rose, exposing his chewed food to whoever happened to look his way.

Benny grimaced and looked away. "Geez, close your piehole, dude. No one wants to see your cud. Anyway, we both went to the DoS counselor and all that. Not being a burden sounded good to me. Rose and I talked about it for a long time and agreed—I thought—to go through with it. Eli was all for it, but not Dakota. She was dead set against it.

"Zane was a couple of years old, and with my bad hip, and Social Security gone..." Benny shrugged. "I didn't want to cause Dakota any more trouble, since she'd be the one to take care of me when it finally came to it."

"What about Eli?" Mack asked before resuming his feeding frenzy.

"I don't know. Maybe he really thought it'd be a good idea to sign up. I can't say he was pushing it so he wouldn't have to take care of me. I mean, the DoS sold the program up pretty well. When it came time to sign over my retirement and pension, I did. She didn't. Now she shows up fancy and I live in a shoe box."

"You should still thank her," Mack said with a smile. "If not for her, you'd have missed out on the joy of knowing me!"

"I could only thank her properly for that by bashing her head in with a shovel. But like you said, you can't kill them. Even in Oklahoma."

"You hurt my soul when you say things like that, Benny," Mack said. "You think she did it on purpose to get you? Or she really get cold feet?"

Benny stared into the distance and finally shrugged. "I don't know. I've thought about it some, which is to say I had imaginary conversations with her where she admitted it and I called her names."

Mack snorted in laughter, but thankfully kept his food from flying out. "Why not just ask her?"

"I'm afraid she'd tell me the truth."

Mack considered the answer and nodded.

Eli, Trina, and Blake wound their way through the crowd and slid in next to the old men.

"Why, Grandpa," Trina said, taking in the mess with an amused smile, "don't they feed you guys?"

"Not like this, darling," Mack answered. "Uncle Samantha don't cook so good."

"It's been a long trip, that's all." Benny didn't want to worry his family, even if Mack was right. Benny overtly stared at Mack, hoping he'd take the hint.

Mack stared back and shrugged. "Now what?"

Eli cleared his throat. "The service is about to start. Dad, you're right up front. Mack, we can squeeze you in up front. It'll be tight. Sorry, we weren't expecting you."

"No, no," Mack said, finally leaning back from his food. "This is family time—I'll find a place in the back."

Eli nodded. "Thanks. Dad, did you talk to Mom?"

"No, thank God," Benny said. "You'd have heard the shrieking."

"She was supposed to talk to you about the service. In her will, Dakota requested that the service only be a few people sharing stories. She especially wanted you and Mom to speak."

Benny looked around with the intent of giving her that look of disgust he knew pissed her off, but she had already left the room. "Even when she's not a screaming harpy, she's still playing bullshit games."

"She's pulling that shit today?" Mack said. "Jesus, Benny. That stinks like a fat German's fart."

Benny rolled his eyes, while Eli and Blake gave perfunctory chuckles. But Trina's eyes and mouth grew wide and she started cackling uncontrollably. A flush tinted her skin from the neckline of her dress to the tips of her ears. When she noticed people watching, Trina tried unsuccessfully to squelch her laughter by pressing her hands over her mouth. Far from helping, it transformed her cackle into a snorting, honking horselaugh. Trina's ears were soon burning red and, with no other obvious options to regain her composure, she grabbed a handful of napkins from the bar and buried her face in them.

Muffled chortling and gasping continued to escape from Trina, her shoulders bouncing in such a way that Great-Aunt Florence came over and patted her back in consolation, cooing, "There, there."

Benny looked over his glasses at Mack and shook his cane.

"What? It's my fault she's got a good sense of humor?" Mack added, "Unlike her gramps."

Trina lifted her mascara-streaked face from now-splotched napkins, waving her hand as if trying to banish the envisioned fart that had set off her laughing spasm currently splitting her sides. Mack looked on with a satisfied smile, nodding. When the onlookers realized Trina was laughing instead of crying—except for Florence who was gossiping about the poor girl to her own daughter—they continued their slow milling to the service.

Benny favored Trina with an uncertain smile before turning to Eli. "Is your mom speaking?"

"She said she would." Eli raised an eyebrow at his daughter, who was now gasping loudly for breath.

"I guess I'll talk then." That made it sound as if Benny was only going to speak because that bitch Rose was going to. Not only did the way he'd made it sound bother him, it also bothered him that it might be true. "I need to use the bathroom. See you inside."

⇒◉⇐

MACK LIKED BENNY'S family. They were nice to him, even if they were only being polite because of the occasion. But he didn't think it was that. For a moment, it made him wish he'd had a larger family. Then again, it would also mean that more kids would have had a shitty dad. What he'd put Ricky through was unforgivable. As it was, he'd only ruined one person's life. Maybe two.

Trina managed to contain herself to a case of the giggles by the time Benny made it to the door. Her father and brother still eyed her curiously, but Benny was beaming. He enjoyed making people laugh, even if it didn't always turn out that way. Trina was a looker, and she looked even better smiling. She had obviously not gotten her looks from Benny.

She took a deep breath, pulled a compact from her slim purse and began doing some damage control on her makeup. "You know, Mack, I asked where Aunt Dakota's cane was. He said he left it at the hotel."

"I wondered about that too," Eli said. "I haven't seen Dad without that cane in years."

Blake picked at a biscuit and nodded. "Yeah, it'd be like him forgetting his leg. Leave your makeup alone, you're supposed to look like you've been crying."

"Not yet, I'm not," Trina said. The levity fell from her expression like a stone mask and when she turned back to Mack, he leaned back involuntarily.

Mack squinted. "What?"

"Do you know what happened to Grandpa's cane?"

Mack stared at her for a second before looking at Eli and Blake. They wanted to know, too, but not as much as she did. He looked back at Trina. "Technically, he's right. It's back in the hotel."

Trina looked over her compact at him and cocked an eye. She wore the same accusatory expression Benny used when looking over his glasses. "Technically?"

"Look," Mack said, "he wouldn't want me to say anything even if I wanted to. You know I have to go back and live with him until one of us dies, right?"

"Do you know what happened to the cane?" Trina asked. Mack looked at Eli, Blake, and Trina in turn again. "Why, yes, yes I do."

11. A Bitch by Any Other Name

The caskets now sat on an old, teakwood dais in one of Drifting Cloud's sanctuaries. The memorial display had been moved between them and soft light from recessed ceiling lamps shone from above.

Benny sat in the middle of the front row between Trina and Eli, while Rose sat on the other side between Eli and Blake. The din of conversation died into silence, except for the occasional cough or sob, when the funeral director took his place on the dais.

"Ms. Dakota asked that her friends and family speak on her behalf, sharing a memory as part of the service." He smiled down at Benny. "Would her father like to share first?"

Benny leaned onto his cane and stumbled forward. Each step seemed to grow heavier, as if Dakota were willing his feet not to approach, to not say the final farewell. He stopped at the steps of the podium, uncertain if he had the strength to carry on.

Trina rose and put her arm around his shoulder. "Do you need help up?"

Benny was too breathless to speak and simply nodded. Trina took his arm and they climbed the few steps together carefully. At the top, the director offered an arm and helped Benny to the mic.

Hot tears rendered the world beyond the podium into an indeterminate, quivering blob. Benny was glad; it was easier to speak to the faceless nebula than the expectant and hurting people who might be looking to him for comfort. The joke would be on them.

Benny took a deep breath. "First, thank you all for coming. It's a heart-warming reminder that Dakota and Zane weren't only special

to me. Second, thanks for the warm welcome and sympathies. It's...
well, I'll just say I've missed y'all.

"Leave it to Dakota to make people talk about her." Soft laughter
rolled through the audience and Benny smiled. "The story that
comes to mind is that of my little girl's battle with the couch dragon.
She'd taken an interest in fairies and unicorns and the like as many
little girls do. But she'd gotten it in her head that she was going to be
a Valkyrie, a divine shield-maiden, when she graduated high school.

"Well, this little Valkyrie would run around wearing this winged
helmet and sword she'd made from cardboard and most of my duct
tape, crying, 'It's a cold wind to Valhalla!' I came home one night and
she's made this dragon out of the couch cushions and every other pillow in the house she could grab. It's all covered with blankets and
she'd waited by the door until I got home so I could watch her slay
the patchwork monster."

Benny had to pause at the tickle arising in his throat. The director
handed him a small bottle of water and waited, smiling, until Benny
handed it back. "Well, she swings with all she has and takes off the
dragon's head, which happens to be my pillow. That pillow flies into
her mother's favorite lamp, knocking it over so it lands on her mother's favorite latte mug, which shatters and spills all over her mother's favorite peace-and-love daily devotional. And her mother immediately ignores everything about peace and love the book had to
say and whups Dakota's hide all the way to Valhalla. All this, and I
haven't even taken my jacket off yet."

Warmlaughter rose from the mourners. Benny's vision cleared
enough to see Rose glaring at him, but he didn't care. That story was
about Dakota, not his ex. Not that he'd mind exactly if it happened
to stick in her craw. He still couldn't work up any sympathy for the
bitch, but he wasn't trying to hurt her.

"She'd learned a little about Norse names and insisted on being called Valkyrie Daddysdottir. I got to be Thor sometimes and that was pretty cool."

Benny raised the hospital cane over his head like the hammer Mjölnir. How inadequate it felt for the task compared to his dear, ruined treasure left in the hotel. He hated it. This piece of trash wasn't worthy to be sending his daughter off. "Ride that cold wind to Valhalla, my baby Valkyrie." His voice broke into high-pitched, staccato sobs. "Ride alongside your brave son."

Tears once again blinded him. When Benny hesitated at the steps, Trina hugged him and took his hand to escort him back to his seat.

The funeral director waited until Benny was seated. "Thank you. I'm quite sure Dakota would have loved that. I like to think of these stories as spoken memento mori. It's easy to understand why the practice has become so popular, and why Dakota chose to have her funeral conducted this way. I'm sure we'll hear many great stories from friends and family today." He turned to Rose. "Would the mother like to share?"

Rose broke down crying into Eli's shoulder, shaking her head. "I can't, I just can't," she sobbed over and over.

Benny leaned forward and looked at Rose. She was going to back out again. Despite the years of riding his ass about never being there for the kids, it was Rose who always flaked out at the last minute, leaving him to clean up her messes and fulfill her commitments.

Eli stroked his mother's hair. Benny half-expected some of it to pull free, despite Eli's gentleness. "It's OK, Mom. You don't have to."

"No, of course not, ma'am," the director said with sympathy. "We're not here to cause more discomfort on an already painful day. Next on the list of those who wanted to share..."

Rose looked at Benny, her rheumy eyes growing steely, almost haughty. Benny's stomach clenched and his bowels grumbled. Why had he kept staring? He hadn't meant to, but she'd seen him and he knew that look all too well. Rose's claws were coming out.

Leaning close to Eli, she whispered something too low for Benny to hear. Eli rubbed her back and lifted his hand to get the funeral director's attention. "Mom's changed her mind."

"Wonderful," the director said. "Whenever you're ready."

Eli guided Rose carefully up the steps. The stoop in her back was more pronounced as she climbed, but when she took her place at the podium, she stood tall and locked eyes with Benny. It was all he could do to keep from looking away. Rose cleared her throat and favored the audience with a hard smile.

"Here it comes," Benny muttered. Trina put an arm around him and pulled him close.

"When I think of how precious my beautiful daughter is... was," Rose said, "I think of the first time I thought she was going to have a funeral. One of the many times her father came home drunk—he was a cop at the time, you see, and was drunk a lot, you see—me and the kids were already in bed and he passed out on the couch. Again." She gave a dry, mirthless chuckle.

"That cunt," Benny whispered. He clenched his teeth but refused to look away, if for no other reason than to avoid seeing how many people would be staring at him in shocked disapproval. Trina squeezed him.

"The next morning," Rose continued, "Dakota's father was still passed out, but Dakota beat me out of bed—she was always such an early riser, that girl—and she came running into my bedroom, playing cops and robbers. Waving her father's gun around, of course, pointing it this way and that, yelling, 'Bang, bang!'

"I'm still half-asleep and it took me a second to realize what was going on. When I did, I started yelling for her to put her father's gun down. Dakota realized she was in big trouble—despite what you may have heard, *I* very rarely screamed at the children. She ran away and hid the gun before I could get untangled from the sheets." Rose waved her hands playfully, pantomiming the struggle to escape her sheets.

"Anyway, I tried to wake her father and of course he won't wake up. I had to threaten to beat Dakota's butt before she would tell me.Guess where? Why, under her brother's pillow of course! Talk about the good times."

Rose's upper lip curled a fraction of an inch and Benny looked away. He knew that look too. The room had gone completely silent, except for a group of teenagers trying to mask their glee at the drama. When Benny looked at them, they were all madly tapping on their voips. Rose's video was probably already on the SafetyNet.

The director cleared his throat. "Yes, well, thank you. It's important to keep in mind that not all memories are pleasant memories. And as long as they are presented respectfully, they are welcome." The man's professionally pleasant smile never faltered and he asked for the next speaker.

There were many speakers. Eli was next. Then Trina, and Blake. Some spoke eulogies fit for a Baptist preacher in timbre—and length. Others popped up to pray or say bye. Friends from school and work spoke of her kindness, and some joked about her ribald side. Zane's father recalled teaching Zane to ride and praised Dakota's charity even after their divorce. It pleased Benny to know that Dakota hadn't grown up like her mother.

The only speaker who caught Benny's full attention, aside from Rose, was Lilly Banks. She was a cute, button-nosed girl who introduced herself as Zane's first girlfriend. This brought gentle laughter from the crowd. She finished by saying she'd also be his last girlfriend, which brought a round of weeping.

Benny hardly heard it. He had retreated from Rose's attack to a place in time where a little Valkyrie swung on his arms and bounced in his lap, hugged him tightly around the neck and shouted "Daddy!" when he got home from work. When he wasn't in that place, his blood boiled and his pulse thundered in his old ears. So he kept going back. Benny wondered if he was remembering scenes that actually happened, or if he was merely revisiting a muddled conglomeration of what his mind could scrape together. It didn't matter. Any where, any when, was better than here.

At length, Eli led him from the service. The rest of the day was a blur, and he was eventually all cried out. The tears didn't come when the two bio-wrapped bodies were taken from the caskets and lowered into the burial garden out back. The tears didn't come when two dour gravediggers covered the bodies with nutrient-rich soil. The tears didn't come as the attendees offered up more songs and prayers and low moans of sorrow.

Benny wasn't even moved by the well-wishers and their heartfelt condolences as they filtered by on their way back to the world of the living, leaving him alone. Did it say anything about him that his sorrow had been replaced with a heavy fatigue? Benny worried that it meant, deep down, he was a selfish prick. If so, it was too late to change now. He wanted the day to be over, and to go back to his hotel and curl up under the blankets. If only Mack would leave him alone...

"I think this bench is more comfy than the chairs inside," Mack said. He took a seat next to Benny. "You OK?"

Benny chuckled.

"What?"

Benny shook his head. "Nothing. Yeah, I'm OK. I think. Everything's twirling and... it's been a hell of a day."

"It ain't over yet, you know. You still got family you could be hanging out with. I just voiped with Jo-Jo. I've got to get back to the hotel tonight, but she said you could stay with family if they're willing to act as your guardians and get you to the station by 10am."

Benny glanced sidelong at Mack. "Did she come up with that or did you ask her?"

Mack shrugged.

"When you aren't being a wart-covered dick, you're pretty all right, Mack."

Mack grinned. "Well, I wouldn't want to spoil you by being such a good Samaritan all the time. Hey!"

Benny pulled himself to his feet using Mack's shoulder for purchase. "Thanks, Mack."

Mack dismissed Benny with a wave of his liver-spotted hands. "You got a real nice family. Shame not to enjoy them while you can."

Benny spent the evening with Eli, Blake, Trina, and their growing generations. They treated him to a fine meal at Maxwell's and stayed up late in their hotel lobby reminiscing. Benny's knees ached from the young ones crawling between and over them, treating him like a jungle gym, calling "Pappi!"

Whenever their parents tried to shoo the children away from him, Benny shooed the parents away instead. He watched Eli and Trish and felt suddenly jealous; they were obviously such better parents than he ever was.

"Did that really happen, Grandpa?" Trina asked. "About the gun?"

"Trina," Eli said, frowning at his daughter. "Drop it. I don't remember any of that."

"Well, you were supposedly asleep," Blake said.

"It's all right," Benny said. "I wasn't the besthusband or dad. I had a few years where I drank too much. And to be honest, I don't remember that happening at all. But it could have. Maybe even probably did. Rose never lies when the truth will hurt more."

"You were passed-out drunk," Blake said. When he saw Eli's glare, Blake added, "According to Granny anyway. You wouldn't remember it."

Eli scooped up a little girl with blond curls who had fallen asleep on the floor. "It doesn't matter. Your grandma only said that to embarrass Grandpa."

"That's exactly right," Benny said. He gave a prodigious yawn and shook his head. "She's earned the right to hate me as much as I hate her, I suppose. I guess she didn't like my story so she wanted to get back at me. She always—"

"Dad, don't," Eli said. "Not tonight. I'm going to run this one to the room and put her in bed. Be right back."

Benny watched the golden curls bounce on Eli's shoulders as he hauled the little girl from the lobby. His son was right. Rose wasn't going to ruin this night for him.

He didn't recall dozing off, who got him into the fold-out bed in the room, or the name of the great-granddaughter cuddled up next to him. But he did know he didn't want to get up.

"Come on, Grandpa," Trina sang, shaking him a bit harder than last time. "You've got a train to catch."

Pain shot up from his hips and knees as he rolled over, causing him to groan. It was a small price to pay for the pleasure of spending time with his family. The hustle and bustle of herding children had been a frustrating chore when Benny was a young parent. Enough time had passed to allow it to bloom into a fond memory, made all the more vivid by the ballet unfolding in front of him.

When the family was packed, dressed, and finished using the small bathroom, Eli shoved Benny into his car. At the train station, Benny was ushered in by his familial horde. Mack and Jodie stood inside, smiling.

"I thought you might have taken my advice and skipped town," Jodie said. "I know I almost did. Here are your things from the hotel."

Mack scanned the family and patted Benny on the shoulder. "You should, you know. Skip town, I mean. Head home with these nice folks and forget about Bile Street."

Benny smiled wistfully and turned to see Eli, Blake, and Trina all whispering urgently into their voips. Well, it was time to go back to their busy lives now that Benny was back with his handler. He couldn't blame them. And he had new memories of his family that he wouldn't trade for anything.

Trina muttered a curse she obviously believed was inaudible to everyone else and thrust her voip into her pocket. She shrugged at Eli. Casting a furtive glance at Benny, she saw him watching her. She gave him a tight smile and a quick wave. A loud voice rang from the door and Trina's expression melted in relief.

Trina's son Willie slid to a breathless stop and handed her a long, gift-wrapped box. "I've got it. You can all stop blowing up my voip now."

"Well answer it for a change then, boy," Eli said. He glanced up at the clock. Benny followed his look and saw two of the ancient LEDs were dark but the time was still readable. It was almost time to go. "Mack told us about your cane, Dad."

Benny glared at Mack, who found a nearby Department of Safety poster to study. Jodie held up the DoS travel bag with the shattered remains of Benny's old cane.

Eli put his hand on Benny's shoulder. "I know it can't replace the one Dakota gave you. But we all chipped in to get you a new one. From us. It even has a DoS pre-safety approval chip installed."

Hands shaking, Benny took the box Trina held out to him. He struggled with the bow until finally asking Blake for help. The family watched him breathlessly until Benny slid a richly carved, oak cane from the box.

The handle was shaped like his other cane but had intricate Celtic knotwork engraved across it for grip. The shaft of the cane was made of twisted wood, so cleverly crafted that Benny couldn't tell if it was made from a single piece or two.

Trina pointed at part of the knotwork. "It's not quite a Valkyrie, but there's an angel worked into the design to remind you of Aunt Dakota."

Benny peeled off his glasses to wipe his eyes. His vision had grown too blurry again to see it. The tiny angel looked like something from the margins of a medieval manuscript. "No. This angel will remind me of my whole family. I love each feather."

He raised his hands and his family drew closer. When Eli and Trina got close enough, Benny put his arms around them. He made sure to get Blake and Willie and everyone he could reach.

The final boarding call for Benny's train echoed through the station and Jodie began urgently waving him to hurry up. Eli started leading his father towards the security gate.

Benny turned a final time and took in his family. "I love y'all."

Jodie pushed him into the scanner, his new cane generating a cheerful bleep from the booth as it went through. The safety officers didn't even turn Benny's way.

He was still emotionally hungover from yesterday and this morning, and napped most of the train ride away. When not napping, Benny stared out the window, stroking his new cane and contemplating everything that had happened on the trip and whatever else popped into his head about his life. By the time Jodie dropped them back off on Bile Street hours later, his hip was throbbing.

Benny and Mack stood staring at the dark, uninviting micro-homes awaiting them. They looked even smaller somehow, maybe smaller than the train compartment they'd spent all day in. How long had he been shoved away in those shitty little closets? There was no way to live in one of those now. The dying light cast a gloomy pall over the entire neighborhood—if it could even be called that.

"Hey, Benny?"

"Yeah?"

"Thanks for taking me. It was real nice to meet your family. They're good peeps."

Benny leaned on his cane. "Yes, they are. And you're welcome."

The two old men in hats continued to stand and stare glumly, as if afraid going inside might erase the experience of the last two days. A nearby street LED flickered to life with an unsteady buzz. A candy wrapper danced down Bile Street in a chilly gust.

"Hey, Mack?"

"Yeah?"

"I hate this fucking place."

12. Benny Gets Another Ride

Benny sat on Mack's porch, rolling his new cane back and forth. In his heart it had replaced Dakota's cane, even though it wasn't as well made as his old one. He knew Dakota's had been custom made and his new one was a stock model. It was a well-made stock model; he was embarrassed about how much it cost when he'd looked it up. Eli, Trina, and Blake hadn't had the time to get a custom cane made. They'd gone above and beyond with what time was available and he loved them for it, and loved their cane.

It seemed Benny hadn't worked out all his tears. February had closed out and March was nearly through and he still had the occasional sobbing fit. But he'd overcome his grieving enough to at least start thinking about Mastiff. His friend still hadn't spoken to him since being invited to the funeral. And now he wasn't talking to anyone.

The comment about Benny not going to Mastiff's daughter's funeral weighed heavily on him. Surely if he'd known, he'd have gone. Benny interrogated other friends, but no one knew anything about it and eventually told Benny in no uncertain terms to leave them alone.

"I'm telling you, Benny," Mack said, "talk to Jo-Jo. Get on the DarkNet if you can't find anything on SafetyNet. See if you can't dig up anything on old Blubba-licious. At least see if his daughter died and we really did miss it. Might start with finding his real name."

"Why don't you search, Mack?" Trance asked as he stretched on his lawn. Recently tilled dirt marked the beginning of his perennial gardening efforts.

"Because personally, I don't give a shit if *Ass-stiff* never talks or games with me again. And if I have to pay Jo-Jo, I'm not going to waste it on his sorry ass. I'd rather watch the crap on the SafetyNet."

"Pay Jodie how?" Benny asked.

"I've told you a thousand times." Mack pinched his forefingers and thumbs and jabbed them at Benny as he continued. "We don't know what she'll want and we ain't supposed to tell anyways. It's part of our contract. I don't want to get Jo-Jo in trouble."

Trance adopted a perfect tree pose. "Or pissed."

"Or pissed," Mack agreed. "Look, stop being such a pussy and fucking ask her. She ain't gonna ask for something you can't give and she ain't gonna turn you in." He hiked a thumb towards Mastiff's house. "Or let it go and ignore that prick. Whatever you decide, stop moping about it like a heart-broke school girl for the love of God."

Benny stared over his glasses at Mack.

"I hate to agree with the Big Mack," Trance said, "but he's right. You need to try to fix it or let it go. It's obviously bringing you down, man. Life's too short to worry about things, or people, out of your control. It's even shorter at our age."

"Thank you," Mack said, motioning towards Trance with an open palm. "Straight from the mouth of Peace and Love, Incorporated."

Heat rolled up Benny's neck and he grunted in frustration. There was no reason not to tell him what she wanted. He had nothing of value to her, only his memory chest and the remains of Dakota's cane. And she knew as well as anyone that everyone on Bile Street had signed over their earnings and retirement to the DoS. He was too long in the tooth for any useful labor and he sure as hell wasn't going to do anything illegal for her. That he was asking her to do some illegal late-night hacking wasn't lost on him, but he wasn't willing to do anything like that yet. Though Jodie was certainly not by the book, she didn't seem like the type to run a crime ring.

He kept wondering if she wanted some sexual favors, in no small part because of the puerile gleam in Mack's eye whenever the subject came up. If so, Jodie was sick and stupid. Even if he could still do something with his pecker besides run old tea through it, her face was a powerful prophylactic.

Benny pointed his cane at Mack. "It's sex, isn't it?"

Mack threw his hands in the air and looked to the sky. "Gah!"

Trance laughed, groaned, and fell on his face. His lanky limbs seemed to collapse under him as if someone had pushed the button of a string doll.

"Whoa, whoa!" Mack said, shuffling to the edge of his porch. "You OK?"

"Yes," Trance mumbled into the grass. He slowly untangled his limbs until he was laying flat on his back. "My new move: downward falling dog."

Benny slipped his voip from his pocket. "We need to call emergency services?"

Trance grunted. "No, they will not be needed. Let me stay in corpse pose for a while."

"Is that some kinda joke?" Mack asked.

Benny put his voip away. "No. That's what that pose is called. In English anyway. It's something like *shivasteroth* in yogi or whatever. You just lay there."

Trance nodded and gave a thumbs up.

Benny looked at Mack and the worry he felt was expressed on Mack's face. They stood vigil over Trance until he rose and hobbled inside his house. With a final glance at Mack, Benny pulled out his voip again.

It was now a well-practiced motion. He'd made it a point to keep in touch with his family since the funeral. Fearful of becoming a pest or coming off as needy, Benny had previously shunned his voip. It often stayed in his dresser, battery dead, for days at a time. He still forgot about it sometimes; his martyr's habits were hard to break. He browsed for new messages and dropped the voip back into his pocket.

But now he was on the message lists of countless family members. Sometimes he found himself in conversations with people he didn't know and they were usually the most fun to catch up with. It was like those old DNA ancestry services before they'd been banned by the Department of Safety when too many people used the results to legally apply for minority oppressed status.

Benny's voip chimed in his pocket. He slid it out again and burst out laughing as he read the message on the small screen. Sharp pops came from the joints of his thumbs as he hunched over and started his response.

"Now that's just fucking rude," Mack said. "You can't laugh like that in front of someone without sharing the joke. Life's too short for that."

Benny finished his message and looked up at Mack. "Well, part of it is for you, I guess. From Trina."

Mack craned his neck towards Benny's voip. As if he could read it from more than three inches away. Benny pulled his voip away.

"What's it say?" Mack asked.

Benny held up his voip. "Farting Germans indeed."

Mack's eyes bulged and he exploded in laughter. Benny did the same and soon they were both holding their sides and rocking. Wiping at his eyes, Mack said, "I like the way she laughs. That was a good day."

Benny's laughter faded away. It had been a good day—and aheartbreaking one.

Mack carried on laughing for a moment, then glanced at Benny. His laughter stopped abruptly and he face-palmed his forehead with both hands. "Man, I'm as sorry as a shit sandwich. I didn't mean... I know... man, I'm sorry."

Benny looked at his friend and gave a half-grin. "I know what you mean. And you're right. It was a good day for the most part. A great day."

The two men sat in silence on the porch. Benny was reliving that day at Drifting Clouds Memorial as he had almost every day since. This time, he was forcing himself only to think of the warm things. Embracing his son. The fried, greasy food. The children climbing all over him.

Mastiff lumbered down the sidewalk in front of them. When Benny looked that way, Mastiff turned his nose up and away a bit more. Benny and Mack watched the big man, nose still held high, until he slammed the door of his microhome. Benny shook his head and turned to Mack, ready to speak.

Mack shoved his palm into Benny's face. "Talk to Jo-Jo or let it go."

Benny opened his mouth to speak again.

Mack looked away. "Nope." With that last word, he shuffled across the porch, into his house, and shut the door behind him.

Benny stared at Mack's door for a moment, then at Mastiff's. A minute later, Mack's door opened.

"And get the fuck off my porch." The door shut again.

Now there were two doors shut in his face. If he wanted to have any friends left on Bile Street, he'd have to resolve this issue with Mastiff. And he wasn't quite ready to give up on his friend. Had he wronged the big guy so badly? He hoped not. Benny drew his voip from his pocket and began typing.

Hey Jodie, this is Benny...

———————◉———————

BENNY STARED AT HIS door like some kid awaiting an ass-whupping when his father got home. Or like an old man waiting for the Grim Reaper. His mind had raced all day trying to figure out what Jodie's price would be. The muscles in his neck ached with tension and the room smelled of Benny's nervous flatulence.

He jumped at the gentle tap on the door, even though he'd seen Jodie's headlights through the blinds a moment ago. She was right on time. Leaning forward onto his cane, Benny stood and took hesitant steps to answer the door. He reached a trembling hand forward but couldn't seem to make it turn the knob.

Another knock on the door made him flinch.

"You shouldn't keep a lady waiting," Jodie said through the door. "I don't want to cause a scene."

Benny jerked the door open. Jodie smiled and started to speak, but he grabbed her hand and pulled her through the door. He spared a quick peek left and right, saw no one, and quickly shut the door.

"I do like an eager customer," Jodie said with a coquettish grin that was ruined by her teeth. Benny looked down at his feet. "How can I help you, Benny?"

She wore her usual drab overcoat that hung down to the top of a pair of cracked, fur-trimmed mukluks. Bright lipstick and dark eyeliner adorned her face, but not caked on as she'd worn it to whatever party she'd gone off to in Oklahoma City. While not subtle, the toned-down makeup left Benny hopeful that she didn't have some old man kink. Jodie's hair was in a frayed bun and there was barely a hint of perfume. It was easy to imagine this might turn out to be like any other business transaction, such as buying insurance or a new voip.

Benny glanced around his tiny house. "I, uh, want to get past the SafetyNet."

"Thought so. Still trying to see what's up Mastiff's ass?"

"Yes." Benny looked at her over the rims of his glasses. "Are you sure you don't know anything about that?"

"Quite sure," she said flatly. "And I'm quite sure I've already answered that one multiple times already. Anyway, once you get into the Archive, a simple search for Mastiff Barkey will get you a ton of hits. There's probably too much if you're looking for something particular."

Benny's hoary brows climbed his wrinkled forehead. "Is he famous?"

"In some circles he was. But we're getting ahead of ourselves." Jodie reached into her coat pocket and, one at a time, withdrew a small red pill, an optical thumb drive, and, finally, a small can of genuine Diet Coke. She set them on the nearby table.

"I'm not running drugs for you," Benny exclaimed in a raspy whisper.

Jodie stared at him for a second before laughing. "Chill, Benny. Listen first, talk last. Jesus. Anyway, I can get you past the SafetyNet to the DarkNet or the Archive for one hour by installing this"—she pointed to the small optical drive—"easy-to-use proxyware. And only an hour because that's how long before SafetyNet security bots detect it. I could push it a bit, but an hour is as long as I'm willing to risk.

"In return, you will take this pill, wash it down with this authentic and delicious soda"—Jodie passed her hands over the items as she mentioned them like a game show presenter—"and we will fuck to my satisfaction."

Benny gasped, got control of his breath, and slammed the tip of his cane on the floor. "I knew it!" he shouted. "I knew it was dirty sex!"

"It's not dirty," she said, frowning. "Did someone tell?"

"Those assholes wouldn't tell me a thing. Oh, I knew it had to be something bad."

"And yet you still called. I'm flattered. Well, at least they kept to their contract." Jodie looked around the place as if she'd never been inside. "Secrecy is part of our agreement, too, by the way."

"You're crazy, woman. Even if you weren't so... if you were my type, I mean, I'm a bit long in the tooth for this kind of shit."

If Jodie was offended by Benny's objections, she made no sign of it. "It's not the length of your tooth I'm interested in, but of your tool." She laughed and caressed the curves of her hips. "And that's what the red pill is for. It's an EM, an Erectus Maximus, you see. Perfectly safe and perfectly legal. Well, legal for me to buy anyway. With it, we can both get what we want. And I'll even do all the work. You only have to lie there. Nap if you want to. I'll even cover you up when I'm done. Win-win?" She gave him a lurid wink and two thumbs-up.

Benny looked at the items on the table. The red pill held his attention. Red meant danger. He'd heard of the EM pills—what a stupid name—but never imagined he'd ever see one, let alone consider using one. A tiny sparkle of blue from Mastiff's window played in the corner of Benny's glasses. Not even thinking about saving his friendship made Jodie's offer appealing.

"I normally save this sales pitch for hard bargaining, but I like you." Jodie pulled open her frumpy overcoat and the bare flesh beneath seemed to light the room. It was the body of a swimsuit model—without the swimsuit. She swung one hip out, then the other, revealing she was freshly shorn below.

Benny took in the full sight of her and felt a measure of pride that his crotch was growing tight with a long-forgotten, throbbing pressure. Jodie's body was, simply put, amazing. It was a bombshell normally covered by the bland garb of the DoS dress code and topped with a face from the Black Lagoon. A small, black cat was tattooed on her inner thigh and her belly-button was encircled with a red anarchist's "A."

"Oh my God," Benny whispered. Heat grew in his loins as he shifted his cane in a feeble attempt to cover his jutting erection.

Jodie laughed and tossed her hair, which caused her breasts to bounce. "Why thank you. I know, I know. My face could stop a clock. What can I say? It's unfair? It's from hard living?" She shrugged, jiggling her tits. I used to offer to wear a mask or a paper bag, only half-joking, but with that pill, it won't matter. Trust me. And if my mug distracts you from these marvelous tits, we can blindfold you."

Jodie shut her jacket and it felt like curtains shutting out the sun. Benny was disappointed to lose the view—and disappointed by his own lecherousness.

"If that doesn't seal the deal," Jodie said, "I don't know what will. I have an opening you can fill. You interested?"

When she smiled this time, her catastrophic teeth and wrinkled face didn't seem so disgusting. Her coat still hung open at the bottom, revealing one curved thigh and the black-cat tattoo. Benny felt his head nod in answer, though he didn't detect any conscious thought that told it to do so.

Jodie purred. "Awesome. I'll install this software. You take the pill and then you can install your hardware in my slot. Fuck, I'm funny." She slipped her coat onto the floor and kicked the mukluks into the nearest corner. When she inserted the optical thumb drive into the computer, Jodie moaned loudly. Benny stared at her as she leaned over to install the hacking program.

"Uh, you can sit down if you want." Benny didn't really want her bare business end on the chair he used for gaming, but the way her ass was waving around seemed indecent, despite what they were about to do. Jodie laughed and began rolling her pelvis in small circles. If she'd started twerking, Benny would have been pleasantly unsurprised. He popped the pill and chugged the soda, finishing with a loud belch. "Oh, excuse me. That was good."

Jodie winked at him over her shoulder. "You ain't seen nothing yet. Strip. At least down to your shorts."

Benny tossed his clothes on the floor; everything except his boxers, which seemed to highlight his raging boner. The longer he stared at her body, the more he got over the shock of her sudden nudity, the more signs of her age he noticed. Small wrinkles were visible on the creases where her shapely ass met her legs. A couple of small age spots dappled her feet. But these were trivialities compared to the package that would make most women a third of her age jealous.

"On the bed," she commanded. "The proxyware is installed and when I turn it on you'll be surfing free from Big Brother's eyes for one hour. I can see you're already turned on. I always figured you for a boxers man."

Benny went rigid as she opened his fly and his erection sprang into view. "Relax, lover," she moaned. The feel of her hand on him was gentle and smooth. With a practiced agility, Jodie straddled Benny and lowered herself onto him. She rose and fell twice before Benny jerked and grunted as he ejaculated.

"Uh, sorry," he gasped.

"No worries," Jodie said, not missing a beat. "That's what the pill is for."

Benny winced as his body was bounced beneath the impacts of her fucking. But his manhood was in the grip of a powerful chemical concoction, and Jodie's hot nethers. Despite the pain and fear of injury, Benny's little man stayed at attention.

Jodie leaned back and the speed of her bucking increased. The twirling of her breasts—they were going in opposite directions now—mesmerized Benny, as did the sexy flatness of her stomach. She'd been right: he didn't notice her face at all. Benny thought he was done for the night, but as he watched her take pleasure from him, a heat started building up again in his balls.

"Jesus," Benny moaned. "Oh, Jesus!"

Jodie massaged her breasts as she continued to bounce. "Oh, talk to me, fuck-stud. I know you want this!"

"Oh, Jesus," Benny cried. "Jesus, my hip!"

Jodie burst out laughing and slowed her pace. "Sorry," she said in a low groan. But she didn't stop. Her hips were now circling around as if trying to make Benny contact every corner inside her. She started rubbing herself, then shuddered, barked, and collapsed on top of Benny, breathless.

A moment later, she carefully got off Benny and slipped into the small bathroom. His erection still throbbed, glistening in the dim light from under the bathroom door. Fear crept over Benny; he didn't know how long the pill's effects would last. And that fear didn't soften him up.

He felt as if he'd been assaulted, which he supposed he had been in a sense. Even if it was consensual. The aches in his joints throbbed in time with his erection. But these worries and discomforts were nothing compared to the dizzying high of his orgasm. His ejaculation had been equal parts pain and pleasure. Whether the pain had been from years of disuse or some effect of the Erectus Maximus, he couldn't say. Either way, Benny couldn't remember the last time he'd been laid like that, which might say more about his failing memory than his lack of sexual escapades.

Jodie stepped from the bathroom and dressed, leaving no skin showing except her hands and face. She smiled down at him. "Don't worry, hero. You're not the first guy to enjoy fucking an ugly chick." She cut off Benny's objection with a chop of her hand and stepped to his computer. "Take a look."

Benny slipped into his undershirt and slacks, the latter effort made more difficult by his lingering erection. Jodie laughed as Benny struggled to find a comfortable position in the computer chair.

"Don't worry," she said, still smiling. "That should settle down in an hour or two. Anyway, look at your screen. The browser works pretty much like they all do, but this one has a tab for the Archive and one for the DarkNet. The Archive is really part of the DarkNet, but focuses more on captured old pages from before SafetyNet came and saved us." Jodie paused to roll her eyes.

"Anyway," she continued, "you'll find old YouTube, Facebook, WeiTang, Merrigold Friends, and pages like that stored around the world. Not every country followed DoS, so you can even find modern stuff that slipped through SafetyNet.

"The DarkNet GUI connects to a lot of actual hacker sites, non-DoS-approved messaging, and such. You might not want to wear your gaming rig to browse them. In fact, I'd completely power your visor down while doing this. There are security exploits everywhere. Of course, not everything on the DarkNet is a pirate base, but better safe than sorry."

Jodie pointed to a red button in the proxyware window. "Once you click that, the timer starts and it won't stop. It doesn't matter if you fall asleep or have to shit. At the end of the hour, or if your terminal reboots for any reason, the program erases every trace of itself and performs a root-level restart. So have paper and a pencil handy if you want to write down a net address."

"I can't cut and paste?" Benny was a gamer, not a programmer or hacker.

"It won't save," Jodie said. "Those addresses stored on your comp will get flagged by a SafetyNet audit, so they get erased too. So paste it and print it if you don't want to write it down. Be done before the bells ring, Cinderella.

"And for God's sake, keep anything you write down hidden and don't write 'Secret DarkNet addresses' across the top or something equally stupid. And I have to say that because not all my clientele are very bright, sad to say. Did you get all that, Benny?"

"Uh, yeah."

Jodie narrowed her eyes. "You don't sound very sure."

"You did just fuck my brains out. They're still scattered."

"You say the sweetest things." She reached down and rubbed his erection once. "One hour." She scooped up the thumb drive, straightened her hair, and stopped at the door.

"You'll figure it all out. We can work our arrangement three times a week in case you can't find what you're looking for tonight. Any more than that and the bots might flag us. Also, you might want to close your curtains. You wouldn't want anyone to see what you're up to." With a final, lurid wink, Jodie left.

13. Goodnight, Trance, My Boy

"So, I saw Jo-Jo come by last night," Mack called as he toddered up the ramp to Benny's porch using a dented walker. The man was grinning from ear to asshole, as Benny's dad would have said. Mack leered at Benny with the expression of the proverbial dirty old man.

Benny leaned forward and glared. "What of it?"

"What? I saw her come over, that's all."

Benny snorted and relaxed back into his seat.

"I saw her come over and over and over, stud!" Mack burst out laughing and started thrusting his pelvis forward and back.

Benny felt the heat race up his face and his clenched fists begin to shake. Mack was now grabbing his sides and gasping with laughter. "I can't believe you," Benny roared. "You, you, pervert!"

Mack leaned on the porch railing for support and wiped at his eyes. His voice was hoarse and breathless. "Relax. You know my eyes ain't so good and you bet your ass I was watching Jo-Jo, not you. What a rack, right?"

Benny jabbed his cane towards Mack. "So you *were* watching!"

"No offense there, champ, but I wasn't able to see much of you anyway, if you get my drift." Mack held up a finger and thumb with a tiny space between them. "Good thing Jo-Jo is easy to please, Millimeter Peter."

Benny put one hand to his forehead. "Aren't we a little old for jokes about dick sizes?"

"Speak for yourself, buddy." Mack leaned as far forward as the walker and his decrepit back would allow and tapped his leg below the knee. "They don't call me 'Packin' Mack' for nothing." He pushed himself up as straight as he could manage and tipped his hat at Benny.

Benny cupped his hand over his ear. "What? Fudge-Packing Mack, you said?"

Mack squinted at Benny. "Oh, so first we're too old, dick shtick, and now with the fag jokes? You fall from your ivory tower?"

Benny flipped Mack the bird and turned away. They sat in silence for several moments. Benny's teacup sat cooling, but his hands were still trembling and he didn't want to drop it. Especially in front of Mack.

"Did you find anything last night?" Mack asked at length.

"Fuck off with your jokes."

"No, tard. I mean on the computer. About Tubby?"

Benny gave Mack a sidelong glance and didn't see the usual stupid grin there that accompanied his stupid jokes. "Some. But nothing much to help our problem."

"Your problem."

"Fine, but I'll tell you one thing," Benny said. "That dude used to be ripped."

Mack's brows raised. "Really? Old Tubbylicious?"

"I shit you not." Benny mimicked flexing like a strongman, but his own flaccid muscles only jiggled like so much pudding.

Mack snorted. "Find anything about his daughter? Not that I give a fuck, mind you."

"He was some big social media celebrity back in the day." Benny cleared his throat. "To be honest, I was still in a bit of shock after..."

Mack gleefully thrust his hips back and forth again. "After the boom-boom-pow!"

"Jesus, Mack, you're a child," Benny said. "But yes. Next time I'll make sure I'm thinking clearly before clicking start."

"So, you gonna negotiate with Jo-Jo again?"

"Yeah." Benny sighed, but to his surprise it felt wistful instead of resigned. It hadn't been all that bad, after all. "I don't like the arrangement. I mean, I almost feel like I'm being forced. Or at least I feel like I don't haveany choice. And that face." Benny shuddered. "And I'll be making sure the blinds are shut next time, Mr. Pervo."

Mack snapped his fingers. "I guess I'll just have to watch the re-run."

"You better not have filmed that!"

Mack started laughing again, but the howl of an approaching ambulance stifled the laughter. The two old men stared down Bile Street as far as they could from Benny's porch. It was definitely coming their way.

"I bet it's Nanny Greene around the corner," Benny said. "I saw some medics at her place a couple days ago."

"Might be Geoff Bettney," Mack said. "Nosey Nancy Braum posted he was having trouble getting out of bed earlier today."

A door slammed behind them. Benny and Mack turned to see Trance stumble from his house and take a seat on the steps of his porch. The yogi's eyes were sunken into folds of deep purple and his whole body was quaking.

"You OK?" Benny called over the wail of the approaching ambulance.

Trance didn't answer. His head drooped down over his lap—the wide-brimmed straw hat knocked against his knees and fell in the grass. Benny called to Trance again, but could barely hear himself over the competing siren. Mack started shuffling over to Trance's yard and Benny followed.

The ambulance rolled into sight, lighting up the fronts of the microhomes and the faces of people who were already gathering to film with their voips. As Benny finally made it into Trance's yard, the ambulance rolled to a stop in front of the house.

Hieroglyph-like graffiti was scrawled above the rear wheel well. Benny wondered how long it had been there. Two medics in their DoS jumpers slid out of the cabin, looked at Trance, and strolled across the yard. Trance held out a trembling arm and one of the medics ran her datapad over his wrist. It chirped loudly after scanning the chip planted in Trance's arm. The medic scanned the screen and Benny knew she was checking to make sure the DoS admin cloud had checked all the digital boxes, dotted the digital i's, and crossed the digital t's on her medical authorization form.

"You OK?" Benny asked again once he was standing over Trance's shoulder.

The medic only looked up from her pad long enough to ask Benny to step away.

Benny patted Trance's shoulder. "They've got you now. They'll take good care of you."

"Just don't pull any shit like Jimmy did," Mack said. When he saw Benny's glare, he shrugged. "What now? You really got to get that stick out of your ass, man."

Benny stepped aside and watched the medics do their work. Mack had walked out of earshot, talking into his voip. After a minute, he dropped his voip in his pocket and stood next to Benny.

"Jo-Jo and Hannah already know," Mack said. "They got notified as soon as Trance called emergency services. He said anything?"

"I don't know if he can," Benny said. As he turned to speak, he saw Mastiff's head peeking from his door three houses down. As soon as Mastiff saw Benny, he closed the door. Benny didn't give a shit about Mastiff at the moment. As the medics finally loaded Trance into the ambulance, Benny had a feeling like a rock in his gut that Trance wasn't coming back to Bile Street.

14. A Dog Named Ugly

U nsurprisingly, the ceiling hadn't changed in the three hours Mack had been staring at it. Counting the little squares hadn't helped him sleep any more than the swigs of cough syrup he'd downed before bed. He considered logging into a game server, but he was loath to spend his precious allotment time as a way to count virtual sheep. Especially since gaming while being a bleary-eyed wreck sucked.

Even if he decided to try playing, the assholes on chat tended to piss him off, which was not useful for an old guy trying to sleep. Playing against Benny was about the best way he knew to bring old Mr. Sandman over—few people were as boring. But Benny was sleeping much better since Jo-Jo's visit and wasn't up playing late these days.

Mack chuckled. "Yeah, Jo-Jo'll do that for a fella."

He muttered a curse as he rolled out of bed. The floor was cool, and light from the flickering lamppost outside peered in around the edges of the blinds. He pulled one of the blinds down to peek at Trance's old house.

The hippy's place had been dark since the meat wagon hauled him off three days ago. A yellow DoS notice of vacancy now fluttered in the night breeze that was pressing desperately on Mack's window. He was glad he couldn't feel it.

That notice told Mack, and everyone else left on Bile Street, that Trance wouldn't be coming back. It said the old hippy was probably already dead. They'd know for sure when the DoS auditors came to clean the place out, probably tomorrow or the day after.

Something ran beneath the window.

Mack bleated in surprise and stumbled away from the window. Tripping over his own feet, he crashed into the kitchen table and barely kept from planting his face on the floor.

"Shit."

A scratching sound came from the front door, followed by the skittering of tiny claws.

"Fucking raccoons. I'm going to turn you into a nice, warm cap."

There was no way he was going to get to sleep now, so he shuffled to the front window. With a gnarled, old finger, he parted the blinds enough to glimpse the porch.

"Gotcha," he whispered. "What the fuck? Ugly Dog?"

The wretched creature on the porch looked around at the sound of its name. It trotted towards the ramp and stopped to look over its shoulder. The dog sat on the porch, wagging its tail. When Mack drew up the blinds and opened the window, Ugly Dog dropped to its belly and crawled towards the window, whining.

"Jesus, boy. I betyou're fucking hungry since Trance left. Have you eaten at all?" The dog's protruding ribs and hip bones told Mack the answer.

The mongrel had been lean, one-eyed, and mange-ridden since Mack had first seen it. One ear had been chewed off in some ancient alley fight. He assumed old Jimmy Flint had named the mutt. Ugly Dog was about the only name that fit this nasty thing. The night wind was blowing a remnant tuft of fur that clung desperately to the dog's head.

Mack shook his head. Pity wasn't usually one of his vices, but he decided to feed the dog once. For Trance's sake. "I'm probably going to fucking regret it. This one time and that's it, dog."

There was a half-eaten ham sandwich in the small refrigerator. Mack grabbed it and a sweater before opening the door. The dog licked its chops and whimpered.

Mack sniffed and wrinkled his nose. "Jesus, dog. You sure as shit ain't coming inside. Here you go, boy." He set the sandwich on the porchand watched Ugly Dog wolf it down.

The dog looked up at Mack, wagging its tail as it licked its chops again. Mack considered reaching down to pet Ugly Dog, but the raw patches of bare, scabrous skinmade him draw his hand back. Nasty. The dog began sniffing for stray crumbs.

"Sorry, buddy. No more. You don't have to go home, but you can't stay here. And I certainly ain't feeding you every night just 'cause Trance ain't coming back." Mack tugged on his sweater. "In fact, I probably fucked up big-time feeding you at all."

Ugly Dog whimpered and looked up hopefully at Mack.

"Go on, now." Mack was satisfied with his little act of kindness and was about ready to go back inside. He spoke in a kind but firm voice. "You ain't getting nothing else."

The dog stared up at Mack, wagging its tail.

"Bah!" Mack said as he turned to go inside. It was too cold and this dog was too ugly—

"Motherfucker!" he shrieked as Ugly Dog tore into his leg and pulled Mack from his feet. Mack landed hard on his elbow and was sure he heard something crack.

"Stop it! Stop it!" he screamed over and over. His legs were sprawled out through the door and on the porch. Pain raced up his leg as the dog kept jerking and tearing at his calf.

Mack caught sight of Ugly Dog's snarling, blood-lathered face and terror stole his voice. He kicked at the mutt's head. It was too feeble to do any harm, but Ugly Dog released Mack's shredded calf to snap at the kicking foot. The teeth nipped painfully into the bottom of the foot, giving Mack barely enough time to draw his legs inside.

Mack wasn't able to slam the door as he'd planned, unable to pull his legs out of the way quickly. But Ugly Dog refused to cross the threshold for some reason as it snapped and snarled from the porch.

Mack silently thanked whomever had beaten the shit out of the dog enough to make it too scared to enter a house.Pulling himself backwards on his elbows, Mack was finally able to kick the door shut. He left a bloody footprint on the white surface of the door.

With the dog's mauling teeth safely on the other side of the door, Mack's voice came back through clenched teeth. "Oh God, you fucking mutt! I'm going to kill you. I'm fucking going to fucking kill you, sonofabitch!"

Mack kicked the door again and scrambled away when he heard Ugly Dog thump into the door in answer, scratching madly to get at him. With a final jump at the door, the dog ran off barking into the night.

"Fuck me," Mack groaned. He couldn't see the extent of his injuries through the blood slick that seemed to cover everything in the cramped house. The pain in his leg was so bad he couldn't even move. He pissed his tattered jammies.

The sheer amount of blood was terrifying. Knowing there'd be a yellow flyer on his door tomorrow if he didn't get his ass moving, Mack pulled himself across the gore-slick floor. His voip was charging next to the bed. He'd have to trust himself to the fumbling hands of emergency services.

Mack hoped traffic was light tonight.

———◉———

"AND THAT IS WHY WE don't allow pets in ward housing, Mr. Francisco." Mack spoke through clenched teeth, in part from the pain and in part from the dumb bitch in front of him. "I told you it's Mack and that little shit isn't my pet." Hannah looked up from her datapad and pursed her lips. "Animal Control will be forced to euthanize it." "Good. Let me pull the fucking trigger." Mack glanced down at the red-tinged bandages around his feet and calf. They covered the eighty-two stitches all the king's horses and all the king's men had fucking needed to put old Mack together again. It would need changing soon.

"And stop tugging at that IV or they'll have to stick you again." He knew the concern in her voice was from her fear of being inconvenienced, not any compassion for him. "You'll have to be here for at least a few days from what they're telling me," she continued. "Hopefully we'll have enough time to get your place cleaned up before then." She slid her stylus into her hair and glanced at Mack's leg. "I'm sure someone will be along soon, Mr. Francisco. Good day."

"Fucking bitch," Mack muttered as the door slowly swung shut behind her. If Hannah heard, she didn't react.

An hour later, a young orderly, as chatty as a houseplant, pushed Mack to his assigned room and helped him into bed. Mack racked his brain for a real zinger to get the orderly to laugh, groan, or at least tell Mack to shut up.

Instead, Mack fell asleep.

He awoke in a new room with new bandages on his legs and a new IV port in his arm. A pretty, middle-aged nurse bustled in, downloaded his vitals to her pad, and perfunctorily asked if he needed anything. She was out the door before he even realized he'd been asked a question.

There were nine other beds in Mack's room. Each was occupied and a couple of the patients chatted with visitors sitting next to them. After Mack had offered various greetings and ice-breakers, only two people acknowledged his existence. Neither one spoke English.

"Fucking figures," he muttered, after listening to the string of foreign gibberish. His family had once spoken the gibberish generations ago. Even his own grand-pappi only knew English. As it should be.

The walls were streaked with dirt and scuffs, and the yellowed tiles of the floor were ringed by piles of dust clinging to the peeling baseboards. Two of the recessed lights in the ceiling were dark.

Each bed was equipped with a small viewing screen. Mack's had several strings of burned out pixels and EFK's initials carved into it—whoever the hell that was. He flipped through the channels and was unable to find anything of interest. The main menu had a settings and preferences screen to explore, but after it took him twenty minutes to turn off the Tagalog captions, he decided to leave the options alone.

Buried two levels down in the hospital information menu was a patient search field. He searched his own name and found it with a note to contact a staff member to arrange visitation with Mr. Francisco K. Townsend.

Despite his best effort, Mack couldn't find any patients named Dick Stroker, Minnie Cox, or Moe Lester. Seymour Butz and Richard, a.k.a. Dick, Hurts were currently in residence however. He laughed until his bed creaked and the gibberish from the other patients stopped as they stared at him.

Once he'd exhausted the list of prankish names he could think of, he started typing in the names of people from Bile Street. It sometimes made him feel bad that he wasn't more attentive to his neighbors. He didn't like any of them, but there was still a part of him that knew he should do better, even if he didn't know why.

No return came back from Trance Adrinac, and Mack wasn't really expecting one because of the yellow flyer. When he remembered Trance wasn't the man's real name, Mack tried Terrence Adrinac and got a hit. The old hippy should be in the hospice death house, not here. The admin-automation scripts probably glitched.

Mack tried to get the attention of anyone in a pair of scrubs. When the sixth person strode by his bed without looking, Mack slammed his fists on the rails of his bed and screamed, "Look at me, dammit!"

Everyone in the room looked at him, including the orderly whose attention Mack was after.

"Do you need to be restrained?" the kid asked.

"I need someone to fucking pay attention for a second." Mack pointed at the screen. "Can I visit my friend here?"

The orderly squinted at the screen and pressed a button with a wheelchair on the wall above and behind Mack's head. "I wouldn't scream at the staff again, sir," the orderly warned, before disappearing into the flow of traffic in the hallway.

Twenty minutes later, Mack was loaded into a chair and raced through the frenetic hallways. Before he knew it, and feeling a bit dizzy, the orderly deposited Mack in a dim room with a single, occupied bed.

"Mack?" Trance spoke in an unsteady croak. "Is that you?"

"In the flesh."

"What are you doing here?"

Mack pointed at his bandages. "Your fucking dog used my leg as a chew toy."

"Ugly Dog? Surely not."

Mack motioned at his bandages with both hands this time. "Surely so."

"Were you kicking him or something?"

"No. I was feeding the little prick."

Trance struggled to get up on his elbow to look at Mack's bandages, but fell back onto his bed almost immediately. "I'm sorry that happened to you, brother. Are you going to be all right?"

"Aside from my two-hundred stitches and fuck-head roomies, I guess so. Hannah said I'd probably be here a few days." Mack paused to vigorously clean out an ear with his pinky. "What about you? They already got your place up for grabs. I figured you'd be in hospice."

Trance managed a weak shrug. "It's too full. So I'm here until they get a vacancy. Here or there, I suppose. I'm about number twenty on the hospice list at last count."

"Shit, man. That sucks like a Harlem hooker. What's the deal? I mean—"

"Cancer," Trance interrupted. "More specifically, bone cancer. I've had it for a while now."

"I didn't know. I never saw you go to treatments or lose your hair and shit."

"I declined treatment."

The very idea was offensive, and Mack prided himself on not getting offended. "Why the fuck?"

"I've seen what those treatments do to people."

"Have you seen what cancer does to people?" Mack waved off Trance's rising objection. "Look, I know. Sorry. That was a fucking stupid thing to say. But you know what I mean."

"I've seen people go into remission just from cleaning up their diet or lifestyle. So I redoubled my efforts, my yoga and meditation." Trance looked away. "Not to mention I'm too old for DoS coverage for cancer therapy."

"Jesus." Mack shook his head. "And none of that stuff worked, huh?"

Trance looked around at the monitors and dingy bed. "Hello? Does it look like eating nature's own diet and daily workouts and calming mindfulness and meditation helped one fucking bit?"

Mack cringed away from Trance's shocking vitriol. He'd never seen the old hippy lose his shit like that. It wasn't as satisfying as he'd imagined. The bed's monitors were beeping out warnings to anyone who cared to listen. "Sorry, man. I didn't mean nothing."

Trance lifted a crooked finger at Mack. "So while you all shoved your fucking faces full of pork rinds and beer until you got too fat to move..."

"I'm not fat," Mack said.

"And poisoned your bodies and minds with pills and porn, it was my body that was eating itself from the inside with cancer." Trance fell back onto his pillow and closed his eyes. "And that hardly seems fair, does it?"

"Hey, calm down, buddy."

"I bet it warms your little heart to see the hippy get his comeuppance."

A flush of hot anger rose in Mack. Like so many others, the hippy didn't get him. He was used to it. Hell, he'd dealt with it his whole life and he'd stopped apologizing decades ago.

The skin on Trance's arm felt so thin it seemed ready to tear merely from Mack patting it. "No fucking way, Trance. Your way ain't for me but I don't want anyone to die. Well, there is one person, and your fucking dog, but that thing ain't a person anyway. Never mind. I don't want you to die, man. No way.

"It might sound a bit hypocritical coming from someone who bitches about things as much as I do, but you can't get bitter. This whole life is so out of our hands, man. All it takes is one asshole to run a red light and bam!" Mack clapped his hands together. "All that safe driving and good living goes down the shitter. And it ain't even close to being your fault."

They sat staring at the same wall, the heavy silence interrupted only by the periodic chirps of the medical scanners.

Trance fidgeted in his bed. "So, it's not my fault? How comforting."

Mack wasn't good with sympathy, but he wanted to do something for Trance. For all his bullshit chakras and tinkly-crystal music, the hippy was all right. "Do you regret it?"

Trance looked at Mack in disbelief. "Getting cancer?"

"No, dipshit. The whole happy-hippy-sunlover act. Cancer sucks, but it always amazed me how fucking cheerful you are about everything. There's probably a good bit of jealousy in there on my part, to be honest. But was it all bullshit? Some act to get pussy or something?"

Trance stared at the ceiling for a long time. "No. I've always tried to do what was best for my body and spirit, knowing they're intertwined. Even fighting my cancer, except for the natural fear of the Big C, I mostly still felt at peace. I remained a happy hippy. So no, I guess not." Trance managed a thin smile. "Though, I do like pussy. And it likes me, too."

"Now you're just bragging," Mack said with a grin.

"Thanks, Mack. Clarity can sometimes come from the strangest places."

Mack looked to the heavens and brought his hands together in a gesture of prayer. "I'm a fucking miracle worker, what can I say?"

They sat in companionable silence for another half hour, until a nurse opened the door and the din of the hallway flooded the small room.

"Time to get you back," she said pleasantly.

Mack patted Trance's arm as the nurse released the brakes on the wheelchair and rolled him towards the door.

"Thanks again, Mack," Trance said. "You know, you're pretty cheerful, too, beneath that cynical curmudgeon act. I bet you're much happier than you let on."

Mack lowered his head. "Naw, that's all jokes and bullshit. All bullshit." He wiped his nose with a sleeve.

"It's not too late to seek peace, you know."

"It is for me," Mack said, stifling a sob. "And I don't fucking deserve it anyway." He wasn't sure if Trance heard his answer over the noise of the crowded hallway.

That night, the old hippy peacefully returned to the universe, feeling no pain.

15. Mastiff Rides Shotgun

Mack waved his hands dismissively. "Why bother with that prick? He ain't coming." "Because he might come," Jodie said. "Terry was the only one of you jokers Mastiff still talked to." Benny scratched his chin. "I didn't think the DoS paid visitation benefits for anyone but family." "Hannah graciously approved me using the office car today because she liked Terry. Not enough to go herself, of course. I'm fine with that though. If the service wasn't local, you guys wouldn't be going." Jodie unlocked the compact e-car with a flick of her fob. Benny and Mack shuffled over and leaned against the car to wait. A peeling decal on its side proudly declared, "This car is powered by the sun!" It wasn't strictly true since the charging station was plugged into the wall in Hannah's office. The maintenance contracts for the solar panels expired two administrations ago.

Pausing a moment to straighten her dress, Jodie knocked on Mastiff's door. A moment later, the door crept open and Mastiff stuck out his head. He glanced at Benny and Mack, then rolled his eyes.

"You said you'd think about the funeral," Jodie said. "In or out? We've got to get going."

"I bet he won't," Mack whispered.

When Mastiff pursed his lips, it made his flabby jowls droop like a cow's udder. "Can I go in a separate car?"

Jodie put one hand on her hip. "No. And I don't have time for any bullshit. Yes or no?"

Mastiff shut the door on Jodie, who simply turned to leave.

"Told you," Mack sang. "I don't think this car could move him, anyway."

Benny glared at Mack as he reached for the door. Mack, for all of his odious behavior, had done right by Benny. But when he started dog-talking Mastiff, Benny wanted to slap Mack silly. Sometimes Bile Street reminded Benny of high school. He shuddered.

As Jodie reached the bottom step of the porch, Mastiff stepped out of his door and slammed it behind him. He wore a garish muumuu covered in purple, red, and orange designs that billowed out behind him. A matching kufi sat on his massive head.

A mocking smile crawled across Mack's face. His lungs sounded almost like bellows as he inhaled with childish glee.

"Shut up," Benny said. "Just don't."

Mack looked confused. "But look at that getup!"

"Shut. Up."

"Fucking fine. We certainly wouldn't want to hurt your boyfriend's delicate feelings now, would we?"

Jodie looked Mastiff up and down once. "Let's roll."

"Shotgun," Mastiff said. The big man started wheezing almost as soon as he was down the steps.

"Like he could fit anywhere else," Mack muttered. Mastiff stopped mid-step and everyone glared at Mack. "Jesus, sorry as fuck."

Benny and Mack slid into the back while Jodie got behind the wheel. As she got in, Jodie's dress hiked up over her knees, revealing her white thighs. Jodie casually pulled her skirt down, leaving her legs exposed long enough for a red lust to build in Benny. He turned away and offered a level gaze to the ghostly reflection staring back at him in the window. It wore a look of disapproval.

The tiny car proved to be a struggle for Mastiff. There was no good purchase for him to grab that would allow him to lower himself with a modicum of dignity. Benny reached for his door so he could get out and help. Upon seeing this, Mastiff shoved his head inside and glared at Benny. When Benny leaned back into his seat, Mastiff continued his efforts.

In the end, the best the bulky man could manage was a semi-controlled fall into the passenger seat that set the car rocking. The car had a noticeable list to starboard when it finally settled.

The silence of the ride to the district burial gardens was uncomfortable for Benny. This was as close as he'd been to Mastiff for weeks and he was missing the chance to speak with his friend. He didn't know what to say. Nothing serious, no "Why aren't you talking to me," or "Stop being a dick." Only some simple chitchat. About the weather? Maybe the scores on the *Battle Master* server?

Benny put on his best smile and leaned forward. Before he could speak, Mastiff glared over his shoulder at him. It wasn't the look of incredulous, joking disbelief Mastiff so often used. There was real anger, a real warning, behind those bulging eyes. The words left Benny and he leaned back in his seat.

But he didn't want to give up, so Benny tried two more times. Each time he was about to speak, Mastiff glared at him, each time looking angrier than before. The final time, Mastiff glared and shook his head. Benny grunted and stared out of the window at the passing slums.

"Man, fuck him." Mack spoke loud enough to make sure everyone could hear. Jodie glanced up into the rearview mirror, but Mastiff didn't move.

Benny looked at Mack and nodded.

The Sunrise Final Resting Home listed several services happening that day, but Jodie quickly found the booking for Terrence Adrinac and led the small pack of shuffling, doddering, and lumbering old men inside.

Crystalline music tinkled from hidden speakers in the ceremony room. There weren't that many visitors in the ancient pews, which surprised Benny, considering how popular Trance had always been. What wasn't surprising was that all the visitors save the three old men were women.

Did Benny really know enough about Trance to make such judgements about who should or shouldn't be at his funeral? For all the talking they'd done, he knew very little about the yogi's personal history. Trance had preferred to live and talk in the moment, in the now. The past wasn't something he tried to keep secret; it never seemed to hold much interest for Trance. Benny sometimes thought Trance was being standoffish, but now he wished he'd listened a bit more. There were definite things in his past he wished he could let go.

The four Bile Street visitors took seats on empty pews, Mastiff sitting two rows away from the other three. Mack drooped his arm behind his pew and flipped Mastiff the bird.

A twenty-something man with a bald head and long beard, wearing loose red robes, sat cross-legged on the floor. Next to him was a biodegradable tree planter, bulging with soil. It made Benny's hip throb thinking about Trance sitting in what he'd called the full lotus position. Benny hadn't been able to cross his legs like that since third grade.

Mack leaned in close to whisper, "Think anyone here's his family?"

Jodie shook her head. "He decided not to have any kids a long time ago. Told me he was worried about all that Malthusian overpopulation bullshit and got snipped." She mimed snicking scissors with her fingers and grinned. "He also said he had too much love to only share it with one woman. He was a good guy."

A deep gong resounded from the hidden speakers and the monk began intoning a slow, repetitive chant. Some of the visitors bowed their heads and placed prayer hands over their hearts. Mack genuflected.

"You're not Catholic," Benny whispered. "And neither is that monk."

Mack shrugged and crossed Benny too. "Can't hurt."

The young monk ranged from high-pitched peals to barely audible thrumming, and into tones Benny couldn't hear. Mack let everyone nearby know he was getting bored by sighing loudly every few minutes, until Jodie jabbed him in the ribs with her knuckles.

The monk's chant faded away and he addressed the audience without opening his eyes. "Today we see our brother Terry back to the Source. He was a man of kindness and joy, at peace with himself, who continually sought enlightenment and constantly shared his smile with all who'd see.

"His flesh gave way, as all our flesh will, releasing the spark within. I invite you to pray and meditate, or come and share a word with me, or pay your last respects to our freed spirit-brother as you feel called to do."

The monk opened his eyes and watched the visitors. Most remained in their seats for several minutes. Some chanted on softly before departing. Another walked forward to thank the young monk. A striking, dark-skinned woman dabbed a tear from her eye and watched it fall from her fingertip into the planter.

"Can we go yet?" Mack asked as the room emptied. He managed to barely scoot out of the range of another one of Jodie's knuckle attacks. "Jesus, fine. But everyone else is just about gone. I don't want to inconvenience the swami here."

When only the four Bile Streeters, the monk smiled placidly at Jodie. She rose from the pew and Benny followed her, not really knowing what else to do. Mack shrugged and followed Benny, flipping Mastiff off as he stood.

Jodie took the monk's hand and leaned close to speak to him. "Thank you. From Brother Terry."

Benny saw her slip the monk a golden ring with some kind of setting that sparkled in the light. It instantly vanished into the folds of his robes.

"Thank you," the monk whispered.

"Hey," Mack blared. Benny flinched and instinctively put his finger over his lips. Mack ignored him and dug a gnarled finger in the planter's soil. "Where's the tree?"

If the monk's inner peace or whatever was disturbed by Mack's crass outburst, he didn't let on. "It will be planted in the monastery to grow. Now it only contains soil, a seed... and Brother Terry's remains."

Mack jerked his finger from the soil and frantically began scraping it against the lip of the planter. "What? In there?"

The monk's smile grew even more placid. "Yes. It's a biochemical process that renders most of the body into fertile dust that is mixed with the soil. We'll name this tree Terrence, for from him it will grow."

Mastiff roared in laughter and pointed at Mack. "What a dumbass."

Mack turned to Benny with raised brows. "What? So he gets a free pass on the insults?"

Laughing himself, Benny handed Mack a kerchief. Mack spat into it and rubbed it vigorously on his finger, which already looked clean.

Mack looked down at the dirt he'd flung onto the floor and grimaced. "Sorry about that."

The monk shrugged. "Dirt here, dirt there. It will all end up in the same place eventually." He made a deep bow, squatted to lift the planter, and hauled it away by a pair of biodegradable handles.

Apparently still afraid of having a trace of Trance on him, Mack was cleaning beneath his fingernails with the edge of his DoS ID card. "Let's get the fuck out of here."

BACK ON BILE STREET, Benny hung back and coughed to get Jodie's attention after Mack and Mastiff had retreated to their micro-homes.

Jodie gave a coy smile. "Yeah? Ready for another ride? On the DarkNet, I mean."

"Well, uh, yes, actually."

"Even after he treated you like that today?"

"Yes."

Jodie slinked a step closer. "I'm starting to think it isn't information you're after, Benny. Tonight?"

"Sure. But that's not what I wanted to talk about. I wanted to thank you for taking us, first off."

"No problem. Second off?"

"Was that ring really from Trance?"

Jodie frowned. "Saw that, did you? I must be getting sloppy. I'm getting too soft. Yes, it was Terry's. He asked me a few months ago to give it to whoever did his service."

"Shouldn't it have gone to the auditors?"

She snorted. "By their selectively enforced rules, probably. But Terry paid me well—very, very well—for my services." She favored Benny with a long, lascivious wink. "And as you know, I never break a contract. See you tonight."

Jodie hiked her skirt up to her upper thighs as she slid into the car. Benny stared after her from his porch long after she'd driven out of sight. This universe he lived in was one crazy place.

16. What Benny Found Out

The timer started on the computer screen when Benny launched the proxyware. He'd learned to wait until his blood cooled before starting his adventures in hacking, but the smell of Jodie—and what they'd done—still hung dank in the air.

This was the fourth time Benny had traded his body for access to the DarkNet and it sickened him. Aside from the sheer ridiculousness of the whole situation, Benny wasn't sure whether he or Jodie was acting more like a whore now. There was still a certain pride in performing, even if chemically aided. But the excitement of rediscovered lust was wearing away; it was a young man's game. And Jodie was still as ugly as sin when she leered down at him with that awful smile. That ass though...

Benny shook his head. Maybe he needed to wait a bit longer before hitting that start button next time.

None of his forays into the DoS-run SafetyNet had turned up anything on Mastiff's daughter. The Archive held many videos of Mastiff's vast YouTube career; it held too many, in fact. Mastiff seemed to have had his recorder going 24/7. There were too many to randomly go through. Benny wouldn't be surprised if Mastiff was one of those people who filmed the food while it was on the table, while he was shoving it in his mouth, and then as it swirled down the toilet bowl.

During the heyday of multitudinous search engines of his youth, Benny could have asked the retrieval gods nearly any question and immediately received a boon of data. But the Archive was different; it had to be, for the safety of its shady lurkers. The search engine wasn't designed for the lowest common denominator among its users. He understood that the Archive wasn't designed for little old men to look at pictures of grandchildren or cats, but he didn't know how many more romps with Jodie he could survive.

He looked away from the monitor. Death would come before he found what he needed on the Archive. There would be no handy 'chat with us' box popping up or virtual assistant on this side of the web, but Benny needed help.

There was someone who might help, someone familiar with the underbelly of the online world. Someone he wouldn't have to sleep with. Hopefully. He tapped his forehead, trying to remember.

Benny snapped his fingers and opened the DarkNet tab in Jodie's program. He typed in 'Phreaky Fellows' in the search box. It had been decades since he'd investigated the hackers' guild, so he wasn't surprised when nothing relevant came back.

Of course, they wouldn't have a blatant site and might have changed their name, if they were even still alive. He tried several variations of 'Phreaky Fellows' and got a few hits on the black boards. None of those he found seemed to be the hackers he was looking for though.

It dawned on him that he wasn't looking for the whole guild, but only a single member. The name struggled its way through the quagmire of ages, not in a flash but in a twinkling muddle—Bromide999.

Bro, as the kid liked to be called, had been picked up for hacking into brick-and-mortar security systems for a gang he thought were his pals. The kid was a pro and covered all his technical tracks. But he learned the hard way the same lesson so many criminals had: there's no honor among thieves. One of his so-called crew got pinched with a stolen plasma monitor and rolled over for a plea deal.

Benny had taken pity on the kid and helped him out of the mess, and received a promise for a favor. It was a favor he'd never expected to collect on; Benny hated calling in favors. But not as much as Jodie's sex face.

It took nearly the full hour to find the Bromide999 he believed to be the one he was looking for. The kid had constantly overused and misused the word "infer." Not that internet talk was known for using correct English, but it was all Benny had to go on. As the timer counted down, he finally found a contact link for Bromide999 on an old board about OS emulators.

Calling in that favor if you're still around, Bro. It's been a while since you got pinched for that plasma monitor in Wichita. I need to know what you can tell me about Jodie Palmer (DoS admin asst) and Mastiff Barkey (old YouTube handle) both in my current district here outside of Chicago. Thanks, Benny Martin.

The timer was down to two minutes when Benny sent the message. Having no time left for earnest searching, Benny hopped back to the Archive tab and clicked randomly on one of Mastiff's old videos.

Benny leaned back to watch the video and winced at the pain in his stiff back. He'd been slouching as he conducted his illegal searches. Mastiff came on the screen dressed like an old Jewish woman, kvetching about her latkes. The one-liners were lame, but the impersonation was passable for the stereotype. Overall, not one of his better videos.

Still, it had received over two hundred thousand hits back in its day, according to the Archive. Apparently, neither the quality nor the content had bothered his loyal subscribers. Benny wondered how many of those people were still alive.

The timer turned red, flashed three times, bleeped, and the terminal went dark. Benny sat in the dark as it rebooted. He didn't know what he might expect from Bro. There was no question that Bro would be able to trace Benny's new account on the hacker board to his DoS account. But he didn't know how, or if, he'd be contacted. If Bro's message didn't come in to Benny's DoS email, it would mean another tryst with Jodie.

Benny shuddered.

There was a tapping on the window facing Mack's place—his Mack window. Benny let out a long sigh. Every time Jodie came over, Mack came to the speaking window. Benny reluctantly shuffled over and opened it.

"Bow-chicka-bow-wow," Mack sang, imitating the porn music of the 1970s.

Benny hated this final cherry on top of every roll with Jodie, but Mack would not be denied his fun, tapping incessantly until Benny opened up. At least he waited until Benny was done with the proxy-ware.

"She's got it going on, eh champ?"

Benny looked over his glasses at his friend. "If you like it so well, why don't you do it for me? You know, since we're such pals and all."

"Jo-Jo don't roll that way." Mack adjusted his ball cap. "And she don't talk to me anyhow."

"Why not?"

"Who the fuck knows," Mack said. "Maybe something I said in the last email. I can't see what would get her panties twisted though."

"You usually can't."

Mack nodded in sage agreement, then screwed one eye shut at Benny. "I see what you did there, prick."

"Oh good. I'd hate to have wasted all that effort." Benny yawned and tapped his cane on the floor. "Are you done being nosey so I can go to bed?"

Mack put a hand over his heart. "I'd almost think you didn't like talking to your old pal Mack."

"OK then, tell me who that guy was in the DoS car that visited you this morning. He looked like a detective."

"Fuck him," Mack snapped. "Some asshat giving me shit about old trucking tickets. Man, those guys never let you go."

Benny gasped. "You didn't obey all the posted traffic signs and safety regulations?"

"Ha-fucking-ha."

"So, is it serious? I mean, that was a long time ago. Unless you've been secretly moonlighting." Benny rubbed his cane along his chin. "But that can't be. All your free time is spent watching me do the wild thing apparently."

"I hope it's nothing serious, but you can never tell with asshole cops." Mack slammed the window shut hard enough to send an echo through the neighborhood.

In the distance, Benny heard a dog bark. It could be Ugly Dog. The DoS Animal Control enforcers hadn't taken more than a few steps from their truck and that had only been to inform Benny to call if he saw the dog again. They made it clear he was only to call during normal business hours.

When Mack turned out his light, Benny did a little victory jig with his cane and went to sleep.

———◉———

THE NEXT MORNING, BENNY was sitting on his porch, enjoying a hot cup of tea and the feel of his cane. The sun was bright and he'd donned his floppy boonie hat. He liked his hat, but not as much as Mack loved his nasty, old lice trap. Thinking of hats put in mind Trance's wide-brimmed straw hat, which in turn reminded him of the yellowed, olde-tyme photo he'd seen of his great-great-grandmother wearing a bonnet.

As Benny was pondering hats, a DoS e-car rolled to a stop in front of Mack's house. Two men in suits stepped out of the car and each gave Benny a perfunctory nod, which he returned. They walked up to the porch and knocked on Mack's door.

Mack was cursing loudly before the door even opened. "What the fuck do you guys want?"

"We need to ask you a few more questions, Mr. Townsend," one of the investigators said, glancing at his datapad. "Can I call you Mack?"

"Fuck, no. You call me Francisco or Mr. Townsend." Mack squinted over at Benny. There was no hint of humor in his eyes. "Only my friends get to call me Mack, and I don't get the feeling we're going to be bosom buddies."

"Shall we talk inside, Mr. Townsend?" the other investigator asked. He glanced at Benny. "Or shall we talk in front of your friend?"

Mack turned and walked inside, grumbling. He left the door open and the investigators followed and shut it behind them. Benny briefly considered trying to eavesdrop at his Mack window, but decided he didn't want to know any details. There was no telling what trouble Mack might have gotten himself into. Benny didn't believe for a second the line about old trucking tickets.

The investigators left two hours later. Benny caught a glimpse of Mack's face the instant before he slammed the door after them. The DoS men offered the same practiced nod to Benny as they had upon their arrival, before driving away.

Benny stepped inside, hung his hat, and set his empty teacup on the kitchenette counter. Once he'd set more water to boil, he tapped on Mack's window with his cane. There was no answer, so he tapped harder. If Mack's expression before slamming the door hadn't been so troubled, Benny would have happily tapped on the window all day long. He didn't have anything better to do. Instead, he stopped after the third round.

"Hey! You all right in there, Mack?"

"No," came the muffled reply. "I'm not fucking all right. Get off my back."

"All right," Benny called back. "I can be as pigheaded as you can, you know. But if you need something, just knock. I'm here all day, every day."

Mack didn't answer so Benny shut his window and sat in front of his terminal. There were a few family messages waiting for him in the in-box of his computer and a few on his voip. Most were thoughtlessly forwarded glurge: rehashed old memes and debunked warnings that had been making the rounds since Benny's youth. He was nevertheless happy to receive them; it meant his family was thinking about him. Or at least he was still on their automated distribution managers. He still struggled to match user IDs and avatars with real faces.

One message was from Jodie. Benny rolled his eyes, expecting another innuendo-laced query about when he'd like to use her services again. When he opened it however, there was a link to a SafetyNet-approved news service. On the other side of all the ads and PSA pop-ups about the great job the DoS was doing for everyone, he was rewarded with a picture of three familiar faces. The headline read, "Train Station Safety Enforcers Found with Bestiality Porn on Their DoS Devices."

The article went on to name them, detail how they were discovered, and describe increasingly uninteresting legal and procedural minutiae. It made Benny nervous.He didn't know if Jodie was bragging, threatening him, or showing him she cared about what had happened. But it was plain she had something to do with ruining the three security workers.

"Hell hath no fury..." Benny muttered.

Had she somehow found out he was trying to get info on her? Not likely, but he really didn't know what her program did. It could send her every keystroke and location. Many years ago, he'd been something of a computer geek, but now he only knew how to navigate a directory, open mail, and play video games. Operating systems had changed greatly in the years since the DoS takeover. Open-source software was vigorously discouraged by the DoS.

Benny wrote a reply to Jodie about people getting what they deserved and deleted it. It read like he was making a veiled threat. He wrote another and came off sounding as if he was fawning over her, which she certainly didn't need to think. Benny's mind went in circles with each reply, afraid of sounding too weak or too uppity or too something. Finally, he wrote "Thanks," and hit send.

He *was* thankful. That big enforcer who'd smashed his cane still popped into Benny's dreams to randomly crush beloved things in his meaty hands. Benny was not normally one to hold grudges, except for that cunt Rose, but those guys deserved what they got.

What if they really were into bestiality? Benny shuddered and closed the email.

Bromide999 was the only one he was interested in hearing from, and there was nothing from him.

———— ✦ ————

COME LUNCHTIME THE next day, Benny was feeling lonely. Neither of his neighbors was talking to him and the family e-chatter was sparse. He stood leaning on the railing of his porch, hip throbbing, waiting to catch Mack or Mastiff coming or going. As he was deciding whether to knock on Mack's door or go back inside, an elegant sedan with gray paint, gold trim, and heavily tinted windows rolled to a stop in front of his microhome.

The car was quiet, but not like the hum of an electric engine. More like a purr. When he smelled the faint but still-familiar exhaust fumes, Benny perked up. It was a combustion engine. Not many of those left around.

The car shut off and a chubby, middle-aged man in a tan suit stepped from the driver's door, carrying a graphite briefcase. He strode to the bottom step of Benny's porch. "Benedict Martin?"

"Guilty as charged."

"I'm Brandon Thain." He hefted the briefcase a few inches. "We have some legal matters to discuss. May I come in?"

Benny looked over the man more carefully, hoping his suspicion showed. "What's it about?"

"You recently made an inquiry of an old acquaintance, yes?"

Benny gulped loudly, nodding dumbly before remembering himself. At least he kept from pissing his pants. Had Jodie found out and reported him to some DoS investigator? Or had someone higher noticed his poking around the DarkNet? Were they about to find bestiality vids on his terminal?

Benny nodded hesitantly and led Thain inside to his kitchen table. "Am I in trouble?"

Thain smiled. "Not from me, Mr. Martin. And not from anyone else I know. I'm merely an overpaid delivery boy."

He set the briefcase on the table, ran his fingers across the identilock, and rummaged through the papers inside. "I'm here on behalf of my aforementioned client. You knew him as Bromide999, I believe? A.k.a. Bro? I love saying a.k.a. It's so cloak-and-dagger."

"Oh. I was expecting something more, I don't know, digital or hacker-like."

Thain chuckled. "I know, right? I'm on retainer and, like I said, a delivery boy. Since SafetyNet can sometimes make it hard to discreetly deliver documents, clients pay for secure, personal delivery."

He pulled out two sealed dossiers, a sheet of paper, and a pen. "I have no knowledge of the contents of those dossiers, nor do I know anything about the sender, aside from the name Bromide999, a.k.a. Bro, and the fact that this entity sent these to me for delivery. Even my fee was paid anonymously. All I know is they are for you and I need you to sign this, please." Thain slid the pen and sheet of paper to Benny.

"It just says," Thain continued, "that you were delivered the dossiers and that any and all debts, rejoinders, and favors are hereby paid in full. You will also henceforth at no time, in any way, for any reason, reach out again to the person you know as Bromide999."

Benny read the short document, which was basically a bullet-point list of what Thain had said. Reading it through a second time, Benny muttered while Thain waited in silence. He slid the paper back, unsigned.

"You can sign it that I agree we're square and I got the goods, but I'm not signing anything for him."

Thain took the paper and loudly scratched some indecipherable letters onto it. "I don't blame you at all. He is a hacker, after all. But this paper doesn't go to him. Please initial here to indicate you instructed me to sign on your behalf."

It was a struggle to make out Thain's writing; Benny shrugged and initialed where indicated. Thain smiled and put the paper in his briefcase. Once that was latched, he handed Benny the two dossiers and stood. "I can see my own way out, Mr. Martin."

Benny stared at the dossiers until Thain's car was out of sight. They were unmarked and slender, made of bland, manila-colored plastic. Being so thin didn't bode well for his favor's usefulness. He ran his finger along the static seal and upended the contents of the first folder onto the table.

Out fell a sheet with a picture of a younger Mastiff Barkey next to a much less flattering, more modern photo. It looked like a sobering before-and-after ad, showing what ten thousand Twinkies might do to a person.

The text below the pictures read: Leonard Evans, a.k.a. Mastiff Barkey, a.k.a. FangedNoodle, a.k.a. ChokeMyBrilliantSmurfBong...

Twenty more online user names were listed, but the dossier listed only one legal name change and no criminal aliases. Notes at the bottom of the page said Leonard Evans changed his name in court almost twenty years ago. The remaining pages didn't add much except the names of some immediate family—including his daughter, Rivka Rey Evans.

Unfortunately, there wasn't anything else about her. It was a unique name, but Benny couldn't know if she was even using it when she supposedly died. He still didn't know when she'd died, or if she even had. Mastiff made it sound like it happened after they'd known each other. Hopefully, the name would be a bit easier to find in the Archive next time he whored himself out to Jodie.

"Speaking of which," Benny muttered as he opened up the second dossier. There were a few more pages in this one, starting again with a few pictures. He sighed. The poor woman wasn't ugly because of her age; she'd always had a face only a mother could tolerate. She probably came out of the box that way.

He shuddered at the thought of some poor teenage boy losing his cherry to her. Text was printed below these photos as well, listing various names and aliases. But they weren't from game servers, they were from the Department of Safety Anti-terrorist Division.

"Shit, Jodie. Good thing Bro doesn't work for DoS."

Nancy Belkin, a.k.a. Tracy B. Nikel, a.k.a. Yara Klibne, a.k.a. Felicity Kargrove, a.k.a. Jodie Palmer.

The next page was a flier announcing Nancy Belkin was wanted for questioning regarding sedition and terrorism activities during the Turnover, which established the DoS as the de facto supreme authority in the United States.

Also listed were four separate anarchist groups she supposedly had ties to, including one in which she was an officer.

"Jesus Christ, Jodie." Benny read the charges carefully, but the details were absent. Sabotage, assault, evading arrest, fraud, identity theft, public criticism of DoS policy, hacking, and prostitution.

It hadn't been uncommon while he was on the force to pile on excess charges on someone'ssheet. Accusations were easy to make and added urgency to get things moving. Some of the things Jodie, or Nancy, was wanted for seemed pretty far-fetched. But he believed the last two, considering he was her accomplice.

That realization tempered his rising indignation at her supposed criminal career. Especially since he was going to be adding blackmail to his own rap sheet.

Lust heated his crotch. Bad girls had always made him hot, though he hated to admit it. He knew it was part of his conflicted feelings about what they'd been doing. She was obviously already a bad girl. Now she was an actual wanted terrorist. Fear mingled with that lust.

It was easy, and popular, to label someone a terrorist. The term was really more of an ad hominem slur than a legal description. If an agency wanted to go after someone, find some sympathetic jurors, a terrorist charge was just the thing, true or not. While procedurally disingenuous, where there was smoke, there was often fire.

He questioned his plans to use this information. Jodie played for keeps, as the goons in the railway had found out. And if this list of charges was even partially true, she didn't only drop porn files around. Jodie apparently had much more experience playing the black hat than he could have expected. She might easily turn his plans back around on him in ways he'd never think of.

And she might really be his friend, a wanted, terrorist, scary friend. Jodie had never mistreated him and had gone out of her way to help him from time to time. He hoped all of Bro's digging around hadn't set off some sort of DoS flag on Jodie.

Benny slid the papers back into their dossiers and drummed his fingers on the table. He was too old to be strong-arming people to get his way. He had no desire to pay, or play, Jodie.

Or get shanked by her.

17. It's a Small World After All

Jodie's perfume wafted in after her like a bride's train as she sauntered to the kitchen. She pulled the three tokens of their arrangement from her coat—this time a tiny Dr Pepper instead of Coke—and set them on the table.

She flashed a lurid smile. "We got lucky tonight. My other plans fell through. So I have an opening you can fill."

Benny gave a mirthless chuckle. He raised a hand as Jodie opened her coat to show off a diaphanous French maid's costume. It did wonders for her cleavage. He reconsidered his objections to the bargain, but only for a second.

"I'd rather you just get me past the SafetyNet, Jodie. Without the whoopee, if you please."

Jodie's smile faltered. "I thought you understood the terms of our arrangement, Benny." She let her coat fall closed and frowned. "And I thought you were having a good time. I sure am."

"I have to admit it was great at the start. And it's nothing personal. But I think we need to renegotiate those terms... Nancy Belkin."

"And what are you going to offer...?" Jodie's eyes narrowed.

Benny could tell by the look in her eyes that he was a dead man. She was glaring at him as if trying to determine where to plunge the shank she had in her pocket. Benny gripped his cane tighter and hoped he could bash her head in if he needed to.

Jodie turned away from him as she buttoned her coat. She was muttering and shaking her head. After a full minute, Benny wrapped his other hand around his cane, ready to swing it like a Louisville Slugger. His bones chilled with the realization that he'd gone too far and he was going to be murdered by a half-dressed, wanted terrorist with yellow teeth wearing a French maid's costume. When Jodie started laughing, Benny muttered a prayer.

When she turned back around, she wore a rueful smile. "OK, Benny. You caught me with my pants down. I must be losing it. So, what's your game?"

Jodie glanced down at Benny's double-handed grip on the cane and laughed. "Put it down, lover. I won't hurt you. The question is, what are you going to do to me?"

"Nothing. I just don't want to have sex any more trying to find out what's wrong with Mastiff. Jesus, I'm too old. It ain't proper."

"That's not what you were screaming last time," Jodie purred. "But that's not what I'm talking about. You obviously found out some things about me. I guess I got careless." She paused to consider him long enough to make Benny squirm.

"Or maybe," she continued, "I didn't give you enough credit and you had some contact on the DarkNet. In any case, what I want to know is if I need to run again. And I won't hurt you if I do. I'd like to get started if it's time to move on."

Benny relaxed his grip on the cane. "All that shit was a long time ago. I don't even remember much about the Turnover."

Jodie scoffed. "The Turnover to the people. Bullshit. More like the Takeover. But that's what they counted on, Benny. People getting used to the new lords. Like boiling frogs."

"I don't care about it and don't know anything about boiling frogs. There were some serious charges against you, but I do know how that works sometimes. I'm not going to say anything." Benny gave a nervous grin. "And not only because I'm complicit."

"How can I be sure of that?" Jodie put the Dr Pepper and Erectus Maximus pill back into her coat pocket. She left the thumb drive in place."I'd like to believe you, Benny. But I've been hiding out for a long time. So-called terrorists aren't protected by statutes of limitations."

Benny tapped his cane on the floor as he considered her problem. "I'll give you the file. I only have one copy."

Horror washed across Jodie's face. She pushed past him towards the door. "Dammit, Benny. If you have a file on your terminal, SafetyNet already has it in an audit."

Benny grabbed her arm. "Relax, woman. It's not on my terminal. I have a hard copy. One hard copy. I'll give it to you."

"Who'd you get it from?"

Benny shrugged.

Jodie pouted. "Was it really so terrible that you tapped a favor so you didn't have to play hide-the-sausage with me?"

"Get me past SafetyNet until I find what I need about Mastiff and I'll give you the file."

"The same rules apply. Only one hour at a time, three times a week. And not during any audits." Jodie put her hands on her hips. "It won't do you any good to blackmail me if I get busted anyway."

"OK."

She poked him gently with her finger. "And you can never-ever, never mention this to anyone. Not Mastiff, not Mack, not whatever god you pray to. But especially not Mack."

"Agreed."

Jodie held up the drive. "Give me the goods and I'll hook you up."

Benny reached into the closet and pulled her dossier from beneath his little treasure box. After peering in to make sure he was giving Jodie the right one, he handed it over.

Jodie immediately opened the dossier and scanned the papers, making the occasional grunt or muttered objection. "Well, not a lot of detail here, but enough to bring me trouble. And enough to make it a good trade. Just keep in mind this makes you a criminal too."

Benny scooted his box back in place and closed the door.

Jodie craned her neck. "Is that another dossier? Is it the goods on Mastiff?"

Benny chuckled. "Wouldn't you like to know?"

"Yes. I'll pay you." Jodie flipped her coat open to reveal her well-shaped thighs and exposed breasts. Benny politely turned away. "Fine. I'll set you up."

Jodie inserted the drive into the computer and fired up the proxyware. "You know where to go from here." She tapped the dossier before tucking it beneath her coat. "This is some really Spy versus Spy shit, Benny. I'm going to have to keep my eye on you." She reached for the door.

"Hey, Jodie?"

"Yeah?"

"Uh, thanks for what you did to those train assholes." Benny rubbed his thumb across the carvings on his staff. "That was pretty kick-ass."

She waved a dismissive hand. "We anarcho-terrorists have to stick together. What they did to you was pretty shitty. You can pull someone's DoS profile easier than you'd think, if you know how. See you."

Benny watched Jodie get in her car and drive away, before sitting heavily in his chair. It took a moment for his heart to stop racing. He'd come into contact with two criminals now, one a wanted terrorist. It wasn't something he was proud of, but it did make illegally accessing the Archive seem less outrageous.

The timer window opened and Benny began searching. After twenty minutes, he'd found several Leonard Evartses, but none that matched his neighbor. There was a Jewish e-car technician, three independent contractors, a piano teacher, and a cross-dressing frat boy. But all his efforts to match Mastiff Barkey and Leonard Evarts came up blank.

Maybe he'd have some luck with the other aliases on the list. The dossier spilled as Benny reached behind him to grab it from the table. He spun his chair, scooped everything up, and looked for Mastiff's daughter's name.

Rivka Rey Evans.

Evans? Benny slapped his forehead. He'd been searching the wrong name this whole damned time.

"Shit, shit, shit." He took three deep breaths and started over. After another twenty minutes, Benny picked his way through a string of false Leonard Evanses: a plumber, an eco-engineer, a band named The Leo Evans Revival, among many others that didn't have anything to do with Bile Street.

"Jesus, there's a lot of Leonard Evanses," Benny muttered.

He started trying to match Rivka Rey Evans with Mastiff Barkey and Leonard Evans. Then he focused on obituaries, funerals, and death notices, since Mastiff's daughter had supposedly died.

With only three minutes remaining, Benny clicked frantically through the remaining search result links. The face of a young black woman, pretty and vaguely familiar, appeared on his screen. Probably some celebrity mingling with the popular YouTuber Mastiff Barkey.

The next picture on the page showed a family gathering with a muscular Leonard Evans before he grew into a rotund Mastiff Barkey. His arms were around two women, one being the familiar woman from the first picture.

Glancing at the text below the photo, Benny let out a sigh of relief when he saw Rivka's name. His heart sank as he read it more carefully; it was dated over fifty years ago.

Rivka Rey Evans, 22, is survived by her parents, Leonard and Alexa Evans. She lost her life in a tragic police shooting during the Wichita riots. Officer Benedict Martin is on administrative leave pending investigation.

The proxyware flashed a warning, then rebooted the terminal. Benny spun away from the terminal. "Oh, Jesus," he whispered. "I didn't go to his daughter's funeral."

The memory of the flashing lights and screaming sirens of that night overwhelmed Benny. Those had been terrible, endless nights. It was the smells he remembered the most: choking exhaust from the armored cars, sickly-sweet wafts of booze-filled vomit, the stinging clouds of pepper spray,the acrid bite of gunpowder. And, of course, beneath it all, the iron tang of blood.

Despite the flood of memories, Benny wouldn't have recognized the girl's face without context—it had all happened fifty years ago. Nor did he feel any unresolved guilt over the incident. She'd pulled a gun and he'd shot her first. He'd known eight of the cops who died that night, and many of the others who'd been injured, trying to hold the line against the mob.

He couldn't even remember what it had all been about. There were plenty of riots in those days, maybe even more than after the Turnover that followed years later.

But he had certainly shot Rivka Rey Evans. What fucking luck that fifty years later, he and her father would become best friends. Not trusting his now quaking knees, Benny rolled the chair over to his bed and collapsed onto the mattress.

"It is a small world after all," Benny muttered. "What the hell do I say to him now?"

18. Mack's Troubles Begin

BENNY SHOOK HIS HEAD and curled back under the covers again. Sleep had been a long time coming last night and, when it did, his dreams offered fear and violence, but little rest. Visions of the riots had disturbed him all night, though now he only remembered impressions of what he'd dreamed. It was his bladder that finally roused him from bed.

He stumbled to the cramped bathroom, took a leak, and scrubbed his face with water. The clumsy attempt to put on his glasses nearly got him a poke in the eye.

An aluminum breakfast tray sat on the table. The nurse, or orderly, or food-delivery temp, or whoever the DoS was using to deliver food these days had woken Benny. It wasn't surprising, considering how tired he was.

He peeled back the lid to reveal soggy soy pancakes drizzled with sugar-free syrup. Now that he was up and shuffling, Benny's belly didn't care if the food was cold and soggy. He finished it with vigor as the electric teapot bubbled. Once he'd finished wolfing down his breakfast, Benny leaned back and sipped from his chipped old teacup.

It took some time for his sleep-deprived mind to remember what he'd found that caused those dreams—and Mastiff's rage. He'd killed Mastiff's baby girl. It was said that time heals all wounds, but Benny couldn't imagine a time where Dakota's and Zane's deaths wouldn't sting. Finding out your best friend killed your child, even fifty years later, had to be a total mind screw.

Now that Benny knew, he had no idea what to do about it.

A car door slammed outside and interrupted Benny's musings. He leaned over and peeked through the blinds to see another DoS e-car parked in front of Mack's place. It still rocked with the weight of whoever had just climbed in. A moment later, it drove away down Bile Street.

Mack was on his porch, flipping off the retreating vehicle with both middle fingers. When it was out of sight, he hung his head and shuffled back inside, seemingly unaware Benny was watching.

Two cups of tea later, Benny still didn't know what to do about Mastiff or Mack. He could at least talk to Mack about what was going on; he feared what Mastiff might do when Benny told him he knew about Rivka. He was too tired for the emotional onslaught that would ensue.

He grabbed his cane and slid open his window. As he was about to tap on Mack's window, Benny heard loud sobbing from next door. He leaned his less-deaf ear in closer—that was Mack inside, bawling like a wrinkled, old baby. Benny waited for a break in the crying, but Mack carried on, now muttering in between gasping breaths.

Benny finally tapped the window hesitantly. The sobbing continued for a moment, then Benny heard the trumpeting of Mack blowing his nose. The window slid open to reveal Mack's bright-red eyes and threadbare ball cap.

"Is everything OK?" Benny asked.

"What kind of dumb fucking question is that? Does it look like things are OK?"

"I suppose not. Would you prefer 'What's wrong?', 'Do you need anything?', or 'Anything I can do?' instead?"

"Fuck if I know." Mack reached up as if to slam his window shut on Benny, then let out a long, ragged sigh. "I'm fucking sorry, man. Thanks, but I don't think there's anything you can do."

"Care to share, carebear?"

Mack made a snot-filled chuckle and flipped off Benny. "I'm not sure. Maybe. I don't... it's all pretty fucked up."

Benny held up his hands. "I don't want to pry. I wasn't even going to ask until I heard..."

"Until you heard me crying like a virgin on prom night?"

"Something like that. Though I think the only virgins we had on prom night were some of the teachers."

Mack merely nodded at Benny's joke and stared at the ground. Benny waited for his friend.

"That what I told you about truck tickets was a lie," Mack finally said.

"No shit?" Benny offered a friendly smile as he spoke. "Look, you don't have—"

Mack glared up at Benny. "They're saying I molested Krysta, those motherfuckers."

"Krysta?"

"My great-granddaughter. Abby's girl. Remember the morning they took old Jimmy away?"

"Oh, right. Jesus, Mack. That's terrible."

"I didn't do it, asshole!"

Benny flinched. "Whoa, whoa. I meant the accusation was terrible. I didn't say you did it."

Mack continued glaring for a second, then hung his head. "Sorry, man. They won't leave me the fuck alone. It's like they already got my coffin measured."

"Have you tried to talking to Ricky or Abby about it?"

"They weren't taking my calls. Now the DoS has my number on intercept and I can't call anyone without fucking permission." Mack made air quotes as he spoke the last word. "Jodie let me use her voip the other day, but Abby hung up as soon as she heard it was me. Now Jodie's number is on intercept and she's all kinds of pissed at me." Mack shook his head. "Fuck me sideways."

"You didn't, uh…" Benny started. Mack's head snapped up, lip curled and brows furrowed. "Uh, hear about a tribunal date or anything yet?"

Mack narrowed his eyes suspiciously, then hung his head again. "Naw, those fuck-stains won't tell me shit. They keep giving me the third degree. I wish I could just talk to Abby or Krysta."

Waves of nausea overwhelmed Benny. If not for the support of the wall and window sill, he was sure he'd have fallen over. There was no way Mack had done that. He acted like a puerile, dirty, old man, but Benny knew it was mostly an act. Wasn't it?

"What are you going to do?"

Mack shrugged. "What the fuck can I do? Except sit here hoping whoever lied about me fesses up before they hang me. Maybe those shithead investigators will actually find out something besides how many dumps I take every day. And I lied to them about that anyway."

The two old men leaned from their windows, staring at the ground below. Benny didn't know what to say and couldn't think of any way to help. So he watched the grass dance in the wind. It was too tall—the DoS Public Works guys should have come already this week. Benny snorted; this wasn't the time to worry about the damned grass.

Mack broke the long silence. "You were going to ask if I did it, weren't you?"

Benny chewed his lip. "Yeah. But not because I think you did it. It caught me off guard, that's all. And it's such a big deal, with detectives and everything."

Mack answered with a curt nod and another long silence stretched out between them until Mack broke it. "I saw Jo-Jo leave pretty quick last night. Forget to take your pill, champ?" Mack followed the question with a short series of pelvic thrusts.

"No. We worked out new arrangements."

Mack gave a knowing smile. "Yeah? Like what?"

Benny was glad to have changed subjects, even if it was to follow Mack into the gutter. "You know I'm not supposed to say."

"Aw, come on. You can tell your old pal, Mack."

"Why the hell should I? You wouldn't tell me about Jodie being a nympho."

Mack clucked his tongue. "Jesus, what a hard-ass."

Benny considered Mack for a moment. The desire to share what he'd found out, even with Mack, was pressing. But Mack had his own problems and didn't care about Mastiff. Benny shrugged. "But I did find out about Mastiff's daughter. She did die and I didn't go to her funeral. Just like he said."

"Not saying I'd go anyway," Mack said, "but I'm sure you would have. If he told you."

"I knew about the funeral. I killed her."

Mack pursed his lips. "Ha-fucking-ha."

"No, really. She died when I was on the force in Wichita. I shot her in the line of duty."

Mack's rheumy eyes widened. "No shit?"

"No shit. During the Wichita riots."

"I think I remember those." Mack lifted his red bulldog cap and scratched his scalp. "Yeah, a whole, long line of trucks got routed around the city for like a week. Jesus, what a mess that was. What were they even about?"

"I don't remember," Benny said. "I didn't even recognize her face when I saw it in the article I found. But it was her."

"Small fucking world, man."

"Yeah."

"So what are *you* going to do?" Mack asked.

"No idea. What can I say to the man? Give him a candy bar and say sorry?"

Mack leaned in closer and lowered his voice. "So, why'd you do it?"

Benny stared over his glasses at Mack. His friend looked almost greedy, like a glutton for bad news. Other people's bad news. But Benny had started it and it wasn't an unreasonable question.

"She drew a gun and pointed it at us. It disappeared into the crowd as soon as it hit the street." Benny shook his head. "I felt bad enough shooting, but then there was no evidence. You never know how those investigations will go. They finally cleared me though. To be honest, I almost planted a gun on her, I was so scared."

"Those were some fucked-up times, man."

Benny nodded. "I'm going to have to talk to him sooner or later. He obviously already knows, though I'm not sure what brought it up all of a sudden. At least he might talk to me about it now."

"Yeah, he was already such a fucking blast to talk to. So... how many people did you waste when you were a cop?"

"Four."

Mack gave a low whistle. "Jesus, Dirty Harry. Did you mean to?"

Benny frowned. "As opposed to doing it accidentally on some rampage?"

"You know what I fucking mean. Righteous shoots or whatever."

"I don't know. Did you stop molesting kids?"

Mack pushed himself as upright as possible on the window sill and screamed, "Fuck you motherfucker!"

"No, fuck you! It wasn't some video game, dickhole. I mostly wanted to stay warm in my car." Benny shoved the handle of his cane at Mack's face. "You think I went out shooting people for the fuck of it?"

Mack shoved the cane away and jabbed a finger at Benny, spittle flying as he yelled back, "What you said was fucking uncalled for. That fucking molester comment."

"Dirty Harry?"

Mack curled back down until his shaking elbows were on the sill again. It looked as if he'd deflated. He took four seething breaths through clenched dentures until he calmed. "All right. My bad. My fucking bad. Sorry."

Benny craned his neck left, then right, getting two loud pops from his spine. "Me too. I was an ass. I just... it's not fun killing people in real life." Benny paused to let a cool breeze blow over his head and neck. "Three."

"Three what?" Mack asked.

"Three were"—Benny raised his fingers to make air quotes—"good shoots. Including Rivka Rey."

"Rivka who?"

"Mastiff's daughter."

"Rivka?" Mack chewed on the name. "Is he Jewish? I think that's a Jew name."

"I don't know if he's Jewish. He never gave me any latkes or anything."

"I fucking love latkes," Mack replied wistfully. "Think he'd make me some?"

"Why don't you go ask? And while you're at it, be sure to tell him we figured out his secret."

"What about the fourth one?" Mack asked hesitantly. "I mean, if you want to tell me."

Benny took a deep breath. He hadn't told anyone in years what had happened that day. There was no reason to tell Mack, who was likely to blab it around and tease Benny about it. Or throw it back in his face. Talking about Mastiff's daughter had put Benny in a confessional mood though.

"I was chasing some asshole that'd robbed a gas station at gunpoint. I lost control and hit another car. It was some pimple-faced boy on his way home after his shift at some fast food joint. He, uh, died in the crash."

Benny pressed his eyes closed. "I knew I should have called it off. But I thought I had him. Crushed my hip and wrecked my career.

I barely avoided jail time on that one. I probably deserved it. I definitely deserved it." When Benny tried to add the final details of that accident, his confessional mood faded. He wasn't ready to share it all.

"Shit, man. That's rough. I've done some shit, but I never killed anyone." Mack looked at Benny and held his hands up. "No, wait. I'm just saying. I'm not fucking with you or anything. Like you said, that's a big fucking deal."

Benny nodded. "Yeah. It's just the shittiest thing that happened on the job. Mostly because it was my fault."

"Sorry I asked, man. I didn't want to... well you know."

"Yeah, I know." Benny grinned. "Great talking to you, Mack. As always."

Mack smiled back. "I'm a regular fucking Candy Man, right?"

Benny hiked a thumb over his shoulder. "Want to hit the servers? Maybe some scrabble?"

"Naw, not today."

Benny nodded and the two old men retreated back through their windows.

19. Doggone

Benny sat on his porch, picking at the soggy sandwich and chips in the foil tray. The orderly had delivered it without a hint of shame. Not that shame was something the DoS felt much of at any level.

But the sun was bright and the breeze warm. It was so nice out that a soggy sandwich wasn't going to get Benny down. Nor would the dismissive glare Mastiff shot him as he walked by. Benny was glad that Mastiff went inside without comment; he wasn't ready for that conversation.

Benny considered blurting out that he knew about Rivka. But how would he phrase it? An apology? Confession? Should he shout it out with emotion or speak somberly? After Mastiff lumbered into his house, Benny returned to the sunny day.

There weren't as many people walking along Bile Street as he'd expected. After being cooped up during the winter, even squint-eyed old gamers and hunched-over voip addicts wanted a bit of sun.

The Bile Street social nets had talked about some people heading to hospice lately. And while Benny could see a few more yellow notes fluttering on doors, it didn't seem as if the neighborhood should be so empty.

Messages from his family had tapered recently, too, so maybe it was some kind of natural lull. Like when a noisy room grows quiet right before someone says something stupid. That someone had been Benny more times than he cared to admit.

Still, he kept his voip nearby, not wanting to miss anything from his family. So he flipped through his conversation trees and flung some emojis at the few relatives chatting today. Someone replied with a googly-eyed poop icon and Benny chuckled.

That's when he noticed Ugly Dog sitting on the steps and wagging its tail.

Benny's breath caught in his throat. He hoped he hadn't gasped. Show no fear, that's what they always said. Was it even true? He didn't know. What Benny did know was that he was about to shit his pants.

"Hey, boy." Benny struggled to keep his voice calm. The dog licked its chops as it lifted its nose towards the food tray.

Benny slowly set the tray on the porch and pushed it towards Ugly Dog with his cane. The dog whined as it began scarfing down the remains of Benny's sandwich, the single tuft of hair on its mange-ridden scalp bouncing jauntily as it ate.

It was when Mack turned his back that the dog attacked him. Benny wasn't going to move. As carefully as he could, he held the cane between him and the dog with one hand and held the voip up to his mouth with the other. Ugly Dog continued to whine and wag its tail.

"Dial Animal Control," Benny said into his voip. The dog looked up at him, a piece of cheese swinging from its mouth. Benny tensed. "Uh, good boy. That's the good stuff."

The dog sniffed and returned to its meal. While the *Connecting...* indicator continued to blink, Ugly Dog scooted the tray against the far railing, trying to get every scrap. With a final slurping sound, the dog whined happily at Benny, licked its wrinkled scrotum, and curled up at the top of the steps.

The dog was all skin and bones, and Benny had a hard time imagining it having the strength to attack anyone. But he remembered Mack's bloody bandages and had seen the scars himself.

Someone finally answered the phone. Benny reported the information in as calm a voice as he could. The dispatcher listened with the indifference of a professional government phone-jerker. At the end of the short exchange, the dispatcher promised someone would be there soon. Benny groaned.

Ugly Dog was snoring loudly now, but Benny was too afraid to move. He prayed, silently, that Mack or Mastiff wouldn't come out slamming their doors and wake the mongrel up. Hopefully, Animal Control wouldn't come rolling in sirens blaring.

Ugly Dog hadn't stirred once by the time the DoS Animal Control van showed up. It rolled silently down the street and Benny almost shouted to get their attention. Instead, he waved his cane over his head, careful not to hit the awning and wake the dog.

Ugly Dog raised its head when the van's brakes squealed, but it lazily scratched its ear and curled back up into a freakish, wrinkled ball. Two enforcers slipped from the van's cab and each grabbed a long pole with a wide, dangling loop. Benny was reminded of Elmer Fudd sneaking through the woods as they crept towards the porch.

When they had made it halfway, Ugly Dog jumped to its feet and snarled. It whirled on Benny with a look on its face that Benny would have sworn was pure betrayal. There seemed to be a promise of payback in those doggy eyes.

While the dog was facing Benny, one of the enforcers lunged forward and got a loop around the dog's neck. The instant the loop tightened, Ugly Dog went berserk.

Benny screamed and scrambled over the railing, landing hard in a tumble with his cane in a small shrub. Ugly Dog was jerked back by the rope around its neck. The other enforcer rushed forward to loop the dog's hind legs, but Ugly Dog was jumping and snapping wildly. It found enough purchase on the confined porch to continue jumping and spinning around the pole's choke. Benny stared through the rail at the beast's outburst of vigor; desperate animals do desperate things.

"Lift," yelled the enforcer. "I'll come from under."

The first enforcer strained to lift Ugly Dog into the air and lost his balance. After three more failed attempts, the second enforcer got his loop around the dog's middle. Ugly Dog whirled and flew at Benny, pulling the pole from the second enforcer's hand. This time, the dog cleared the railing. It dangled by its neck only two feet from Benny's face.

The leap had left the dog-catching poles crossed and tangled with the porch rails. The enforcers struggled to free them, but Ugly Dog continued to snarl and snap at Benny, causing the dog to bounce and twirl even harder.

"Get the latches!" the first enforcer yelled. But when he tried to undo the small latch at the back of the pole, it wouldn't come free. The pull from the strangling dog was keeping the latch shut.

The other enforcer tried loosening the loop near Ugly Dog's neck, but the dog snarled and snapped at the hands trying to save it even as it strangled. The rope bit deeper into its neck with each twirl.

By the time the Animal Control enforcers managed to disentangle the poles from the porch and push the whole mess over the railing, Ugly Dog had stopped struggling. Benny stumbled backwards as the dog landed at his feet, its eyes and tongue bulging grotesquely from its lifeless face. The last tuft of hair on its scalp had come free in the struggle, leaving Ugly Dog dead and bald.

The first enforcer knelt to undo the loop, the distaste clear on his face. "Should have shot the fucker to start with."

"No shit," the other answered. They hefted the dog's body into the back of the van and rolled away without a word to Benny.

Benny started at Mack's voice from over his shoulder.

"What a clusterfuck, eh? Glad that little shit's dead though."

20. Mack's Troubles End

It was turning into another sleepless night for Benny. One in a long string of them. To the left was a friend being investigated for being a child molester, and to the right a friend whose daughter Benny had shot to death. Yet it was Ugly Dog that had been keeping him awake for the last week.

That mongrel had been a pitiful thing, mangy, starving, with no real reason to carry on that Benny could see. It lived by begging and probably digging through trash. Even with the vision of the blood all over Mack's deck, and the terrible scars on his legs, Benny felt sympathy for the rancid, old dog who'd died so horribly. The sight of that bulging tongue and eyes wouldn't leave Benny alone. He agreed with Mack though: Benny was glad the poor dog was gone for good.

An orderly strolled in, talking loudly on her voip and letting in the cursed sunlight. Benny didn't remember falling asleep. She didn't bother to acknowledge Benny or her bad manners, dropping the breakfast box on the table and slamming the door on her way out.

Despite nightmares full of dog carcasses, Benny was starving. The soggy blandness of the food didn't slow him down one bit as he wolfed it down. He'd shared his experience with Ugly Dog the night it happened, and people were still showing gratitude that he was OK and making comments about what his balls were made of. Adamantine was his favorite, though he thought it was from some comic book.

After two cups of tea, Benny had made his way through his morning chat replies. A couple of people offered to come visit after his close call with the dog. He'd love that but hatedputting the burden of traveling to Bile Street on anyone. His family lived so far away.

Then they'd have to find a place to stay. And they might meet Mack. Benny politely declined.

With a steaming cup of peppermint tea in his hand, Benny made his way to the porch. The sun was out but the wind was a bit chilly. As he was about to get up to grab a sweater, a DoS car pulled in front of Mack's place. Two uniformed enforcers, no investigators this time, stepped out and pounded on Mack's door.

The door swung open and the enforcers stepped inside without being asked. Benny stood and leaned against the railing, watching and sipping his tea. Observers sometimes made cops more cautious in their treatment of suspects. Sometimes.

Benny was getting cold waiting for something to happen next door and set his cup down to fetch his sweater again. In doing so, he noticed a tuft of fur caught in the boards of the railing. It waved in the breeze, as if greeting him. Benny hesitantly reached out and pulled it free, casting the last bit of Ugly Dog to the wind.

Mack stepped through the door, followed by the enforcers. He was handcuffed, staring at his feet as he shuffled along. The enforcers glowered at Benny before helping Mack down the steps. Without noise or scuffle, without looking at Benny, Mack got in the back seat of the DoS car and they drove away.

"Shit," Benny whispered. He didn't need a sweater—he needed to go back inside.

Benny was waiting for his dinner delivery when he heard the slamming of car doors. Peering through the blinds, he saw Mack standing on the sidewalk and a DoS car pulling away from the curb. Benny got up and reached his porch at the same time as Mack reached his.

"Are you..." Benny started, then reconsidered. "Anything I can do?"

Mack stopped and gave Benny a sidelong glance. He seemed about to say something, but only shook his head and went inside.

Benny stood on his porch, staring after Mack, considering his friend. Nothing useful came to mind so Benny went inside, too, and put one of SafteyNet's random approved streams on the monitor.

No matter how he tried, Benny couldn't listen to the Barbie doll on the screen. Though probably a beautiful woman with millions of followers, her vapid expression and asinine script left Benny shaking his head. There wasn't really any point in trying another channel so Benny clicked the terminal off.

Even if he'd found one of those rare DoS entertainment gems, he wouldn't be able to concentrate on it. Mack's hangdog look as he came home had Benny worried. He'd never been good at dealing with drama queens, which Mack certainly was. But Mack was also in a lot of trouble. If the enforcers were hauling him away, it was serious. Benny wished he could help somehow.

Or did he? What if Mack was guilty of those monstrous charges? He'd said he wasn't, but Benny knew most people lied when first charged. Did he want to help a monster?

And who was more monstrous? Would the boy Benny killed choose to be dead over having been molested? Trying to prioritize their sins and offenses had Benny's head spinning.

He shook his head. He'd already assumed Mack's guilt, it seemed.

Guilt and sin comparisons aside, Benny was angry. Here he was, having beaten Jodie at her own game and solved the riddle of Mastiff, and now he had to worry about Mack's bullshit.

No, not bullshit. Mack's problems were real and more pressing than either Benny's or Mastiff's. Mack had been there for Benny. And as Benny considered recent events, he realized Mack had been there for him all along. Benny had once been in the middle of having three good friends all at once. Now he only had one. Benny sighed.

There was no answer to his tapping on Mack's window. "Mack?" He waited and tapped again. Shouting and banging on the window wouldn't send the I'm-here-to-help vibe Benny was trying to send, so he ducked back in through his window.

Mack's silhouette materialized against the blinds and, a second later, his window slid open. "Hey, Benny."

"What's up?"

Mack let out a quivering sigh. "They've opened the tribunal. They're fucking charging me."

"Shit."

"I know, right? It's fucking bullshit. They pulled me in today and fucking grilled me. I don't know if I tripped up or if they were just fucking with me before pressing charges."

"Now what?"

Mack laughed bitterly. "I fucking wish I knew, man. They read me the riot act and had me thumb-scan a shit-ton of forms. Then they took every biometric sample they could think of. Not to mention speaking to me in a very unkind and unprofessional manner before dumping my ass back here."

Mack pounded his fist against the wall. "I guess I wait some more. Oh, and they revoked my travel status and all licenses pending outcome."

Benny nodded. It was all he could do. No words of encouragement, no sage platitude, seemed appropriate. They'd often described Bile Street and the retirement-ward system in general as jail, but Mack was facing the real prospect of spending the rest of his life in a literal jail. And that life wouldn't be long.

"Shit," Benny said. "Man, I don't... I don't know what to say."

"Me neither. And that doesn't happen often."

"No shit." Benny chuckled, then put his hand to his forehead. "Oh, sorry. Not the time for joking."

Mack grinned. "It's true, though. The me-not-knowing-what-to-say part."

"You maybe want to do a few rounds of *Galactic Showdown* to take your mind off it?"

"Naw. I'd just end up being a prick. Thanks, though. I know how much you hate that one." Mack nodded towards Mastiff's window. "You tell Fat-ass yet?"

Benny shook his head. "I started to but keep wussing out."

"Stop trying to be so clever. Fucking blurt it out."

Benny glanced over his shoulder. "I might do that, but I don't want to make an ass of myself."

"Fuck him. Even if you did that, it was what, fifty years ago? And that don't excuse his shit when Dakota died. I wouldn't give a shit about what he thought."

Benny snorted. "Whose thoughts do you give a shit about?"

"Good point. I guess you're about it, and then only sometimes." Mack lifted his face into the cool breeze and blew out a loud breath. "Thanks, man. I'm going to go take a dump and think about shit."

"All right. You know where to find me." Benny slid his window shut against the now gusting wind.

Benny flicked the monitor back on. Barbie had been replaced by an equally asinine host of indeterminate gender. It was possible Benny was looking at a virtually rendered celebrity. Programmed or live, it was an idiot. Everyone on every channel Benny flipped through was an idiot, so he shut it off again.

Next to the terminal were two books he'd checked out from Bile Street's scant library. To call it a library would be putting on airs. It was a dusty bookshelf in a break room in Hannah's little admin building. Benny picked up an old sci-fi book and flipped through it. It had a cool cover, but the description on the back was a lame-sounding list of overused tropes so he put it down. It had been the only sci-fi book in a pile of zombie-romance and planning-for-retirement titles.

Even if it hadn't looked so lame, Benny wouldn't have been able to read it. There was too much on his mind. His only choices were to work something out about Mack or Mastiff, either one would do, or sit drooling at the monitor. Trance would have offered up the third option of meditation, but Benny felt pretentious and silly the few times he'd actually tried it.

Stoicism, the actual philosophy as opposed to the Hollywood version of grim Spartans and laconic gunslingers, was popular when Benny had been on the force. At its core, it was an easy set of ideals to understand, but difficult to live by. One of the most important ideas was not worrying about things that were out of your control.

What had happened fifty years ago with Rivka Rey was now out of his control. It might have been out of his control even then. Whether Mack was found innocent or guilty, whether he actually *was* innocent or guilty, was completely out of Benny's grasp. Being able to keep that in mind had helped keep him sane at times.

"Not my circus, not my monkeys," Benny muttered. In the growing dusk outside the blinds, he convinced himself, if only temporarily, that none of it was his problem.

The lie helped him get to sleep.

THE STACCATO TAPPING on the window wouldn't stop. Benny didn't know how long it had been going on before jerking awake in his chair. He also didn't know where he was exactly. But since his hip wasn't screaming, he knew it hadn't been a long nap. Everything else would come later. Benny's head lolled back against the chair.

The tapping gerw louder. Benny looked at the window through bleary eyes. It was dark through the blinds.

"Benny?" Mack called in a loud stage whisper. "You awake?"

Benny straightened his glasses and wiped his chin before stumbling to the window. Mack's face stared back at him through the blinds.

"You rattle my window and then decide to whisper?" Benny asked after sliding his window open.

Mack flashed an embarrassed grin. "Oh, yeah. Sorry about that. Hey, look, can I use your, uh, your voip?"

Without thinking, Benny's hand went to his pocket. "If anyone finds out I let you use it, they'd put mine on intercept too."

"They won't find out. Come on, man. I need a solid here."

"How'd they find out about Jodie?"

"Jodie?"

"Jodie," Benny said. "You told me they put her voip on intercept after you used it. If anyone knows how to get around that, it should be her."

Mack lifted his ratty hat and scratched his scalp. "OK, so they might find out. But I really think they're going to haul me off tomorrow. For good this time. I might never get to talk to my family again. Come on. Please." Mack held out his hand.

"You'll get to see them, even if you go to tribunal. Even if you end up in jail, they can still visit. I mean, even if it goes that far."

"And what if they don't come?"

Benny frowned. "Why wouldn't they?"

Mack's face twisted in rage and he slapped the window sill with both hands. "I need to call them! I need to explain. I need to fucking apologize before they put me away." Mack hung his head. "They won't want to see me then."

Benny's stomach clenched. His jaw fell open. "What... what are you saying, Mack?"

Mack slid down until only his head and arms were sticking out of his window. His head bobbed in time with his wet sobs and he made no effort to wipe the tears or snot from his face.

Benny's head swam as Mack's words came in a nearly unintelligible moan.

"I fucking did it, Benny. Oh God help me. Oh fucking Christ..." Mack's confession trailed into heaving blubbering. He wrapped his face in one flannel-clad arm.

Benny recoiled. "Jesus. How could you...?"

Mack cupped one hand upwards and wiggled his middle finger in the air. "That's all I did. That's all I could do, even if I wanted to do more. Without Jo-Jo's pills, I mean. Nothing works down there, I can't even piss right."

"That's not really what I meant," Benny whispered.

Mack continued as if he hadn't heard. "When they haul me in tomorrow, I'm going to confess. It was the only time, but I'm going to put it all out there and let the fucking cards fall where they will."

Mack blew two streamers of snot from his nose into the grass below and wiped it with a sleeve. "They won't want to see me after I fess up. I need to apologize. To Ricky and Krysta. And to Abby for what I did to her baby girl. I've got to..." He broke down crying again.

"They'll give you a call in jail," Benny said.

"You think they let criminals call their victims from jail?"

"Have your advocate arrange it."

Mack shook his head. "I already tried. Look, I'll tell them I stole your voip when you weren't looking. Man, that'd help me out before I go. Fuck, Benny. Don't look at me like that."

Some of the disgust and horror Benny felt must be on his face. He hadn't meant to show his feelings. It was all so crazy, and Benny knew people sometimes confessed to things they hadn't done for some strange reasons. There was no way to know for sure about Mack and Benny was trying to keep a poker face. It must not be working.

"Jesus," Mack whined, thumb and forefingers pinched together. "Come on! I know I'm a fucking monster. And I'm turning myself in. I ain't asking you to forgive me or lie! I only need a last favor, man. Ain't I been a friend? Just ain't I?"

"You do want me to lie, about the voip."

Mack put his face in his hands. "Don't leave me fucking hanging, man."

"I-I can't. And I can't believe you did that." Benny's arms felt leaden as he slid the window shut in Mack's face.

"Oh, you mother fucker!" Mack's cry was muffled through the window, but must be echoing down Bile Street. "You fucking motherfucker."

Benny stared wide-eyed through the window. Mack's face was twisted in rage and spittle flew from his lips as he screamed. The hate in those eyes, the terror, made Benny quail. Mack flung his ball cap against the window, making Benny flinch.

"Calm down!" Benny yelled back.

"Let me call them," Mack shrieked.

Benny closed the blinds, eliciting more vitriol from Mack. The tapping and pleading started through the window, alternating with Mack's fiery curses.

Fearing that any movement would be taken as a sign of possible consent, Benny remained frozen. After minutes of onslaught, Mack's window slammed shut.

When Mack's front door crashed open, Benny's back went ramrod straight. He stared at the front door and relaxed only a little when he could see it was locked. Mack was shuffling outside his window now, probably looking for his hat.

A girlish squeak escaped Benny when the window rattled beneath Mack's fist.

"Come on, man," Mack pleaded hoarsely. "Come the fuck on, man. One call. I swear. No one will even know." He tapped gently on the window.

"Lights out," Benny whispered. The computer didn't hear. "Lights out," he whispered louder. Nothing. "Lights out!" he finally blurted. It went dark.

"Fuck you!" Mack screamed at the window. "You. Fucking. Prick!" Mack's voice broke and everything that followed was too raspy to understand.

Benny flinched at another thump against the window. The blood thundered in his ears as he prayed for Mack to leave. The cursing and slamming moved next door, letting him know his prayers had been answered.

Hoping Mack was no longer watching, Benny slid onto his bed and lay frozen. When the adrenaline dump was finally over and his heart had slowed to a dull pounding, Benny fell asleep, still clutching his cane.

It was still dark when a crash from Mack's place woke Benny. "Mack?" His voice was thick and heavy.

His hip screamed as he sat up to peer through the blinds. The whole episode around Mack's horrible confession came back to him. He moved one blind as cautiously as possible, fearing Mack might notice it.

The blinds next door were down, too, but Benny could see Mack's silhouette moving in some feeble interior light. Fearing discovery, Benny let go of his blind. Nature demanded a trip to the toilet, and his hip demanded the shoes he'd fallen asleep in come off. Benny was afraid of even flushing, but gratefully fell fast asleep once he'd sneaked back into bed.

BENNY SAT UP IN BED, this time woken by the sudden pounding on Mack's door.

"Open up, Francisco!" bellowed a deep voice. The command was followed immediately by more pounding.

Benny twisted his blinds open. The two enforcers had been there before, but he couldn't remember which time exactly. Their expressions no longer held the pretense of benevolent public servants there to help. Benny recognized the set of their faces, the furrowed brows, the clenched jaws. They were here for some state-sanctioned violence.

After two more rounds of bellowed commands, the enforcers drew pistols. One swiped his badge over the door and it swung open. They rushed inside.

Benny's heart raced. He expected screams and crashing as Mack made some stupid attempt to resist or cause a scene. But there was only silence once the enforcers came to a stop.

Not being able to make out the muttered conversation, Benny quietly raised his blinds and window. Mack's blinds shot up, a meaty hand gripping the drawstring.

Benny screamed.

Mack's body swayed gently inside the window. It spun slowly, probably disturbed by the bull-rush of the enforcers. The old bulldog hat had slipped from its usual place, the tattered bill thankfully hiding the dead eyes beneath. Benny had worked suicides before though—he knew what they would look like. Mack's eyes would be staring, bulging. Empty in death.

The hat didn't hide the purple tongue pushing its way between Mack's white lips or the way the rope was biting into his neck. There was something else that looked wrong and it took Benny a moment to realize what it was: this was the first time he'd seen Mack's back straight.

Benny nearly vomited. He imagined the cap slipping from the top of Mack's head while he thrashed, fighting for air, as he reconsidered his decision.

That had been the crash he'd heard last night. That had been what he'd seen cast in shadow against the blinds.

A neatly drawn sign hung on Mack's chest.

I'M SORRY!!!

Benny leaned out of the window and vomited.

The enforcers turned to stare at Benny through the window, framing his hanged friend's face with their scowling ones. They looked at each other, then closed the blinds without reprimand or comment.

The ballet of a Department of Safety crisis scene slowly unfolded. Within twenty minutes, an ambulance rolled up, followed by two more enforcer cars, and finally a tiny shift-supervisor cart. Soon, flashing solar-powered lights and drone-scrambler screens surrounded the area.

Benny watched it all from his porch, teacup in hand and a wet rag on his forehead. Hannah eventually showed up and tapped datapads with the site supervisor.

The food orderly chattered at Benny about all the excitement, having shown up in time to see Mack's plastic-shrouded body get loaded up. She dropped Benny's breakfast on the bench next to him in her attempt to pull out her voip. She left, cursing the enforcers under her breath, when her voip wouldn't record due to the scrambler field.

Benny sat staring all morning, leaving his breakfast untouched. He didn't even feel like refilling his teacup. The heat against his palms would have felt good, but he was so numb, he wasn't sure he'd even feel that.

By lunchtime, the DoS vehicles had all left except that of the two enforcers who'd come to make the arrest. They finally came out onto the porch, slamming the door behind them. The bigger one tapped his datapad with a note of finality and tucked it away.

"All done," he said. "I knew it. We should have just shot that fucker from the get-go."

The other nodded. "At least this saved us a bullet and some paperwork. Bonus is that we don't have to testify before the trib."

Benny didn't know if they'd forgotten about him in the slow commotion, or if they didn't give a shit that he was there.

Either way, he was glad to feel so numb. That kind of heartless talk would have fired his mouth into getting him in trouble otherwise. It was no way to talk about his friend. But should he consider Mack his friend, knowing what he knew now? Should he be upset about comments made about a confessed child molester hanging himself?

"Fucking pedo," said the first. He spat on the porch, locking eyes with Benny for a split second.

The other enforcer looked over at Benny. "At least the kid's safe. How could someone do that to their own family? Or any kid?"

Now they were both looking at Benny. He shrugged. Without further comment, they got in their car and drove away.

As Benny watched them go, he saw a splash of red on Mack's porch. It was his tattered, bulldog ball cap, shoved between two slats of the railing. Benny hobbled over on stiff joints to get it.

It had Mack's smell on it. Years of cheap cologne and strong coffee clung stubbornly to those tattered threads, mixed with hints of medicine and death. In all the years of knowing Big Mack, Benny had never examined his friend's totemic hat.

Yet it had always been part of Mack's presence. In some ways, it was a parallel to the old trucker: ragged but sturdy, keeping to its nature no matter how worn it became.

Benny shuffled back towards his house, nearly running into Mastiff. He shuffled around Mastiff, who took up nearly the whole sidewalk. Before opening his door, Benny turned back. They stared at each other in silence.

Mastiff's face might have been a little softer than it had been lately, his eyes maybe not so baleful. But there was no warmth there, no pity. Benny didn't have the strength to chase Mastiff today, so he merely looked on, waiting for some words.

When none came, Benny went inside and closed the door slowly behind him. "Mack's right," he muttered. "Fuck him."

Benny took a final look from his window, wondering when the yellow paper would show up. All the DoS horses, and all the DoS men, hadn't been able to put Big Mack together again.

21. The Last Mack Truck Stop and Grill

"Because he was my friend," Benny said.

Jodie smirked. "Even after what he did? I mean, he confessed it to you. It's not like you can claim it's hearsay."

"That doesn't really matter now. He's dead."

"And I hope he's burning in hell this very instant," Jodie said. "Not that I personally believe in hell."

"He may be burning, but I need to go. I see him swinging everywhere I look." Benny looked away from Jodie, down the street. "I don't know if he'll see from on high, or down low, but if I don't go..."

"You're afraid he'll haunt you," Jodie said, no mockery in her voice.

Benny nodded. "Not necessarily like a real ghost kind of thing. But I'm afraid that vision won't go away. That some id or superego bullshit will make it worse. And yes, I know what he did."

"You're lucky the family allowed the DoS to do it locally. Cheaper that way. Free cremation with every DoS retirement ward. Anyone else around here want to go?"

Benny snorted. "I posted it on the Bile board and got nothing but hate in the comments. The few people I asked in person just stared at me."

"You ask Mastiff?"

"No."

"You might want to." Jodie shrugged. "You never know."

"I do know. Will you ask him?"

"I'm done getting in the middle of your bromance."

"Will you come?"

Jodie laughed acidly. "Fuck no. That dude was a pedo-perv. I'm still amazed you're going."

"You slept with him."

The glare on Jodie's face made Benny gulp. He was hoping he hadn't lost his ride. "That's my business. And it was before..."

"Before you knew?" Benny finished.

Jodie sighed. "If we're going, we need to leave soon. Are you going to ask Mastiff, or not?"

Mastiff did not answer Benny's voip message so Benny pounded on his door. "Will you come to Mack's funeral with me?"

Benny wasn't sure he'd heard Mastiff move so fast. When Mastiff opened the door, he was short of breath.

"I ain't going to no kiddy-diddler's funeral. I hope that pervert rots in hell." Mastiff slammed the door. It swung open again before Benny had a chance to move. "And fuck anyone who be wanting to go. And fuck anyone hurting kids." He slammed the door again.

"At least he talked to you," Jodie said as Benny approached the car. "And you get shotgun. There's always that."

Jodie dropped Benny off at the funeral home with instructions to send her a voip when he was ready for pickup. As long as it was during normal working hours.

Federal Funerary Garden 12 in the Chicago district was definitely a DoS facility. Two bored enforcers sat behind their stations, scanning people as they entered and left. It was a drab and heartless place, full of cracked concrete and carpeting left over from 2020. The one concession the bureaucracy made to mourning visitors was to make the enforcers dress in dark suits matching the employees. They didn't fool anyone though.

Benny held his cane up with the DoS approval chip towards the scanners and ready to point it out to anyone trying to take it. Neither guard gave it, or him, a second glance.

The inside was cavernous, though well lit. It wore the typical DoS, lowest-bidder décor, accented with cheap, artificial floral arrangements. The place was so huge, Benny didn't know if he could find Mack's service, let alone be able to make the walk.

An usher in a small electric cart pulled up in front of Benny. "What service are you here for, sir?"

Benny grinned in relief. "Mack, I mean, Francisco Townsend."

"I'm very sorry for your loss, sir. I can take you there." The young man smiled and stepped out to help Benny into the cart.

Benny got in and examined the boy. It must be nice to have such a cushy DoS job so young. Probably some district administrator's nephew. But it was unfair or, at least, unkind. Benny didn't know a thing about him. He remembered being the kid, being the new guy. And he'd not been treated any better than the way he was thinking about the kid helping him now.

Benny leaned over and read "Phil" on the driver's DoS employee badge. "Thanks, Phil. This place is huge."

"Oh, yes, sir." Phil took a look around before smoothly accelerating the cart. He pointed to large signs as they passed. "We have several wings here. This place is used by all branches of the DoS. Enforcement, Admin, Utility, to name a few. We even get folks from out of state. Sometimes even military members. Those usually go to military gardens, but some want to rest closer to home."

"It's like an airport in here, except the carts have real drivers."

Phil laughed. "Yes, I guess it is. I've never been to an airport, but I've seen the vids. We used to have auto-carts, but the people that know how to fix them are too greedy. Good thing for me, eh?"

Benny grinned and nodded slowly. Phil drove on in silence, his face engraved with a mild smile. Turning away to try to read the signs passing by, Benny kept silent too.

The cart tilted when Phil took a sharp right, causing Benny to clutch the seat. It was nothing compared to the car chases of years ago; they were barely moving. But Benny's eyes and balance weren't what they used to be and his body didn't like the sensation of anything that threatened its limited time left on Earth. How frail could he get?

"Sorry about that, sir," Phil said. "I'll be more careful."

Minutes later, the cart rolled to a stop with a soft squeak of the brakes. The nearby door had a digital marquee that read:

Francisco Townsend, 10am

Clusters of visitors chatted around the door, blocking the way in. There were a lot of people here for Mack, way more than he'd expected for a crotchety, foul-mouthed pedophile. A crowd of angry protestors would have seemed more likely than the relatively normal people here. Of course, Benny knew and had still come.

Phil stood next to Benny, offering his hand. "There we go, sir. Service should start in about twenty minutes." He pointed to a nearby bench. A large orange button with a cart icon glowed on the wall. "Press that button and have a seat and one of us will be along shortly."

Benny took the hand and got out. "Oh. Thanks, Phil."

Phil smiled and waved before tooling back down the hallway.

Benny approached the door and removed his hat. A heavy, middle-aged man with a wild beard and swinging braids stepped from his conversation and opened the door for Benny.

"Don't worry about the hat, old brother. We don't care about that stuff here." The big man nodded as Benny entered. "Hey, I dig that cane, pops."

The gathering inside was even more eclectic. There were mostly well-behaved truckers, bikers, barstool cowboys, tatted-up musicians, and other vagabonds. As the man had said, many wore their hats. There were the more traditionally dressed mourners, too, scattered in the crowd.

It wasn't quite standing room only, but Benny understood why so many were standing outside. So many people, for Mack? He was starting to question if Phil had stopped at the right door, when he caught sight of Ricky and Abby chatting with a leather-clad, old woman. His fear of being at the service was allayed, if not his wonder.

Despite the ride in the cart, Benny's hip was throbbing. There were no seats nearby, but he saw a heavyset boy of about ten sitting at the edge of a row of mismatched chairs. Apparently, the directors had been surprised by the turnout too.

A couple with similar features and clothes to the boy sat next to him on the crowded row. Benny sidled up to the boy and groaned. He leaned heavily on his cane as he shuffled past. Nothing. Benny frowned and tried again, feeling as though he was yelling to get over the din.

"Jerry," said the father. "Jerry, give this man your seat. Show your manners, son."

Benny waved his hand. "Oh, don't worry about me. I'll find a place eventually."

The mother put her hand on Jerry's shoulder. "Get up for the man."

"But, Mom!"

The father leaned over his wife. "Don't you back talk, boy. We taught you better."

"But, Dad!"

The father stared at Jerry and finally hiked a thumb. Jerry got up with a whine. He spared Benny a disgruntled, but not unkind, look before stepping around the row to stand behind his parents.

"Why thank you, son," Benny said with an added quaver to his voice. He didn't feel bad—the younger should make their respects when able. There'd have been a whupping involved if Benny had been that child. Besides, he was doing the fat kid a favor. Jerry needed all the exercise he could get.

A muffled voice came over the speakers to announce the service was starting. The raucous assembly slowly moved to find whatever sitting or standing place they could. Benny's seat was well to the rear, but that was OK.

A well-muscled man in a skintight black shirt stepped up to the podium. The thick, white collar didn't quite cover the tattoos around his neck. There was no eulogy, only a short and somber, vaguely Catholic-sounding sermon. The prayers were more energetic, with the audience hooting and shouting whenever it seemed to suit them.

The priest continued to speak about the need for kindness and turning things over to a higher power. The crowd answered the best lines of the sermon with eruptions of laughter or cussing. The priest continued without comment, even joining the stadium wave that went through the crowd.

While occasionally funny, Mack had never seemed more than a bitter old man. Certainly not the type to attract so many people. Especially so many happy people. How could he have been so wrong about his friend?

The priest set the urn on the podium and prayed over it, ending with the old "ashes to ashes, dust to dust" line. The room grew relatively quiet during the prayer, but once it had ended, the priest began shouting blessings and praises on Mack and all present. The blessings crescendoed into a scream that belonged in a thrash metal concert. With a final, thunderous cheer from the crowd, the service was over.

The visitors split into two ambling groups, one headed towards the podium and the other for the exit. Benny stayed in his chair, waiting for the crowd to thin out. Getting trampled at Mack's funeral wasn't how he wanted to go.

The attendees were milling around longer than Benny had hoped. He wanted to speak with Mack's son, Ricky, and make a delivery. But he wasn't sure how the delivery would be received. So Benny was happy to scroll through the messages on his voip, watch the asinine videos, and exchange texts with Trina. She was concerned about him losing a close friend and kept mentioning how much she'd liked Mack. Which was why Benny had never mentioned how Mack died... or why.

Benny wanted someone to remember the Mack he wanted to remember.

"Hey, Benny."

Benny started at the voice. Ricky was looking down at him with a weary grin and red eyes. If Ricky hadn't stopped by, Benny would have missed him. It was too easy to get sucked in by his voip.

"Hey, Ricky."

"I didn't see you come in through the crowd."

Benny smiled. "No problem. Hard to see a wrinkled old man in a crowd like this. I have to admit, I'm amazed so many people showed, considering what an ass he could be. And, well, you know."

Ricky sat heavily in a chair in the row in front of Benny and turned to face him. "Yeah. Everything else aside, Dad was the type to help anyone. Even if he didn't like them. And these people"—Ricky panned his hand around the room—"were his type of people. A lot of them are from his trucking days. Just people he helped out with jobs, or rides, or bar fights. He liked you a lot, Benny, but he thought you were a bit too straitlaced."

Benny chuckled. "He was never shy about telling me that, though not usually so politely." He lowered his voice. "Do they... know? About, you know?"

Ricky let out a long breath. "Some do, but most don't. The story made the SafetyNet local feeds, but who watches those?"

"Think it would matter?"

"Maybe for some. I'm sure no one would condone what he did, but there's not too many halos in here. And speaking of not having a halo, hello, Abby."

"Like father, like daughter," Abby said. She held Krysta's hand and guided the girl to sit in a chair across the aisle. "Hello, Benny."

Benny tipped his hat. He stared at Krysta, unable to look away. A wave of nausea rose from Benny's belly as he remembered a pleading, soon-to-die Mack making his confession with a terrible wiggle of his finger. Benny tore his eyes away, afraid Krysta would see and think he was staring at her in disgust.

"You OK, Benny?" Abby asked. Her eyes were filled with understanding. She'd seen him staring.

"I'm fine." Benny cast a furtive glance at Krysta and whispered, "How's she holding up?"

"She's a trooper," Ricky said. "But it's been hard. I should have..."

Abby rubbed her father's shoulder and said, "No."

As the silence drew on, Benny felt he should say something. Maybe that Mack wanted to call them that night. But they might ask why Benny didn't let him. Better to hand it over and go home.

"I have something, but I'm not sure how you'll feel about it." Benny reached a hesitant hand behind his back. "I don't want to cause any harm, but it might help. It was special to Mack. Do you want it?"

Ricky and Abby glanced at each other, then nodded in unison. Benny pulled the tattered bulldog cap from his waist and offered it to them.

"He was wearing it when they found him," Benny said.

Abby recoiled from it. Her lip started to tremble. "Of course he was."

Ricky reached out and gently ran a finger along the weathered old bill before pulling it from Benny's grip. "They said anything left in the house belonged to the DoS as per the contract."

"That's true," Benny said. "You can register mementos, as long as they're not too valuable. I don't know if he did any of that, but this got left on the porch and I took it. Not real sure why though."

"They said Dad never filed anything like that," Ricky said. "He was never good at keeping track of things like paperwork."

Benny nodded. "For what it's worth, kids, I'm very sorry for your loss. I know things have to be confusing."

"Thanks," Abby said, looking over at her glowering daughter. "I've got to get Krysta fed. Dad, I'll see you in a bit."

Benny tried to sound sympathetic. "Bye, darling. It was good seeing you."

The girl's eyes widened and she rushed to hide behind her mother's leg.

"It's all right, honey," Abby cooed. "Let's go get lunch." She offered Benny a sad smile. "Sorry, Benny. She told me to never trust old men in hats. They're scary."

"Smart kid." Benny watched Abby go, Krysta casting hateful glances back at Benny as she went.

Ricky wrung the hat in his hands. "Thanks for coming, Benny. And thanks for this. As much as I don't want to get back up, the day ain't done, as my dad would say."

Without knowing he was doing it, Benny reached out a hand and put it on Ricky's arm. "Can I ask you something?"

"Sure."

"How do you feel about your dad?"

"What do you mean?"

"I mean just that. How do you feel about him? I don't know how you two were before, you know. But he worried he'd been too hard on you as a kid." Benny looked away. "He was afraid he'd somehow made you gay."

Ricky's smile was replaced by a stony jaw. "Are you asking if he molested me too?"

"No, no, no," Benny said. "That's not what I meant. Mack was one of my best friends in the ward program. First on Clarke Street, then on Bile. Your dad really came through for me a few times, I guess like these folks here. Like when my daughter and grandson were killed.

"But I'm having a hard time deciding what to make of him. Despite the monstrous thing he did, I still think of him as a friend. So I guess I'm really asking about me." Benny adjusted his hat. "What am I supposed to think about Mack? Where is that line between man and monster?"

Ricky looked up. It made him look exhausted. "And you think I've puzzled it out, eh?"

"Hoped."

A handsome man close to Ricky's years approached and got their attention, keeping a respectful distance. The man raised an eyebrow at Ricky.

Ricky smiled fondly. "I'll be right there."

The other man offered Benny a warm smile and melted into the dispersing crowd. Ricky's gaze followed the man.

"If I'd have caught Dad in the act, I'd have put a bullet in his head on the spot. If he'd confessed to me after the fact, looking for help or forgiveness..." Ricky shook his head. "I don't know. To be honest, I'm glad I don't have to worry about that scenario.

"When I left home, I stole nearly every dollar that son-of-a-bitch had. I called him in desperation after getting arrested in Utah. Dad left that very night and drove all the way from Newark and signed away everything else he owned to help me out." Tears welled up in Ricky's eyes. Benny had to look away.

"If you'd asked if I can forgive him," Ricky continued, "I did that long ago. But what do I think about him? He was a man who did good and evil. Do you have regrets? I know I do. And I think Dad regretted the things he did. That doesn't pardon him, but it gives me hope that he wasn't just some monster. That he was weak, not wicked."

Ricky let out a quavering sigh. "All that to say, I don't know what to think. But I can remember the good, without worrying about him hurting anyone else."

"You know, he wanted to call you guys to say he was sorry. He was all tore up, crying and cursing, and begging to use my voip." Benny put his hand over his pocket. "He'd have done it for me. But I was afraid of helping..."

"A child molester?"

"Yeah. And he sort of dropped it on me like a bomb. I didn't know what to do, but I was mostly afraid of my voip getting put on intercept. And now..." Benny's throat ached and his eyes grew wet with tears. He rubbed them with the hanky all old men should carry.

Ricky nodded. "And now you can't help wondering if you could have stopped it. Me too. He tried to get hold of me several times, but I couldn't bring myself to answer. What if his son had taken the calls from a desperate father?

"I didn't, partly because of what the lawyers told us. No contact whatsoever. Mostly it was me hating the fucker for what he'd done. Every time I saw the text, or call, or email was from him, my stomach went sour."

Ricky looked down at the hat. "But I don't think either one of us could have stopped him. Even if he'd gotten on his hands and knees and Krysta forgave him. I think the horror of what he'd done would have been too much. He'd just have done it later in jail. Or maybe I'm hoping that's true so I can say there wasn't anything I could do."

Ricky stood and arched his back. "Look at me running off at the mouth. Thanks for coming, Benny. And thanks for the hat. Sorry I don't have a better answer for you than I do for myself."

The handsome man returned and took Ricky's hand, leading him away through the crowd.

Benny wiped his eyes and shoved his hanky back into his pocket, unsure if he was glad he came.

22. Benny pwns Lenny

The yellow flyers on the abandoned microhomes next door danced in the gusts that blew across their porches and into Benny's face. The flyer on Trance's old home rustled gently like a sunflower. Mack's whipped like a panicked bird caught in a snare. Benny knew it was only a result of how they were taped on the doors of the dead men's homes, but the contrast seemed too fitting for mere circumstance.

At one time, the retirement ward homes would have filled up quickly. A day of cleaning and some paperwork, and someone new would be there. Yellow flyers dotted Bile Street now. It seemed no one was moving in. Benny felt old in body and spirit.

He'd spent much of his time out on the porch staring at the dead men's porches. Death terrified him. It was approaching him, as it did all people. He hated the way his knees trembled and his heart raced when he thought about it. Not very manly; definitely not Stoic. He was weak and always had been.

He couldn't help thinking of death as he looked at Mack's home. He'd been staring for two weeks at that porch. But he kept the blinds facing Mack's window down. He never looked through that window. Even a glance planted the image of Mack swinging with that bulging tongue in Benny's mind. That, or Mack's vile, wriggling finger.

Mack's voice was everywhere, usually cursing. Especially when he was thinking about Mastiff. Then he'd think about one of Mack's stupid jokes, or how Mack had come to Dakota's funeral. And he'd find himself staring at Mack's porch, then about death again. It was a paralyzing cycle. Benny saw himself wasting away on this porch until Death came for him.

Benny knocked himself on the forehead with his cane several times. "Enough already!" He didn't have time for moping and he missed his living friend. Tugging on his boonie hat, cane firmly in hand, Benny shuffled over to Mastiff's door and rapped on it with his cane.

The door opened to reveal a blinking, surprised Mastiff. He tried to slam the door in Benny's face, but Benny jammed his cane in the door.

"I'm sorry about Rivka."

Mastiff jerked the door open and lumbered out, almost pushing Benny down the porch steps. "Don't you even say her name, mother-fucker. And don't you ever talk to me again." He stepped back inside.

The slamming of the door made Benny flinch. He didn't care if Mastiff killed him, Benny was going to get through to his friend. The spare key card Mastiff used to keep tucked away between two boards was gone. So Benny pounded on Mastiff's door.

The dull throb in Benny's hand forced him to stop after a few minutes. "Fine."

Mastiff might be able to close this door on him, but Benny knew where Mastiff was going, and the rules there were a little different. Mastiff couldn't hide from Benny there.

Back at his terminal, a steaming cup of tea at his elbow, Benny cracked his knuckles. The DoS provided access to the servers, but nothing like a real rig. That was fine with Benny; VR headsets made him sick. They were crutches anyway; he'd been online since the 1990s. A big screen and a decent mouse was all he needed.

Benny hadn't been playing much online lately, so his DoS allotment hours were high. Certainly higher than Mastiff's. The games seemed pointless lately and he hadn't wanted to play. But as he saw the gaming library loading, a grin spread across his wrinkled, old face. A quick check of his friends list showed him where Mastiff was playing. With another satisfying cracking of knuckles, he logged in to the *Blood Castle* server as theEasterBenny.

Benny didn't need the dossier to recognize Mastiff's game name. MonsterDawg was Mastiff's favorite profile and theEasterBenny began hunting him down. The sheer joy of racing between the virtual towers, dodging digital traps, and hiding from the invulnerable dragons that flew overhead had Benny laughing. Not only were the graphics awesome, it was like coming home, in a sense.

Booze hadn't been his only escape. He'd hidden from his children, his wife, his job, and his woes by jacking in and losing himself in game worlds. He preferred games with story lines instead of death arenas, but the types of games like those on the DoS-approved list were heavy-handed propaganda pieces or so bland the in-game ads were more interesting than the story.

If only he still had his Vision EXG VR rig.

But he wasn't here for the game. He was here for his friend. He was here to destroy his friend in the arena. Watching the scenery roll by, Benny promised himself he'd be back after he'd settled this business with Mastiff.

The four of them—he, Mastiff, Mack and Trance—used to have so much fun together on the servers. Dakota's death had taken the fun from everything in a way he hadn't realized until now. He'd never been one to clown around much but, after her death, he didn't allow his friends to make him laugh. MakTrukFkuk had liked this game. Maybe Benny would make some new friends and lighten the fuck up.

Since he wasn't going for high kills, kills-to-death ratio, or last survivor, Benny avoided everyone he could. There were a few heads he had to sever before finding MonsterDawg, and that was OK.

MonsterDawg was camping in his favorite place near the crystal garden, hiding while the horde thinned out. TheEasterBenny crept along the ridge above the garden, sword in hand. When he was about to jump down and end MonsterDawg, some unseen shit killed Benny with a crossbow. It was a good shot, right through the head.

"Dammit," Benny muttered. He rolled his head and loosened his shoulders as he waited to respawn. It was like riding a bike. The rust was quickly falling from his fingers, his old skills coming back. This time, he fragged three players on his way to his real prey.

At least MonsterDawg was moving. But not fast enough. Benny lined up his shot and a digital axe flew from his screen and buried itself in MonsterDawg's digital face.

A message flashed across the top of the screen: *theEasterBenny axed MonsterDawg! Headshot!*

Benny laughed when he saw it scroll by among the other kill notifications. He ran to Mastiff's favorite respawn point and spawn-killed MonsterDawg before he'd taken two steps.

TheEasterBenny speared MonsterDawg! Nutshot!

Benny slapped the desk with glee and the hunt was on again.

theEasterBenny axed MonsterDawg!

theEasterBenny tossed MonsterDawg from the tower!

"Leave me the fuck alone!" came Mastiff's angry cry over the speakers.

"Talk to me then."

MonsterDawg has left the game.

"Oh no, you don't," Benny muttered. He took a sip of tea and began logging into Mastiff's favorite stomping grounds, looking for familiar account names.

Benny grinned. "There you are..."

theEasterBenny dominated FangedNoodle, +1 kill

"Fuck off!"

FangedNoodle has left the game.

Benny half-expected Mastiff to report him to a DoS admin. Instead, Mastiff bounced off the server as soon as Benny logged in.

Benny started using secondary accounts that didn't have "Benny" in the user name. He had to create noob users on some servers.

RickyPapaGravy slaughters ChokeMyRighteousSmurfBong! Awesome! Ricky

Mastiff's voice came in whiny over the speaker. "What the fuck you want, Benny!"

"I'm guessing I have more hours than you do, man. I can do this all day." A quick glance at the clock told Benny he *had* been doing it all day. It was almost dinner time. "I understand if you hate me. But you're my friend. We need to talk."

CarrotCakeEater234 lobbed a rocket into Benny's lap, leaving his screen to rotate around a pile of bloody giblets. A prompt appeared for Benny to select his spawn point. He watched the gory, life-like remains on his screen as he waited for Mastiff's reply.

"I can't."

"I'm going to frag you on every server until you can."

"I... can't, man. Not face-to-face. I'd kill you. Hold on."

A moment later, a chime sounded on Benny's terminal, accompanied by an invitation from ChokeMyRighteousSmurfBong.

"Head over to FreeWorld," Mastiff said. "Link's in the invite."

ChokeMyRighteousSmurfBong has left the game.

FreeWorld was new to Benny; he'd never spent much time on the social servers. They usually didn't have any gaming, only rooms for chatting, emote swapping, avatar dress-up, and yacking. Lots and lots of yacking.

He took a few minutes to gather his thoughts and make an avatar that looked something like him. When he'd finished, the terminal displayed a simple stone room with another avatar named M.Barkey. The avatar was sculpted to look like a much younger Mastiff.

"Hey."

"Hey. What the fuck's so important?"

Benny took a deep breath. "That you're my friend and won't talk to me. I only found out about Rivka after trying to figure out what you meant about her funeral. I had to sleep with Jodie to do it."

Mastiff's avatar flipped both middle fingers up, but said nothing.

"I get it, man. But why not say something? Why not go batshit crazy and beat the shit out of me? Break my hip? Something besides the cold shoulder?"

M.Barkey continued staring; the only changes on the avatar's face were the eyes that blinked every few seconds. If they had been using VR immersion rigs, the facial expressions would perfectly mimic that of the wearer. Benny let the quiet stretch out, hoping Mastiff would grow uncomfortable enough to start talking. Once a cop, always a cop.

"Mostly because I don't want to beat the shit out of you," Mastiff finally said. "And I didn't know what else to say. The more I tried to think about what to say, the more pissed I got and the less I fucking wanted to talk to you at all. Oh, Lord Jesu, so pissed." The avatar reached out with both hands to emote choking Benny. "I been killing you in my head every day since I found out you was in Wichita. Found out what you done."

"I... I understand."

"You think you understand?"

Benny leaned back in his chair and closed his eyes. "Yes. Every time I thought about you refusing to go to Dakota's funeral, about how you wouldn't even look at me, I wanted to kick the shit out of you."

"I'm sorry about Dakota. Damn sorry. But I didn't kill your girl, Benny."

Benny bit back a sob. Not sure if he could bite back the next one, he muted his mic. The sincerity in Mastiff's condolence took a weight off Benny's chest. It felt as if he could suddenly breathe, not having realized he couldn't in the first place. He remembered the look of relief old Asthma Ernie would get when he huffed his inhaler back on the playground. That's what he felt now. Mastiff *did* care about what had happened.

But Benny couldn't let the accusation stand. "Thanks, man. But you say that like I just went up and shot her. She pulled a gun."

"That was never found."

"There were like two hundred people there," Benny said, trying not to sound confrontational. "Any one of them could have taken it. She had it, man. I didn't go John Wayne out there. I hope you know that."

Mastiff's avatar was now punching Benny's in the face. "You was a cop, and that all the reason you need. And when it comes to the so-called thin blue line, cops cover they asses."

"True enough. I saw some dirty shit. But I promise you, Mastiff, she had a gun."

"The hell she did. Just more pig bullshit." On the screen, M.Barkey put a hand on one hip and waggled a finger under Benny's nose.

She did have a gun. He'd seen it as clear as day. During the trial, he was questioning himself by the time the defense team was done. But he *had* seen it, and he had shot Rivka Rey Evans. Benny didn't know how to respond without fanning any flames.

M.Barkey's shoulders slumped. "Look, man. I'm dead tired. There's a *Blood Castle* tourney tomorrow. Maybe I'll see you there."

"Sounds good."

"But don't fucking kill-spam me, man. Cool?"

"Cool. Be sure to have your hanky. You're going to be doing some crying."

Mastiff laughed. "You bring your game, sucker. I'm going to light you up."

Benny wanted to ask if he could come over so they could talk in real life. But he was afraid that might blow out the tiny ember of hope he'd worked so hard to ignite. It wasn't the time to push it. "OK, see you."

"See you, Benny."

Benny fell asleep smiling, hearing that laugh in his mind over and over.

23. An Airing of Grievances

B enny didn't win the next day's tournament, but he sure beat the hell out of Mastiff. GiGiMonkeyToes dominated, but Benny came in a respectable fifth. Not bad for an out-of-practice, old coot. Mastiff came in third from last. For the sake of all the effort he'd put in to make things up with Mastiff, Benny kept the trash talking to himself. Mostly.

The two old gamers spent the day on their favorite servers. Benny hadn't played them in so long that it was like visiting old friends. And it was much more fun to play with Mastiff than to play just to piss him off. Because Benny had been away so long, and Mastiff had still been using up his DoS allotment every month, Benny figured Mastiff would have the edge. He didn't.

They shot each other out of the sky, bloodied the Colosseum of ancient Rome, razed mystic elven kingdoms, and scuffled in the modern, gang-infested streets of London. In the afternoon, they played co-op against AI xenomorphs and dinosaurs.

Benny rubbed his burning eyes and looked at the clock. It was close to midnight. If he kept it up at this rate, he'd burn through his allotment too. He didn't want to antagonize Mastiff, but it was past his bedtime. "That's it for me tonight. I can't stay up like you whippersnappers."

"Weak, Benny," Mastiff said. "Very weak."

Despite the dis, there was warmth in Mastiff's voice. Like the old days. Benny knew there were miles to go before their friendship was like before, if indeed it could ever be like before. But it was a good start.

"Goodnight."

"Night, man."

———⊂●⊃———

THE NEXT FOUR DAYS were much of the same. Benny and Mastiff ran together through procedurally generated landscapes like kids in a park, hopping from server to server as they grew bored of the game or of the other gamers. Or if they were getting their asses kicked too badly. Getting destroyed by some twelve-year-old kid from Guatemala was never good for the ego.

The SafetyNet constantly monitored all text and voice chats for Wrongspeak. Expressing opinions that the DoS determined some-one, somewhere, might take offense to was forbidden. As was any-thing subversive or otherwise critical of the people's government. People learned how to speak around these restrictions, using new words or code phrases to express their views. SafetyNet algorithms then eventually banned those words, and the cycle continued. Some considered the resultant gamer pidgin a modern lingua franca.

Wrong opinions were strictly censored and fined in the social feeds and nets, but not so much in gaming chats. Gamers weren't generally trying to influence public opinion as much as they were trying to insult each other.

After a week, the fun was wearing off. Benny was a lifelong gamer, and his interest had lulled from time to time. But it felt differ-ent now. Like sexing the ex: it felt great at first but, as time wore on, everyone remembered the reasons for the break up.

Benny missed chatting with his friends in real life—IRL as it was still known today. The way he and Mack used to; the way he and Mastiff used to. And he still preferred playing single-player games. He liked an immersive story and it was hard to get into that when your wingman was named BuTtLiCkEr1984. But Mastiff preferred online arena-type games, even though he sucked at them. Not wanting to lose his hard-won toehold in Mastiff's good graces, Benny played on with nocomplaint.

The following Monday, Benny set his steaming cup of tea next to his terminal. With a deep sigh, he logged in to see what Mastiff wanted to start playing this morning. But there was no instant message with attached gaming itinerary waiting for Benny this morning.

Mastiff's online status changed to **away** and there came a tapping on Benny's window a moment later. Benny rose, willing himself not to say something stupid. This was the first time Mastiff had reached out to him at all since their falling out. It might mean it was time for the big fight. He opened the window to see Mastiff's bulk filling the frame of his own window.

"Hey."

"Hey, Benny."

They stood there looking at each other for a long moment, then they both looked away. For all of the imaginary conversations Benny had held in his head with Mastiff over the months, for all the moving monologues and fiery rebukes he'd practiced, Benny couldn't think of a damned thing to say.

Mastiff grunted and thumped his chest a few times with a fist. It was as good an ice-breaker as Benny had come up with, so he took the cue.

"You OK?"

Mastiff's chuckle shook his belly and seemed to rock his tiny microhome too. "Yeah, real bad heartburn. I sweet-talked Jodie into getting me some spicy burritos a few nights ago. Been killing me ever since."

"You mean like wink-wink sweet talk?"

"Ain't none your damn business, Benny. Mack done rubbed off on you."

"You shouldn't have left me all alone with him for so long then. It's good to see you IRL."

Mastiff shrugged. "Allotment's out. I can usually make it closer to the end of the month, but we been hitting it like the old days."

Benny smiled. "I'll take what I can get. I've still got plenty of time left if you want to watch a movie or something."

"How about a walk?" Mastiff asked. He slapped his belly, sending a blubbery wave across his belly. "I've been trying to work some of this off. You may not believe it, but I used to be shredded, man."

"No shit?"

"No shit."

Benny grinned. "I know, Leonard. I watched a ton of your YouTube vids on the Archive, uh, researching."

"And I was funny as hell."

Benny waggled a hand. "A little. You were definitely ripped though."

A walk sounded nice. But his damned hip could flare up at any time and the thought of not being able to keep up with his morbidly obese friend was embarrassing. At least Mack wouldn't be around to see it.

"It be good for you, too, Benny."

"All right," Benny said hesitantly. "Let me get my hat and cane, and I'll meet you outside."

It only took a few moments of ambling along in silence for Benny to realize his fear of not keeping up was unfounded. Mastiff moved ponderously down Bile Street, with plenty of rest stops.

"The lawns look like crap," Benny said.

Mastiff nodded. "Yup, getting worse too. These weeds be growing up through the pavements now. DoS ain't careful, they going to have a bunch of old folk with busted hips."

The street was filled with wind-strewn piles of trash, choking the gutters and the corners of the porches. Benny shook his head at how people let their homes get so rundown. Even though DoS retirement age had increased to seventy-two, people could still do something.

They were too busy plugged into their voip or the SafetyNet. Even if DoS Public Works had fallen down on the job, again.

Then Benny saw why no one was cleaning the houses. Yellow flyers on the doors waved at him like friendly crime scene markers. Many of the houses were empty. Benny paused and craned his neck to scan all the porches up and down the street.

Mastiff was wheezing, and Benny realized the big man might be having trouble keeping up with him. "Need a break?" Mastiff said. "OK, I'll oblige you."

Benny waved his cane to encompass the neighborhood. "Where is everyone? I know I don't get out much, but damn."

"You must not be getting out much. This been going on for months. But hell, man, we old. We all old up in Bile Street."

"I get that, and I've seen some of the notices on the Bile board. But shouldn't they be moving new people in? There used to be a long waiting list for any ward openings."

Mastiff was still panting heavily as he looked around the deserted street. "Don't know, man. I been hearing ain't no money for new motherfuckers."

"Hope they don't run out of money for us old motherfuckers."

Mastiff's eyes grew wide and he nodded. He started walking again. "I hope this don't turn into some banger-ganger hood. They squat wherever the hell they want, you know? Good thing we out in the burbs."

Benny walked on, trying for a pace that wouldn't push Mastiff. Despite his earlier misgivings, Benny was enjoying himself. It was a beautiful day and being with Mastiff's cheered him. They pointed out squirrels, rabbits, and small birds to each other. Each pause to observe the neighborhood wildlife was also a good excuse for a breather.

Mastiff stopped suddenly, almost falling over. He looked away and sniffled loudly, rubbing his eyes. The rumbling sobs in his chest were like the thunder of a distant storm. Benny stopped and averted his eyes.

Mastiff spoke, his breaths still heaving. "Man, I really thought I was over Rivka. Thought I had forgave and forgot, turned the other cheek, let it all go on by, and all that shit.

"But when you said you a Wichita cop and I looked you up? Oh, man. It all come back like it were yesterday. I mean, what the fuck? I know it's a small world and shit, but damn. You? Out of the million fucking people could be my neighbor, my friend, and it's the pig that shot my baby girl. Lord Jesu, done did me with that."

The despair in Mastiff's voice made Benny want to reach out and hug the big man. Benny stood gripping his cane, his eyes still averted. He would listen, listen to it all. Let Mastiff get everything off his chest, even if he cursed Benny seven ways to hell. It's what friends did.

Mastiff held his hands to the sky. "I hated you, even hated God for a bit. Thought about killing you, or maybe see if Jodie take a contract on you. She shady, you know? She got the booty, but she shady as shit.

"But old God cured me of them thoughts right quick. He helped me know that mostly I was fucking pissed with myself. And then, Lord Jesu help me, I didn't know what to say. I still ain't got no love for pigs, whether they call theyselves police or enforcers. But what happen was my fault." Mastiff's voice cracked into a ridiculous, warbling tenor. "My very own fault."

Benny reached out to touch his friend, but withdrew his hand. "No, man. No matter what you do as a parent, they make their own choices. They're their own person. I've seen kids grow up in the same house, and one grow into a peach and the other into a bad apple."

Mastiff pinched his left nostril shut and blew a string of snot from his right. He shook his head. "No, I mean it was my fault. I was so proud of her standing up, I mean. Things were bad, Benny. Even if you couldn't see it. Even if you was a so-called good cop. For us, there was no winning. If a black man put up with shit, it only got worse. If he push back, he whining or being a thug."

Mastiff turned to Benny and wiped his eyes. "You white folk just get jealous when people actually stand up to the man. When y'all get upset, you post some links on your social page, eat some tacos, and go back to sleep like nothing happening. Y'all got normalcy bias for blood.

"But I done the same, man. I only wanted to make my vids and get my ad revenue. I loved making those vids. I had it good and I didn't want to lose it."

Mastiff turned to watch a flock of birds dance overhead. He was obviously considering his words. "When Rivka decided to take a stand, man, it made me realize what a pussy I was. A chump. I not only working for the man, I was going down on the man. Patted myself on the back for making little skits with political commentary. But Rivka? She got up in your ugly faces and told you to fuck off. That she wasn't going to listen no more."

"It wasn't only blacks cops beat up, you know?" Benny said. "Or that were at the protests."

"Yeah, I'm sure they lattes even got cold before they went home. How many of them did you shoot?"

Benny spoke gently. "None of them pulled guns on me. But I can see why you'd be proud of her standing up."

"Proud... and ashamed. Ashamed because I didn't have the fucking balls to go with her. I didn't want to get tazed, or shot, or locked up."

Mastiff staggered towards the uncut grass next to the sidewalk. Benny did reach out to him this time and put a hand on his shoulder. They stood there in silence for a minute.

"I know she had a gun, Benny," Mastiff said at length. "It was mine. I gave it to her and told her to cap some fucking bacon if they gave her any shit." His voice cracked again. "I helped kill my baby! Oh, Lord Jesu."

Mastiff fell like a slow avalanche onto the grass.

Over the protest of every joint in his body, Benny sat down on the grass next to his friend, making sure he wasn't sitting in any snot. He sat there quietly, rubbing Mastiff's back with his free hand, feeling the sobs rise from deep in Mastiff's chest.

Benny waited a long time as Mastiff rocked back and forth in the grass, beseeching Lord Jesu for succor and comfort. When Mastiff was finished, the old men helped each other up and shuffled home in silence.

24. Faces in the Window

B enny was enjoying the week before Mastiff's gaming allotment renewed. They took long walks and had long talks. They hung out on the porch, discussing the state of the Union, the weather, church, Jodie's tits, and anything else they could think of. They played some of the lame-ass board games from the main office, but most were missing pieces. Once the DoS brought the tax-hammer down on independent game designers, the industry had dried up.

Playing the board games with Mastiff was still better than playing video games. Benny had grown weary of the pseudo communication offered by texting on his voip. So few wanted to actually talk, even when their voip was right in their hands. Trina asked him if he'd forgotten how to text once. Ever afraid of becoming a pest or a burden, Benny went back to letting his thumbs do the talking.

"Who the hell talks, Benny?" Mastiff asked after Benny complained. "She right. Why can't you just text like everyone else in the universe?"

By tacit agreement, they didn't speak about Rivka. Mastiff had gone silent about his daughter after his breakdown. But they did talk about Dakota. Which is to say, Benny spoke at length about Dakota and Mastiff listened in earnest.

Benny caught his friend wanting to add something about Rivka from time to time, but Mastiff bit off the words before opening up. Even when Mastiff was being taciturn, he was more comfortable to speak to than Mack had been. Benny didn't want to dismiss the support Mack gave, but even forgetting the terrible things Mack had done, Mastiff seemed more genuine. Mack hadn't been all prurient jocularity and profanity, but it was hard to get to him through it.

At least, it felt that way now.

"We went to this big daddy-daughter dance at the Century Convention Center," Benny said as he and Mastiff leaned on their porch rails. The sun felt wonderful on his face. "I don't remember when exactly. Sometime around 2020, maybe? Anyway, they had this huge brass band, real brass, not synth, and Dakota loved it. So did I."

Benny held up his cane like a trombone and mimicked working the slide. "Most of those types of things made your ears bleed with their huge speaker. Not that time. That band had class.

"Anyway, she's standing on my feet dancing and we're having a good time. I'm actually having a good time, which I wasn't expecting since I didn't want to go. And it wasn't only being away from Rose. But I hear this noise from the ceiling and Dakota points up—"

"And they a whole lot of glowing fairies up all over the place," Mastiff finished. His head was inclined and his eyes closed as he spoke.

"Were you there? I think they only used those things once."

"Oh, yes. Those fairy drones were pretty slick. Rivka was a bit too old to stand on my feet, but I sure remember it, Lord Jesu, yes." Mastiff smiled, his eyes still closed. "I was amazed how much a little girl she looked again as she hopping and laughing. Oh how she was laughing. And right before, she was carrying on about how she too old for this and how it were for babies."

Benny laughed. "I don't think any of those little girls cared about old Dad when the fairies started buzzing around. Well, except one. She was holding on to her dad for dear life, crying about Satan's angels coming to get her. Her dad had this satisfied smirk I wanted to slap off his face. Poor girl. Funny what you remember."

"Truth."

"I think they flew the fairies to give the dads a break. Then they had to put them away so the girls would start dancing again."

And like the sun burning through an overcast February day, the two old men relived their memories as if their daughters weren't dead.

BENNY PRETENDED TO be asleep until the food orderly left. Once he heard the door close, he hopped up, took his morning piss, and dressed. A quick peek out the window showed that Mastiff was settling down on his porch to eat. Benny grabbed his cane and breakfast, and headed to the porch.

Mastiff finished rolling the aluminum away from his breakfast tray and looked up at Benny. "Morning, Sunshine."

"Morning." Benny returned the smile. He took a seat and set his tray on the wide porch railing nearest Mastiff. It was a little too tall compared with the seat, but it was close enough. Benny didn't mind not being able to see what was in the tray anyway.

Before Benny had his tray uncovered, the aroma of spiced sausage wafted over from Mastiff's tray. Benny lifted his nose and sniffed deeply. Then he lifted the corner of his aluminum and sniffed. The pleasant aroma wasn't coming from his breakfast, that was for sure.

Benny craned his neck, trying to peek into Mastiff's tray. "What you got there, Mastiff, old buddy?"

Mastiff gave an embarrassed smile. "Oh, uh. It's vegan sausage and spiced apple oatmeal."

Benny frowned, poking his own bland, lumpy oatmeal and grease-laden soya patties with a spoon. "And why do I have the usual Bile Street shit? I didn't see Jodie over last night..."

"And it ain't none of your business if she were. But that ain't it anyway." Mastiff raised a succulent-looking sausage substitute, took a bite, and closed his eyes as he slowly chewed it.

Benny stared at Mastiff. "I'm glad you're enjoying your feast there. Would you mind sharing how your good friend might get that, instead of this?"

"Man, this good."

"That's enough."

Mastiff broke out laughing, a deep, rich sound that fit the beautiful, sunny morning. "You just request it. They get some vegan contractor to make it and it's fresh and a hell of a lot better than the shit you got. Man, I don't even miss the meat. Not that you have real meat there anyway." He stuffed a scoop of apple-filled oatmeal into his mouth. "Talk to Jodie—she'll hook you up. Without a booty call even."

"I thought all this food was made of soya?"

"Not according to Trance. He say most of it GMO soya, but it mixed with some kind of meat slime by-product or something. He showed me a few vids."

Benny thought back to last night's faux lasagna. It had certainly been slimy. "You get something for every meal?"

"Twenty-one squares a week, man. There's a page you sign up on every week. I ain't got but one nasty meal from these guys, and it was still better than that shit you eating." Mastiff narrowed his eyes. "Now get your nose away from my grub."

Benny lifted his tray. "Trade?"

"Oh, hell no, boy. I ain't putting that slop in me for the rest of my days." Mastiff shoved another faux sausage into his mouth and winked at Benny.

Benny looked forward to his daily walks. They'd become the highlight of his day. He was up to managing two trips a day and his hip was no longer screaming at the end. But it was still sore. It was good to have Mastiff with him, and not only because Benny didn't want to be alone on the street if his hip broke or something. It only took one stumble. And calling emergency services was as likely to get him run over by the ambulance as put inside.

Mastiff stopped their walk in front of what used to be Mr. Deinkin's microhome to stretch his back. "Who that?"

"Who's who?"

Mastiff nodded to a house with a yellow flyer on the other side of Bile Street. "There, looking out that window."

Benny squinted across the street. He saw two dark faces staring back through a grimy window. The front door of what had been Emma Gooding's home stood ajar, creaking in the breeze.

"I'll be damned," muttered Benny. "There goes the neighborhood. Squatters."

"Let's go," Mastiff said.

Benny cast furtive glances over his shoulder as they finished their walk home. He knew the population of Bile Street had been dwindling, but the presence of these strangers made it dangerous. How many were there, and how many would come before the DoS did anything about it? If they would do anything about it.

"You going to call Hannah, or you want me to?" Mastiff asked.

Benny pursed his lips. "I called her once already, going on about where everyone had gone. She'll think I'm being melodramatic if I call her about this. You call. Besides, she's one of you."

Mastiff's eyes bulged and he lolled his head to stare at Benny. "Oh, hell no. What the fuck that mean?"

"You know." Benny spread his hands out in front of his stomach. "Fat. Wait. What did you think I meant?"

Mastiff continued to stare for a second, then burst out laughing, sending the birds in a nearby tree into the air. "You crazy."

Four hours later, a DoS enforcer patrol stopped by and told Benny and Mastiff they'd run off the squatters and Bile Street was as safe as ever. That didn't particularly comfort Benny.

25. Game Over, Man. Game Over!

Benny fired up his terminal the following morning to check his messages and the weather for walking, and to clear out his various DoS and corporate sponsored ads. The request form for his vegan breakfast said his meals wouldn't be delivered until the following week. But he was looking forward to eating with Mastiff on the porch anyway.

When he opened the final DoS notification, his shoulders sagged. Gaming allotments had been replenished. Moments later, Mastiff's online itinerary appeared. It seemed Mastiff had given the schedule a good deal of thought as it was as full and convoluted as anything he'd ever seen, squeezing every second possible from the day. They would be jumping from tournament to raid to grind session, and back to another tournament, and so on. All day long.

Benny took a loud sip from his chipped teacup. "Shit."

But he logged in and waded through the digital domains his friend had planned out for them. Benny did enjoy killing Flaming_Armpit_Bomb in the first tournament, but everyone got ass-stomped by the appropriately monikered IWILLUKFCK-INGDELETEYOU. When it came time for their morning walk, Benny was ready to log out.

"Let's walk."

"I'm not really feeling it this morning, Benny." Mastiff's voice was distracted, and Benny could imagine his friend was hastily jumping to the next server on the itinerary. "And I'm not feeling good, you know."

"Oh, come on. You don't want to spend all your minutes in one day."

"No," Mastiff said. "Maybe after lunch."

Benny grunted. "I'm going for a walk."

"OK."

Benny gritted his teeth. It wasn't realistic to expect Mastiff to join him out of guilt, but Benny hoped he would have. Benny logged off, snatched his hat and cane, and stepped out into the sun shining down on Bile Street.

He'd talked himself out of walking alone more than once already, and for good reasons. Those reasons were still valid, but the day was so nice and he was enjoying the relief in his hip the exercise provided. The birds were chirping. A spry-feeling Benny took it all in as he shuffled along.

"Hey! You deaf, Pappi?" a voice shouted.

Benny started from his reverie and realized the voice had called him at least twice before it had registered. The voice was heavily accented, but Benny couldn't place it. Definitely not local. Maybe Middle Eastern or Indian.

A young, scruffy-looking man stood on the porch of the house Benny and Mastiff had seen the squatters in. He wore a tattered, black jacket and an untucked, red shirt that hung below the crotch of his dingy, grease-streaked jeans.

"That's right," the man said when Benny looked his way. "I'm talking to you, Pappi. You fucking call the enforcers on my friends, old man?" The man motioned to the house. Two faces were peering out through the door.

The man splayed his arms truculently. "Didn't do much good, eh, Pappi? You want to keep your nasty dentures in your mouth, you don't call them any more. Mind your business, you old fucker. You got me?"

Benny's heart raced. He looked around for signs of anyone else and caught glimpses of at least three other people staring out at him from nearby houses. Trying not to show fear, Benny stared at the young man.

"You go deaf again, Pappi? Yeah, you see we ain't alone. We know where you and your fat friend live. And it's easy to get into these houses. You getting me, old fucker?"

The kid didn't look like a real street tough, but he was tough enough for Benny. Hell, a troop of grumpy Child Scouts that had missed their nap time was tough enough for Benny. But the kid was stupid. Tough could be reasoned with. It was hard to tell what a dipshit with an attitude would do though.

"Got it?" the kid screamed.

"Yeah, I got."

The kid offered a fuck-you smile. "Good. Maybe we can be friends, Pappi. We can be good neighbors. You can be a good neighbor too. Don't fuck with us, we don't fuck with you. Easy, right?"

Benny nodded, not trusting himself to speak. His stomach was jelly and he feared his voice would crack to reveal the scared old man he was. He turned away and hurried home before the squatters could see the thin stream of urine running down his pant leg.

He felt as if he was being watched the whole way home. When he got in, Benny changed his pants and logged in to tell Mastiff what had happened.

"Just some punks, but you prolly shouldn't go alone no more," Mastiff said, the distinct sound of key and trigger clicks coming over his mic. "If they give us any trouble, we call the enforcers. And this time they ain't just squatting, they threatening violence. They haul them off this time."

It was no surprise that Mastiff didn't want to walk after lunch. He was in the middle of a big guild war that only happened once a week. Benny didn't join in, but he didn't go for his walk either. He didn't know if it would be safe even if Mastiff was with him.

Instead, Benny opened up one of the books that had been gathering dust since he started playing with Mastiff again. It was some hackneyed, old, zombie-apocalypse, urban-fantasy romance that jumped from tired trope to tired trope. Benny loved it. He fell asleep one chapter from the end and had disturbing dreams filled with zombie erotica.

Benny went through his normal morning routine, happily when the food orderly delivered breakfast in one of the vegan food tins Mastiff enjoyed. The steaming stack of pancakes smelled delicious and the organic orange juice tasted only slightly of concentrate.

There was no ingredient list. The DoS occasionally let its corporate slip show. The pancakes were probably made of some of that hippy shit Trance had gone on about. Wheat germ or quinoa or almond flour or something. Trance called everything he considered healthy superfood. It came from the foggy depths of Benny's memory that maybe Trance had told him about the vegan food program.

Benny shrugged and took another bite. Whatever the pancakes were made of, they were fresh and utterly delicious.

After stuffing himself, Benny sat back and ignored his terminal. He kept patting his full stomach with surprising satisfaction. Most DoS meals seemed to only last a few minutes.

When he'd digested his meal to his satisfaction, Benny poured a fresh cup of tea and reluctantly logged in to his terminal. After clicking through the usual morning shit, he pulled up Mastiff's chat connection. There was a notification blinking at the bottom.

M.Barkey is typing a message...

Benny watched the window for five minutes and it never updated. The old fool had probably fallen asleep on his keyboard again. Benny got up and tapped on Mastiff's window with his cane. There was no answer.

Benny shook his head and grinned. "Wake up, Princess," he called. He banged louder, this time on the window frame so as not to break the glass. Nothing. He could see a hint of that blue light in the dank shadow behind Mastiff's blinds.

Worry roiled in Benny's gut, ruining his fine breakfast. He shuffled over to Mastiff's door and pounded on it. When there was still no answer, Benny reached for Mastiff's spare access card, which had been put back since their friendship was on the mend. He paused to make sure no squatter was watching him, before pulling the card from between two boards and letting himself in.

Mastiff's bulk lay on its stomach in the middle of the floor like a great, sleeping bear. His head was turned towards Benny, revealing a twisted, pain-filled grimace and lifeless eyes. The strong smell of urine wafted from the puddle around his wet pajama pants. A thin sheen of perspiration glistened on his upper lip and forehead, but he made no reaction to Benny's entrance.

"Oh, shit," Benny whispered. He fell on Mastiff, slapping him sharply on the back and cheek. Not even a flinch. The skin was still warm, but clammy. "Oh, shit. Oh, shit."

Benny grunted as he strained to roll Mastiff onto his back in hopes of starting CPR. He couldn't even budge the huge man. Leveraging his cane beneath Mastiff, Benny managed to get his friend onto his side. But the cane slipped when Benny tried to reposition it and Mastiff rolled back in place like an avalanche. A huge, black arm flopped as the body rolled, knocking Benny's glasses from his face.

Tears rolled down Benny's face as he slid downMastiff's body. He didn't even care about the growing wet spot on his back as he leaned against Mastiff's mountainous form. "Don't leave me here," Benny whispered. "Jesus, please don't leave me alone."

The breakfast tray was on the table, untouched. That meant Mastiff must have been OK when the orderly came. Or, at least, Mastiff hadn't been lying on the floor. But Benny couldn't be sure; the orderlies weren't the most observant lot. Emergency services might still be able to do something if they hurried.

Benny pulled out his voip and connected. The dispatcher gave him a string of instructions that were all beyond his capability. Even if Mastiff hadn't been so huge, Benny didn't know if he could have performed even half of the instructions. Once Benny finally got it through the dispatcher's head, the dispatcher concentrated on keeping Benny calm.

Benny rubbed Mastiff's shoulder each time the dispatcher asked if he was still on the line. "Yes, I'm still on the line. No sirens yet. What's taking so fucking long?"

He looked around the house for something that might help. Since he didn't know what might help, Benny knew it was a pointless gesture. But he had to do something. "Yes, I'm still fucking here."

Blood-scrawled letters rotated on Mastiff's screen.

You're Dead!

Benny shuddered. A picture of Rivka Rey in her twenties, perhaps close to the time Benny would kill her, was taped to the side of the monitor.

"We'll get you taken care of, man," Benny whispered. "You'll be fine. Yes, I'm still here."

Mastiff wouldn't be fine.

When emergency services rolled up some twenty minutes later, Benny was hunched over Mastiff's desk, face in hands. His glasses, voip, and Rivka's picture were in a little pile by his elbow. He listened without turning as the medics grunted, cussed, and strained to roll his friend's body over. The work would be even harder in the cramped microhome.

"Allah," one panted. "I'm surprised this fellow made it this long. I wonder how much we had to pay for his food?"

They went through the lifesaving checklist with perfunctory ease. They knew, as Benny did, too, the man on the floor was long past saving. But the DoS had its forms and those who didn't get all the boxes checked, didn't get paid.

Benny didn't even turn at the horrendous crash as the medics tried to roll the massive corpse onto the gurney. The wheels and floor creaked in protest when they finally rolled Mastiff out of his final home.

Someone tapped Benny's shoulder. "Mr. Benny? Are you OK?" Hannah asked.

Benny looked up at her, unsure how long he'd been sitting there. He rubbed his eyes and saw Jodie standing behind Hannah. "I guess so. I think Mastiff's dead."

"I'm sorry, Mr. Benny. There wasn't anything emergency services could do. They called me a bit ago."

Benny nodded, willing the rage building up in him to go away. Instead, it burst like a pressure cooker. He slammed his fists repeatedly on Mastiff's desk, sending a half-empty water bottle rolling onto the floor. Curses spewed from his mouth as if spoken by Satan himself; or worse, the Big Mack. Hannah and Jodie looked away.

The fit left Benny trembling. He let his hands fall open to his lap. "Sorry. We... we were friends again. Shit. And now he's left me alone."

Jodie put a hand on his shoulder and Benny held it. "Sorry, Benny. I know how hard you worked to fix things up."

Benny looked up at her over his glasses, searching for a hint of mocking subtext in her works. Her expression was genuine and he squeezed her hand.

"I know it's too soon for arrangements," Benny said, "but is it possible to get a travel chit for his funeral?"

Hannah's brow furrowed and she exchanged a furtive glance with Jodie. "I'm sorry, Mr. Benny. We don't have authorization for that in the budget. And that comes from the very top."

Jodie scoffed. "Yeah, they can't even pay—"

"That's enough," Hannah said. "Mr. Benny doesn't need to worry about the bureaucracy now."

Jodie rubbed Benny's back with her free hand and leaned close to him. "It's not like anyone could really stop you if you found a ride though. I can't, but I'll send you the arrangements when we get them."

Hannah pursed her lips. "And we certainly won't try to stop him, Jodie. I will issue a travel pass and make sure you get the information as soon as it's available." She withdrew a yellow flyer and her face fell. "I'm afraid I am going to have to ask you to leave though, Mr. Benny. And... please don't take any mementos. DoS needs everything it can get."

Jodie flipped a finger up at Hannah down low where only she and Benny could see it. He barely noticed. The chair was shaped to Mastiff's huge ass and Benny needed Jodie's help to get up. He adjusted his glasses. The picture was right below his fingers for a second and he considered grabbing it, but could see Hannah watching him in the terminal's reflection. So he took a final look around the latest of Bile Street's crypts and limped home, his hip screaming.

<hr />

"LET ME SHUT DOWN MASTIFF'S terminal," Jodie said, watching Benny through the window. "Poor old Benny. I think he's the only one left on Bile Street. Except that filth moving in down there."

"They aren't filth," Hannah scolded. "They're people."

Jodie turned to face Hannah to make sure the other woman could see the eye-roll. "You walk by them alone some night and in the morning you can tell me what kind of people they are. If you make it back. Mastiff already called the enforcers on them once. I'm going to call again when we get back to the office."

"That might not be such a good idea."

"I bet Benny is terrified. When are they going to move him? Surely it's not economical to leave him here alone."

Hannah sighed. "They aren't. All transfers except medical emergencies have been frozen."

"That's some bullshit."

Hannah pursed her lips momentarily, but then softened into a look of sad resignation. "It is."

Jodie watched her boss for a moment before turning to Mastiff's terminal. It was too bad Hannah was such a DoS cheerleader. The woman had a good heart beneath all that bootlicking. What a tool.

The reflection in the terminal let her know when Hannah wasn't looking and Jodie slipped the picture into her pocket. She didn't know who the girl was, but she'd seen Benny's fingers shake as if he wanted to take it. There was no reason for the DoS to have it. It would only sit in the crammed warehouse with the rest of the shit the non-elected grave robbers took. The DoS hadn't paid rent on that building in almost six months. Jodie wouldn't be surprised if the ripped-off owners found themselves the subject of an ass-clenching audit.

"All done." Jodie powered down Mastiff's terminal for the final time. She walked out on the porch and watched Hannah close the door and tape the yellow flyer on it. Hannah pulled out her administrator card and locked the door and windows. They walked towards the e-car.

"Where you going?" Hannah asked as Jodie broke off and stepped on Benny's porch.

Jodie pointed at Benny's door. "Here."

Hannah got in the car without comment.

Benny opened the door but didn't say anything.

"Just checking up on you," Jodie said. She slipped the picture into his hand. "Hide that until we leave. I'll make sure you get the info. Mastiff was a good man." She gave Benny a peck on the cheek and got in the car.

BENNY WATCHED THE WOMEN go, leaving him alone with the skulking faces he saw in every window. It was hard to tell if they were real or imagined. Or both.

With a trembling hand, he placed the photo gingerly in his memory chest. Rivka and Dakota now stared up at him from the top of his pile of memories. He imagined the girls playing together as children as he and his dead friend looked on, laughing at the fairies.

Benny cried himself to sleep, feeling his heart couldn't take any more. It was all too much. He was ready to go now too. His heart continued to thunder in his chest. It felt as if it would burst, and Benny prayed it would. Was this the real curse of old age? Watching his family and friends die, leaving him behind in the world all alone?

Waking up the next morning didn't seem all that wonderful to Benny now.

26. Big Mamma Tells it True

B enny settled back into the luxurious seat in the back of the van. It was a sunny day and the scenery flying by outside the window was a rich green, so he'd adjusted the digital tinting level to zero. Benny wanted to see it all.

The van's tires rumbled on the pitted and crumbling roads, as they had all through Illinois and Missouri. But it was beautiful outside. And they were over halfway to Wichita, the landscape thinning into the plains of Kansas.

Grinning out of the window, Benny spoke up. "Thanks, again." He didn't expect an answer; they'd given up responding to his repeated, fawning thanks over an hour ago.

Putting out a call for help had been hard for Benny. He hated it, always had. But Mastiff deserved it. The family that still lived in Wichita hadn't even been born when Benny moved away. A few great-nephews and -nieces of kin long dead and cousins he couldn't even remember were about it. But he put out the call anyway.

Need ride from Chicago to Wichita for friend's funeral. No money for gas or hotel.

The near-immediate reply shocked him.

Got your back. Send details.

And true to their word, they had his back. They had it so completely that Benny still felt weepy. It was easy to pretend he didn't really need help when he wasn't trying to do something. But his poverty and creeping decrepitude were impossible to ignore. Amazed gratitude and embarrassment filled his heart.

Even as Daniel and Jayna rang his bell early that morning, Benny was having a hard time believing it.

"I like the digs, Benny," Jayna had said. "Very eco-tastical."

Benny wanted to comment about it not being so great to live in, but he didn't want to come off as a whiny ingrate. Which was why he didn't complain too much about Bile Street. The stories he did tell about how much life there sucked were wrapped in wry humor.

Describing his digital adventures didn't interest Daniel or Jayna, but they listened when Benny spoke of his dead friends. He couldn't tell if they were being polite or genuinely interested in these people they'd never know. They at least weren't scanning their voips as he spoke, but who was he to judge them? They'd driven across the god-forsaken country to give an old man they'd never met a ride. Daniel and Jayna could do whatever they wanted.

As they approached the loop around Wichita, Daniel shut off the autocruise and took manual control. The RoadNav system complained in a petulant voice about losing control. The familiar skyline of Wichita rose from the horizon like a haunted forest, waking Benny's memories like moaning phantoms.

Traffic was traffic as it had always been, and they slowed. Each metropolis touted its advanced grid control system, but that only meant that cars were stuck in computer-caused gridlock instead of human-caused.

"Every flipping day," Daniel muttered as he turned down the nearest off-ramp.

The RoadNav system chimed in over the van's speakers. "Please return to the highway. The traffic control grid is more efficient and safer for all drivers when vehicles remain on the primary roads."

Benny stared at the stalled traffic on the freeway above them. "At least we know it isn't true artificial intelligence."

Jayna laughed and spun her seat around to face Benny. "Yeah. I've always figured some programmer told it to say that. Easier to gather data points if everyone's in one place."

"And pitch directed advertising to a captive audience," Daniel added. He turned onto Montare Street, then zipped into the turn lane for Broadmore.

"Please return to the highway—"

Jayna spun back around and thumbed the RoadNav controller to off. It sounded almost offended as its voice faded into a digital warble. "It always says that. Every freaking time your turn doesn't put you on a prime road."

The dusky streets rolled by outside the window. Electric billboards, LED tube signs, and streetlights were beginning to flicker to life. Wichita, pronounced "Witch-ta-tas" by Eli as a child, hadn't changed much in the decades since his last visit. Not really. The facades were more worn and stained, and the graffiti declared new street players since Benny's time on the force. But he could still see the city's heart through the changes.

Clean streets couldn't hide the essential weariness of the city. A civic improvement here, a metro station there, stood in stark contrast to what Benny remembered waiting for him every night. He knew the streets still held the same dangers. No amount of fancy lights or paint could give this city a proverbial new-car smell.

Daniel pulled to a stop in the parking area of their housing complex. While the access to their apartment was adequate, Benny's hip was very stiff and Jayna had to help him a couple of times. Their place was cozy, and Jayna prepared leftovers while Daniel set up a fold-out couch. Benny was looking forward to some more face-to-face conversation, but dozed off shortly after dinner.

Before he knew it, a ray of morning sun slipped through the curtains and tickled his nose until he sneezed himself awake. He looked around with bleary eyes and saw Jayna smile at him and motion to the plate on the table. With a slow, pop-inducing stretch and prodigious yawn, Benny sat up. He felt pretty good.

"Morning," she said. "Are you sure you don't want us to come?"

Benny stumbled to the table and shoved a piece of Fakin' Bacon in his mouth. "Oh, no. I couldn't even think to ask. You guys already drove halfway around the world for me. I'll just voip a cab."

"No, voip us and we'll get you," Daniel said as he walked in. "We're glad to help. St. Frank's Methodist is in a pretty nice sector so there shouldn't be any trouble. And it's close. It won't take long."

"I hate to impose."

Jayna patted Benny's arm. "He's just going to sit around picking lint out of his navel anyway. Feel free to use the shower. It's almost time."

———◆———

DANIEL WAS RIGHT ABOUT the neighborhood. Row houses lined the street leading to the massive church. The buildings were free of graffiti and the streets free of trash. The houses were clean and the small yards tidy. Many had warmly colored hedges or trim.

Turning down a final offer from Daniel and Jayna to accompany him, Benny waved them on and shuffled up the ramp to St. Frank's. The parking lot was filled with vehicles, and parked cars lined the street.

A middle-aged Latino couple smiled and opened the crystalline door for Benny. He tipped his hat, then removed it as he walked between them and into the church.

The woman handed him a small pamphlet. "Brother Mastiff's viewing is through the door right there. The service will be in the main sanctuary over there, a bit after lunch. Have a blessed day."

"Thanks." Benny moved aside, making sure not to block the doorway. He never understood why people did that, oblivious to the other people trying to get through. Good Christians should not block the doorway. Not that he was a good Christian. He knew there was some sort of creator, but he'd lived too long to pretend he understood it.

But he did like churches, if not necessarily the congregation or preacher. Especially old churches with stained glass and old, beloved, wooden furniture. When he was a child, churches began looking like cafes or convention centers. St. Frank's looked as if it was trying to play the middle. Benny remembered Jesus saying something about being neither hot nor cold and being spit out, but that wasn't his business. And he loved the smell of food and flowers that filled the lobby.

A cluster of multi-colored children raced by, nearly bowling him over. The man at the door scolded them, but the kids were off again before he could finish. He offered Benny an apologetic smile. Benny didn't mind. It was good to see children running and playing. Their antics cheered him, though he'd have felt differently if they had broken his hip.

Sunday school artwork lined the walls and tables. Bible heroes in finger paints fought God's enemies and saved the righteous. Stick-figure apostles marched across colorful construction paper. He'd painted such things when he was a child. What would those children believe when they were his age?

The faith of his youth had been comforting and a sudden grieving for its loss washed over Benny. He sniffed loudly and wiped his eyes. It was a fine thing to believe Jesus loved you.

He wished he could still believe it.

As he shuffled towards the viewing line, Benny passed a rack overflowing with colorful tracts, displaying what he supposed were the spiritual concerns of the elders of that church. Abortion, gender swapping, racism, environmentalism, impending AI singularity, faith, baptism, the Papacy, corporate greed, the rich, the poor, the best Bible, and the fate of non-believers were arranged on one side of the rack. He didn't bother looking at the other side.

As he took a place in line, a young, black woman dressed in a white pantsuit offered him one of the church's wheelchairs. The line was slow and meandering, and Benny considered it for a moment. At length, he politely declined.

The line moved in fits and spurts and, before long, Benny could see a young, black man in a dark suit and black shoes shined to a mirror-like polish. He sat at a small table near Mastiff's casket, scrawling names and information into a white visitor register. A bright sticker on his pocket read "Anton."

"Hi," Anton said as Benny approached. "Would you mind if I write your name in the register?"

"Sure." Benny spelled out his name and answered the couple of simple questions Anton asked.

"And how did you know Mastiff Barkey?"

"I lived with him in the retirement ward on Bile Street. I, uh, found his body."

Anton stopped writing and looked up at Benny. "That must have been terrible."

"Yes. Yes it was."

"So you lived next door to him?" asked a fortyish-looking, black man behind Benny. "Up north?"

Benny turned and squinted at the man. "That's right. We were neighbors for quite a while."

The man cast Benny a sidelong glance and stormed away. The line was relatively short after Anton's table and Benny was at the casket in a few more minutes.

The casket was huge. It had a bright, white finish that matched Mastiff's suit, highlighting the man's dark, placid face. Benny suppressed a laugh at the unbidden recollection of an ancient Jell-O commercial from the depths of his TV-scarred, childhood memories.

Benny now wished he was at the end of the line. It felt as if there wasn't enough time to say good-bye, and he wanted to speak to his dead friend, but not where others could see and hear. People were waiting behind him, but Benny hoped his age would afford him some grace from those waiting.

On the drive down, he'd spent hours engaged in the age-old tradition of telling his dead friend all those things he should have said while he had the chance. Benny's internal, and occasionally muttered, monologues had been long and sagely, witty and relevant. But now all he could do was place his hand on the cool casket and sigh. He mutely stepped away and looked for a place to sit until the service started.

No sooner had Benny made his way to the sanctuary and found a comfortable chair in the back, two men walked in front of him and stopped. They were crowded so close that Benny had to scoot the chair back to be able to look up at them.

One was the man from the line and he leaned close to Benny. "So, you're the guy who lived next to Mastiff in the old fuckers' home?"

Benny's heart raced and he gripped his cane tightly. The man was angry about something and looking for a fight. "Yup."

"So that mean you the fucking pig that killed Rivka Rey Evans, right?"

Benny looked away, but said nothing.

The man sucked air loudly between his teeth. "That's what I thought. You know she were my cousin, right? Right, you fucker?"

Benny didn't answer and, after a moment, the man turned to his companion. "Hear that shit, man? He ain't got nothing to say now. I bet he had all sorts of shit to say to Rivka Rey before he shot her ass."

Anton strode up the aisle. "Jesse, leave the man be."

"Oh, if it ain't our fine young gentleman here to save whitey."

Anton shoved in close, shouldering the two men back. "Big Mamma wants to talk to him."

The two men exchanged wicked glances. "Oh, she going to fuck you up," said the second man in a gleeful, high-pitched voice.

Anton offered Benny a hand. "She is not. Big Mamma, that is to say, Uncle Mastiff's mother, would like you to talk to her, if you will. She really appreciates you coming. Especially since you were the last to see him alive."

"Probably shot his ass too," Jesse said.

Benny glanced at Jesse, then took Anton's hand. "Does she know?"

"About Rivka Rey?" Anton asked. "Yes, sir. She's not angry. She just wants to meet you. Uncle Mastiff used to voip us all about you."

Benny let Anton pull him up and followed him towards a door behind the main stage. Jesse and his companion followed, ignoring the glares from Anton. Anton opened the door for Benny, but let it close on the other two. It didn't stop them.

They entered a room that was quiet with age. It smelled old, too, filled with the tangy hint of hidden mold and tearful prayers. The furnishings were dark wood that matched the panelling on the walls. Oil paintings depicting tales from scripture hung around the room. Jesus and Moses stared beatifically across the room at each other.

Oak bookshelves sagged under the burden of cracked, long-unopened concordances, bible studies, apologetics tomes, and olde-tyme hymnals. This august room had obviously been the heart of the church, swallowed by the electric modernity that now defined the place. Benny liked this part of the church—it was at least a bit more honest.

The woman sitting in the afghan-covered wheelchair beneath Jesus had to be Big Mamma. Her face was gaunt, deathlike, with eyes that shone brown over bony cheeks. Time had ravaged her body, but Benny could tell from the keen look in those eyes that it hadn't taken her mind. She smiled up at him, revealing perfect, white teeth that looked too large for her mouth. The wheelchair creaked as she rocked back and forth in it.

Big Mamma motioned for him to come closer with her skeletal hands. Benny shuffled forward and, when he was close enough, she wrapped her rail-thin arms around him.

"Mr. Benny." Her voice creaked like a comfortable rocking-chair, rolling from between her spit-speckled lips in a drawl, with no pause between her words. "Would it be all right if I called you Benny? Leonard called you Benny when he spoke of you, boy."

Benny couldn't help but laugh, and not only at being called boy. Given her age, he didn't mind. Especially since there was no trace of vitriol in that sweet, cracked, old voice. "Yes, ma'am."

"Call me Big Mamma, Benny. They all do. Anton, be a doll and scootch that chair over here for my friend Benny so's he can sit and talk with me."

As Anton stepped to grab one of the worn leather chairs that must have supported thousands of holy bottoms in its time, Jesse stormed past and stopped in front of the wheelchair.

"Big Mamma! This fucker killed Rivka Rey. We should be beating the shit out of him and tossing him to the curve."

"Don't be so rude, child," Big Mamma said calmly. "And it's curb, Winston, you ninny."

"Whatever," he said, glancing at Benny. "Call me Jesse, Big Mamma. You know that's my street tag."

"Winston, you know Jesse James were a white boy, right? That lame-ass street name wasn't cool when you was eight, and it ain't cool now. I saw your backside slide out your mamma and I'll damned well call you by your given name, child."

"Big Mamma," Winston, not Jesse James, whined, "I'll bust this dude's ass right here for what he done to Rivka Rey!"

Benny hefted his cane at Winston as the man rounded on him. "I'll shove this cane right up your ass if you don't step off. Winston."

Big Mamma cackled, slapping her curled hands on her knees, and bent over laughing in her creaking chair. Winston glared at Benny, then at Big Mamma.

"No wonder Leonard liked you so much, Benny." She turned her wrinkled face to Winston. "Child, you weren't even born when Rivka passed."

"You mean when she was murdered by this motherfucker?"

Big Mamma's frown pulled the wrinkled mask of her face down. "You need to run along now, Winston. It's a shame you didn't listen to your daddy when he were teaching you manners."

Benny saw Mastiff in Big Mamma's scowl. Winston sneered at Benny, but left with the other man with no further comment. Shaking his head, Anton set the chair close to the wheelchair and helped Benny sit.

Big Mamma reached over and patted Benny's leg. Her hand was warm and leathery. It reminded him of his mother's hand on her last day.

"Sorry about that, Benny. Winston's heart is in the right place. I mean, you did kill his kin, even if he never even met her. But he don't care about Rivka Rey. Her name ain't nothing but a slogan to him, a well-worn family motto.

"Every time someone in our clan has a run-in with the law, they call on poor old Rivka's name like some Papist invoking one of their blasphemous saints." She chuckled for a second, then looked Benny in the eyes. "I'm very sorry about your daughter. It's hard to lose a child. I know. I've put four in the ground already. Leonard will make five."

Benny took her hand and patted it. "Thank you. They say parents shouldn't outlive their children."

"Well, I think they are full of shit." Big Mamma laughed again. "Three of mine died because they were dumbasses. They turned from God and started playing in the Devil's alleyways and crack houses.

I did my best, but sure don't want my candle to go out early just to avoid seeing their folly."

Big Mamma let out a quavering sigh and dabbed at her eyes with the afghan. "But Leonard—Mastiff was such a damned dumb name—he was a good boy. Took good care. And Lord Jesus forgive me because Leonard probably wouldn't want me to tell you how bad, how rotten, he felt after not going to your daughter's funeral."

"We talked a lot about that, and other things," Benny said. "He apologized."

"I'm sure he did." Big Mamma pulled out her bright teeth and smacked her gums. "I hate those things."

Without dentures, her face shrank even more and Benny couldn't tell if she was harder or easier to understand. "But," she continued, "I bet he didn't tell you he called me up crying like a baby about how he done you wrong. He loved you, Benny. Called you his best friend. It weighed so heavy on his heart." A thin tear rolled down her leathery cheek. She clutched her hands over her chest. "Oh, his heart."

"I'm so sorry about Mastiff," Benny said after a moment. He looked away. "And Rivka, too. I didn't want to shoot her, you know. It was all so long ago. So crazy then."

"Thank you, Benny. And you're right. It was a long time ago. We told her she were running with the wrong sort." She offered Benny a toothless smile. "And I told that fool son of mine to keep his gun away from her. But we knew she had that gun because someone there snatched it up before you pigs could find it."

"So you knew she had a gun?"

"Sure we did." Big Mamma squeezed his hand. "I drove it out somewhere and scattered the pieces in the river myself. You must understand that to our thinking, what she did was stupid, but not wrong. And I still don't think she was wrong. Just bad planning because of those fools she was running with.

"She was right to fight. More of my people needed to fight. You cops were a bunch of assholes. But let's not pick those scabs. As you say, it was long ago. Let the kids fight it out and grant us old-timers some peace."

Benny nodded and they sat in silence until Benny asked, "Why Jesu?"

Big Mamma cackled and pointed to a portrait on the wall of a man in a suit. "His granddaddy put the fear of God in poor Leonard. Being a preacher, that was part of his job after all. But especially about taking the Lord's name in vain. Leonard were almost too afraid to even pray by the time he were six years old. Poor child."

Her old throat was not quite up to the task of imitating her son's baritone. "'Oh, Lord Jesu!' he'd say to get around the letter of The Law. But that never fooled my daddy or God."

Benny smiled. "Thanks for talking with me, Big Mamma. I like this room. It's what a church should look like."

"You know, I was a deaconess in this church for almost thirty years and this was always my favorite room. This is where my daddy worked." She winked at Benny. "I was a preacher's daughter, and you know how much trouble we can be. I come here to think about him and the times when St. Frank's brought the spirit of God to men instead of the spirit of shiny Babylon. They mean well, but I'm afraid they left the narrow path."

"*Mene mene tekel upharsin.*" He thought those words were funny as a child and they'd always stuck in his mind. It felt good to use them.

"Praise the Lord and amen," Big Mamma cheered. "Just so, Benny. Just so. Anton, take good care of Benny here, would you, darling?"

"Of course, Big Mamma."

"And send in your daddy with some tea and lemon cake, too. That's a boy." She turned back to Benny. "He's a good boy who knows the value of his name. If you need anything, ask and he'll take good care of you."

An overwhelming urge came over Benny to kiss her on the forehead. He could neither explain why nor resist it. Benny leaned over and planted a gentle kiss on her forehead. It felt as though he was kissing his own mother again, one last time. "Thanks, Big Mamma."

She squealed in delight and coyly waved herhand at Benny. "Fresh."

They heldhands for another moment before Benny allowed Anton to lead him away. He felt the uncomfortable stare of several people and wondered if Winston had been out here dog-talking him. Anton led Benny back to his chair and brought him an eco-foam cup filled with dark, steaming tea. Benny closed his eyes and let the tea warm his throat and belly. Fuck Winston. Let them stare. He wasn't here for them.

The service was boisterous. Not quite as chaotic as Mack's had been, but the attendees cried and prayed openly and without shame. A choir that was larger than entire congregations of Benny's childhood belted out a cappella spirituals, singing hope and comfort over the audience like a divine thunderstorm. The choir robes swayed like a giant satin curtain caught in the wind as the men and women moved to the rhythm, clapping their hands.

The stares and his aching hip kept Benny's own booty-wagging to a minimum. He saw massive speakers, laser lights, and disco balls hanging silently behind the stage, not partaking in the celebration. That was probably Big Mamma's doing, if Benny had to guess.

After countless songs, a doughy Latino wearing a dark suit and an earpiece with a mic took to the stage. His voice boomed from the speakers as he prayed, and blessed, and called on the name of Jesus. The congregation responded with barks of "Amen!" and "Yes, Lord!" The preacher spoke fine words about Mastiff and his family, and commended his good works to Heaven above. Benny found himself enraptured by the man's words, despite his usual ambivalence about preachers. Mastiff would have probably been embarrassed at all the praise.

Benny looked for Big Mamma during the service, but only caught sight of her once through the writhing crowd. She was right outside her door, waving her arms over her head. Later, after the service when Jayna was helping Benny into the van, he saw Big Mamma in the lobby, watching him through the door. Anton was behind her, holding the handles of her wheelchair. Big Mamma raised her hand a final time as the van's door closed.

Benny never saw Big Mamma again, but he thought of her, and his own dear mother, often after that. He thought of them all the way back to Bile Street. He thought of them to the end of his days.

27. The Welcome Wagon Strikes Back

B enny looked at his voip in disbelief. He wanted to scream into it, wanted to smash it against the wall. He wondered if it would be better to hang up and talk to the wall instead. Bile Street had gone to hell in a handbasket in the weeks since Mastiff's death.

"What do you mean you can't do anything about it? If anyone who was actually supposed to be here left a single piece of trash in the yard, it was citation time. Now there's thugs who aren't supposed to be here, breaking into houses, running around like cockroaches and tearing things up, and nothing happens?

"I can't even sit on my porch without someone rushing over to harass and threaten me! Some little shit threw a rock at me yesterday as soon as I opened my door. I have it right here. Want to see it?" Ignoring Hannah's protest, Benny picked up the rock and held it in front of the voip's camera. "See that? That almost caved in my forehead."

"I'm very sorry to hear that, Mr. Benny," Hannah said. "I've already called the enforcers three times this week."

Benny dropped the rock back onto his table. "Have they arrested anyone? I see what they do. They drive through as fast as they can, the squatters hide and come back out when the enforcers speed away. Last time, they didn't even bother hiding and the patrol didn't even bother stopping."

"I can't control what they do, Mr. Benny."

He thought the sympathy in her voice was genuine, but that hint of irritated resignation he heard pissed him off. Those thugs probably weren't pounding on the windows of her district office. But he knew she was right. What could she do?

"Have you seen this place in the last few weeks?"

"Yes, sir. I have."

"Then you saw the huge cocks painted all over the place? You saw the huge pair of tits someone sprayed on Mastiff's place?"

Hannah hesitated for a second. "Yes, Mr. Benny. I saw that."

"You shut off the plumbing when a place is empty, right?"

"Yes."

"Imagine what those crappers look like now, Hannah. Where do you think those squatters are squatting? I can smell the shit coming from everywhere." Benny paused to wipe his eyes. "How am I supposed to live here?"

"I'm very sorry, Mr. Benny. I'll see what I can do about the patrols."

Benny couldn't keep the sobbing stutter out of his voice. "Did you know I've missed two meals this week?"

"Yes," Hannah said. "You mentioned that. I'm working on getting replacement meals."

"It won't do any good, Hannah. Don't you see? These punks are chasing the delivery people away. Or even robbing them. I have a contract right here on file. I'm supposed to get three meals a day, every day, atno cost, including two snacks if requested. Portion size provided as per section 42.A-C."

Benny kicked the table leg, sending a spike of pain up his leg. "I've been a good ward and I don't deserve this. I signed every fucking thing I had over to the DoS and the DoS is supposed to be taking care of me."

Hannah sighed. "I know what the contract says. I've been an administrator for seven years. But I can put you in contact with DoS Legal if you—"

"Goddamnit, Hannah! What I want is to be fed like you guys agreed and I want to be able to rest in my own goddamned home without being terrified by some gang-bangers. I want to be treated like a human fucking being. Surely there's other housing that isn't overrun with muggers and thieves. Move me. I'm about the last one here anyway."

Hannah's teeth clacked over the phone. "I told you already the budget's been frozen. No moves are authorized for non-medical reasons."

"I'm starving and scared shitless. My stress levels are through the roof. That sounds like a medical condition to me."

"Not according to Accounting. And you know they don't care about self-diagnosis."

Heat raced up Benny's neck. They were going to leave him to die here. He raised his cane, ready to smash it into something nearby, when an idea occurred. "Schedule an appointment then. You can do that, right? I should be in my quarterly check-up window."

He squeezed his eyes shut, listening as Hannah tapped away on her keys.

After a few moments, Hannah answered. "OK, Mr. Benny. It is close enough. I've got you scheduled for Thursday. The shuttle will be by to pick you up at 8:30am. If your doctor agrees the situation warrants a medical intervention, I'll put in the move request. And I will continue working on the food and enforcer patrols."

Benny's chest relaxed and he rubbed his burning eyes. The next two days would be hard, but it was something. Or, at least, a hope of something. "Look... I'm sorry for yelling."

"It's been... challenging lately, Mr. Benny. For all of us. They're not giving us any money."

"Thanks, Hannah. I know you'll do what you can." Benny moved his thumb to disconnect his voip and added, "And, just to be clear, I'm requesting my two daily snacks, please." He hung up without waiting for her reply and sat sobbing into his hands for a while.

Tiny feet stomped across his front porch, followed by a loud thud on the door. Benny jerked up with a cry. There was no telling what he'd find on his porch if he dared open that door. There had been dirt clods, rocks, and pieces of wood torn from nearby porches. He'd even found a door knob from one of the Bile Street micro-homes.

Childish voices laughed and jeered outside his door in some hateful, foreign gibberish. A voice echoed from somewhere up the street and the kids ran off the porch.

Every call, laugh, or other noise set Benny's heart racing. Texting on his voip provided no distraction. He couldn't focus long enough to follow even a short text chain. Every meme was unimportant, every joke fell flat. He didn't want to text about what was going on around him and he knew he'd fall into gibbering histrionics if he tried to call someone. The only thing he hated more than listening to whiners was being a whiner. Suffering in silence had worked for him so far.

Benny lurched upright in his chair at the heavy knocking on the door. His heart was racing and, before he could say or do anything, the door opened. In swept a pretty, young woman with black hair and brown skin. She looked Indian, maybe Latino. There was no ac-cent when she spoke, so Benny couldn't be certain.

"Lunch, Mr. Martin," the girl said. She immediately peeked through his front blinds. Muttering something under her breath, she raced to the table and dropped a lunch tray there.

Benny still had his hands over his chest. He let out a nervous tit-ter. "Jesus, you scared me."

"Sorry, sir. I'd be jumpy living out here too." She strode to the door.

"How's your day been?"

"Look, Mr. Martin. They're going to jack my shit if I don't get out there." She opened the door and paused before stepping out onto the porch. "Oh, I almost forgot these." With a careless gesture, she pulled two bags of corn chips from her coat pocket and tossed them on the nearest chair.

The woman ran outside, leaving the door open behind her. "Get the fuck away from my car!"

Benny pushed to his feet, using his cane, and hobbled to the door as fast as his hip would allow. Afraid of being seen, he closed the door, except for a crack that allowed him to see outside.

The woman was cursing and shaking her finger at a group of children running around her car. One boy refused to move from in front of the driver's door. Instead of moving, he cupped his grubby hands on his chest and jiggled them around as if they held large breasts.

The woman grabbed the kid by his unruly mop and threw him into the street. The other children ran to the other side of the car and started slapping it repeatedly. She jumped in her car and pulled away from the curb.

A group of men stood watching. Two of them broke out laughing and slapping each other on the back. One grabbed his crotch and yelled with a thick accent, "Suck this, my princess!"

"I'll give you all you can take," yelled the other.

The woman reached out of her car to flip them off and sped away down Bile Street, trailing a string of curses behind her. Benny was still watching through the door when one of the men looked straight at him and flipped him off and shouted something at him.

Benny locked the door. He stood there frozen, waiting for any repercussions. Nothing happened. The crowd of hooligans dispersed and Benny allowed the aroma of his lunch to seduce him. The vegan sweet potato casserole was delicious. He was sure the cookies were gluten-free or made with almond flour or something like that, but they were pretty good too. The bags of chips were still on the chair. Benny considered eating one of them, but stashed them away instead. The young woman probably wasn't going to be back any time soon.

Stomach full and adrenaline rush fading, Benny logged in to his terminal to tune in and zone out with the true opiate of the masses. Things didn't seem so bad for a while.

Despite his concerns, dinner was delivered on time and without incident, though it wasn't the woman from earlier. The food was good, but Benny could only pick at it. What was the point of eating it? He was waiting, trying to survive until Thursday, which seemed like a long time. But then what? All he had was the hope that some doctor would declare him unfit to live alone. Otherwise, it would be straight back here Thursday afternoon. Then it would be back to the same, old, terrifying shit. He forced half of his dinner down and left the rest in his fridge. Not much else to do than try to sleep.

Pounding on the wall woke Benny, though he was too exhausted and groggy to scream in surprise. By the time he blinked his sleepy eyes open, he wasn't sure what had woken him. Whatever it had been, his bladder was screaming for attention now, so Benny clicked on the light and stumbled off to the bathroom.

When finished, he eased back into bed and waited for his thudding heart to slow. Sleep had protected him from the terror of the pounding, but now he realized someone was probably outside. They liked to wait until he turned the light off and give him just enough time to fall asleep, before kicking the door or screaming. Benny feared breaking the silence by using voice commands to turn off the lights, so he clicked the lamp's button with a trembling hand.

He felt it before he saw it: a bloodshot eyeball staring in at him through a slot in the blinds. Benny turned his head to look and screamed.

Laughter came from outside the window.

Benny slapped the blinds, trying to get them to fall back in place and hide the eye. "Get away!"

Two or three other men joined in the laughter outside. "Good night, Pappi," one yelled. A fist thundered against the glass. The jeering trailed away and Benny was too terrified to move until it was completely silent.

It was going to be a long day.

28. Benny Gets a Reality Checkup

Benny woke up Thursday morning feeling well rested. No pounding, blaring music, screaming, or fighting outside his window disturbed his sleep. Not even his bladder had demanded action last night.

Which figured; today was the one day he needed to look and feel shitty. Only a bad prognosis would get him out of this hellhole.

If the squatters had been taken away once and for all by the enforcers, Benny would be OK with that too. He didn't want to go to the hospital. But he knew better. The squatters must have been too drunk or too cold to bother him last night. Or it was some holiday of theirs where their god forbade them to fuck with old men. Maybe they were urban nomads and they were off terrorizing some other poor folk. Wherever they were, it wasn't thanks to the DoS.

Benny knew they'd be back sooner or later. The thugs had invested too much time marking up the neighborhood.

A knock came from the door, causing him to jump. But it was only the food orderly. He walked in and set the steaming tray on the table, along with a bag of cookies and a bag of chips.

"There you go, sir," the young man said. "We heard there was some trouble with the deliveries. Some are refusing delivery runs to Bile Street. I almost freaked out when I saw the schedule, but I didn't see anyone."

Benny lifted the lid and took a deep sniff. Showing up at his doctor's malnourished would probably help, but Benny couldn't turn down the aroma of whatever was in that breakfast casserole. "Thanks, man. Can you guys request enforcer escorts?"

The orderly shrugged. "I guess. But the patrols don't want to come here either."

Benny spoke around a mouthful of food. "Well, I hope you guys can do something."

"I'll ask my supervisor, for all the good it will do. You know you're like the only one left on this street? Why don't they move you?"

"Good question. I'm hoping they will after my appointment today."

The orderly knuckled his forehead and pulled a small card from his pocket. "That's right. This says you have an appointment at Mercy today. Take this and the cafeteria will redeem it for a meal."

Benny smiled gratefully and took the card. Hannah or Jodie usually provided the food chits for his appointments, but he hadn't seen either one in person for at least two weeks. Not that he could blame them. There was no telling what the squatters would do to a woman they caught alone. But a little flame of resentment burned in his gut when he thought about it. They should be here for him. It was their jobs.

"Well, have a good day, Mr. Martin," the orderly said as he moved towards the door. "I hope they take good care of you at Mercy."

Twenty minutes later, three cheery blasts from a horn sounded from the street. Benny peeked through the blinds and saw a small, white e-bus in the street. No one else was in sight, so Benny snatched his hat and rushed as fast as he could out of the door, afraid the driver would leave him.

As soon as Benny made it onto the porch, the driver yelled from the window, "Hey, buddy. You need a wheelchair?"

Benny barely kept from putting a finger to his lips to shush the man. Instead, he shook his head and shuffled to the bus's door. The driver lifted a latch and opened the door.

"Welcome aboard, Mr. Martin. Two more pickups and we'll be on our way to Mercy Hospital."

"Pickups on Bile Street?"

"Hm? Oh, no. They're at Tucker."

Benny nodded and fell into his seat. Bile Street looked like a filth-strewn, inner-city slum as it rolled by outside the windows. Which he guessed is what it was now. Broken windows and splintered doors lined both sides of the street. Knee-high weeds held the piles of trash in place against the breeze.

The sight caused his throat to tighten and ache. He'd never liked Bile Street for what it was, for what it represented. But the neighborhood had been nice, once. Now it was an alien landscape, nothing like the place he and Mastiff had walked in those final days before his friend's death.

Sobs threatened to rise from his chest, so Benny turned away and closed his eyes.

Once the ruin of his neighborhood was behind him, Benny allowed himself to relax in the sun and the gentle rocking of the shuttle. The other streets they drove on were cracked and falling apart too. But they weren't his home. The shows on the SafetyNet didn't show streets that looked like this on their news feeds. It was comforting, in a way, to know it wasn't only Benny's home suffering.

Twenty minutes later, the shuttle turned off the express and into a rat-warren of cracked, pothole-filled streets. The neighborhood felt heavy and silent, melancholy with its encroaching demise. Few people were out on the sidewalks, but he saw several faces peering at the shuttle through grime-encrusted windows.

Benny perked up as the Tucker Care Home appeared around the final corner of the maze of streets. He'd been researching places to which they might transfer him after Bile Street closed. The newly inaugurated Department of Safety had declared Tucker unfit, and launched a series of studies and projects to find a solution. Years later, a less idealistic and more budget-conscious DoS reversed its decision, satisfied with some minor renovations. It was still better then Bile Street at this point.

The driver turned in his seat to face Benny. "It'll take a few minutes to get the ladies. There's a head inside if you need it."

"I'm good for now, thanks. I like to keep my options open though. You never know."

"I hear ya! I've almost lost this job twice 'cause I gotta piss about every five minutes." The driver stretched his back, generating two loud pops. "Oh, here they come."

A pale, cheery-looking woman shuffled along in a walker, supported by a diminutive teenage girl. The other woman was in a wheelchair. Her face was so wizened that her heritage was indeterminable. A middle-aged woman, speaking angrily into a voip headset barely visible beneath her hair, pushed the wheelchair.Both women—in the walker and wheelchair—looked older than Benny.

The driver walked to the rear of the shuttle and flipped a lever. The whine of a motor filled the bus as the back door and ramp unfolded. Offering each woman and their nurses friendly smiles, the driver lifted the women into the bus one at a time and led them to their seats. He set the pale woman across the aisle from Benny and locked the wheelchair into a space next to the rear door.

Benny nodded to the pale woman as the bus pulled away from Tucker. "Howdy."

"Howdy yourself," she said. Her smile lit up her face. "It's a fine day to get out of the dungeon. I'm Stormi. With an I."

Benny winked. "I just bet you are."

"Oh, go on."

Benny bowed as best as he could in his seat. "I'll try. My name's Benny. And it is a nice day, even if I'm on the way to wait at the hospital all day."

"And where do they have you tucked away, Benny?" Stormi's voice was thin and crinkled, like paper. Benny had to lean in to hear her.

"Over on Bile Street in a microhome. It used to be pretty nice, but not now. I'm the only one there who's supposed to be there."

"What a terrible name." Stormi leaned towards the woman in the wheelchair. "Did you hear that, Liz? Bile Street. What a terrible name."

Liz didn't respond.

"Pretty apt name, these days," Benny said. He motioned to the building now behind them. "How's your place? I wouldn't mind living in Tucker."

Stormi's smile faded. "You might. If you like staring at SafetyNet trash all day, hoping the nurses don't forget to feed you. And it is warm enough, when they pay the heating bill.

"What's funny, Benny, is that I keep trying to get into a place like Bile Street. They keep telling me I'm not mobile enough. Not self-sufficient enough." Stormi snorted. "That tells me the people upstairs don't realize how much I have to do for myself because of my lazy nurses."

She paused to wipe drool from her chin. "I asked about it again last week and they gave me some story about all transfers being denied for money."

Benny nodded. "That's what they keep telling me too. The only transfer I can get is a medical one."

Stormi leaned towards the wheelchair. "Liz? Didn't Paul tell you they even froze medical transfers?"

There was still no reply from Liz.

"I don't know if she can even hear me," Stormi said. "She never talks or moves, but I don't want her to be lonely. Why do you want to move, Benny?"

Benny motioned towards Liz. "Because I'm lonely." He snapped his mouth shut and held his breath, savagely fighting back his tears. After a moment, he continued, "They all left me alone."

"Who?"

"My friends. Everyone on the block. They haven't moved in any new wards to replace those who have passed on or got sent to the hospice house. The only people in them now are squatter thugs."

Stormi reached out and took Benny's hand. "That's terrible. Two of my dear friends passed away last month. And I'm not sure how many are left in Tucker. Surely not as many as before. Say, that's a nice cane."

Benny held up his cane, turning it to show off all the carvings. "Thanks. My family got it for me at my daughter's funeral a few months ago."

"That must have been horrible. I pray to God I don't have to go through that. But I've got over thirty grandkids and great-grandkids. All of my *kids* are all old farts themselves." She smiled fondly into the distance. "I don't think I can even remember all their names. Shhh, don't tell."

Benny chuckled. "Thirty? You've been fruitful and multiplied."

"You could say that. And all from the same man too. Don't see much of that anymore."

"True enough," Benny agreed. "He must have been a hell of a man."

She beamed at Benny. "Oh, yes. Kevin was that and more. So good, I never remarried. It wouldn't have been fair to the poor slob who tried to replace him."

Benny waited for her to continue, but she was mumbling now. The distant twinkle in her eyes and the girlish giggle told him Stormi was lost in reverie with Kevin. There was no acknowledgement of the shuttle or anyone on it now.

Benny smiled and turned to look out of his own window, not wanting to intrude on a private conversation between old lovers.

Mercy Hospital towered above the surrounding skyline, visible from the expressway as the shuttle exited to the side streets. It was one of those hospitals that looked more like a business complex than a vast cathedral. The parking area was huge, with drop-off and pick-up lanes like those at an airport. Such a setup was needed to handle the massive number of patients that called such DoS-run hospitals their second home.

The shuttle fell in line behind other vehicles, many bearing decals showing what facility they were from. Benny could see license tags from at least three counties and seven different logos from retirement or treatment centers.

The driver turned to face his passengers. "Sorry, folks. Now we wait. Good thing we got here early though." He pointed to the mass of vehicles shoving their way into line behind the shuttle.

Benny grunted. He hated waiting, especially when he was waiting to get in line to wait somewhere else. But the comfy shuttle seat was far better than being at home, so he rolled his head around to relieve the tension and took a deep breath. Any place was better than Bile Street.

From a distance, the sparkling windows and sleek curves of the hospital complex were impressive. But up close, Mercy had the same worn look as everything else in the city. Bits of trash hung snarled in the shrubbery and the outside facade was covered with the ghosts of graffiti still visible through the half-hearted attempts to hide it. Similar to how that bitch Rose had looked at Dakota's funeral: there wasn't enough makeup in the world to fix that disaster.

Thirty minutes later, the shuttle driver was helping Liz onto the small lift and lowering her to the curb. A smiling orderly scanned the DoS chip in Liz's wrist and pushed her through one of the many doors leading inside.

The driver gently shook Stormi and helped her to her feet. She looked at Benny and smiled.

"Hello. I'm Stormi. With an I. It's good to meet you...?"

"Benny. It's good to meet you too, Stormi with an I." He stood and stretched his back. "Maybe I'll see you later."

Stormi patted his arm. "That would be nice, Kevin."

The driver gave Benny a shrug and led Stormi to the lift. Another orderly sat Stormi in a wheelchair and scanned her chip. With an exasperated glance at the line of waiting vehicles, the orderly hurried her inside.

The driver moved to the shuttle's front door and hiked a thumb over his shoulder. "You want to use the lift?"

Benny looked at the steps to the door and considered the chances of his pride going before a fall. "I'll take the steps, thanks."

Cane held tightly in one hand and the rail in the other, Benny started down. The driver stood one step in front with his arms outstretched like a father waiting to catch his toddler. Benny grunted when he made the final step to the concrete. It had been farther than he'd expected. Going down steps was hard.

The driver got in the shuttle and gave a friendly wave to Benny before driving off. Benny took a moment to catch his breath and shuffled up to the nearest, waiting orderly. He held out his medical card and the orderly scanned it. Benny's chip had failed four years ago and the DoS deemed it too expensive to replace.

The orderly was a pretty, young Latina. She smiled and read Benny's information from her datapad. "Would you like a wheelchair, Mr. Martin? You have plenty of time to get to your appointment if you prefer to walk. It's not far."

"I'll walk, miss. Thanks."

"Sounds good. Elevators are right inside. Head up to the seventh floor, go right, and you'll find room 744. If you get lost or have any other problems, any staff member can scan your card and help out."

Benny tipped his hat and walked through the sliding doors. They clattered shut behind him and he had the sudden feeling of being swallowed.

The line for the elevators mirrored the line of vehicles outside: slow moving and seemingly endless. Benny reminded himself that he had plenty of time and that Mercy's lobby was still better than being home. When it was finally his turn, Benny was shoved to the back of the elevator by the crowd. He noticed the young Latina was pushing an old man in a wheelchair.

The pretty Latina pushed her ward out of the elevator on three, but every floor had a stop and a noisy exchange of passengers. An obese woman wearing athletic pants stretched too thin for Benny's viewing pleasure began cursing when she realized she'd stepped onto an up elevator instead of a down. Fortunately, they only had to listen to her for one floor.

As seven approached, Benny was struck with the fear that he might not get off before the doors shut and that he'd have to get back in line on some distant level of the hospital. He pushed through the crowd as politely as he could, accidentally stepping on a barrel-chested, black man's foot.

The man looked down at Benny and smiled. "You need off, sir?"

"Uh, yes. Please."

The man traded places with Benny and held the elevator door until Benny was off.

"Thanks, man."

The man popped a lazy salute as the elevator doors slid shut. "No problem. Love the hat, man."

Benny found the check-in kiosk and swiped his card. A digital clock appeared on the grungy screen, spinning as it processed his info. Curses and crude images of genitalia were scratched into the touch screen, but it still seemed to work. The clock was replaced with a window giving him a customer number and an estimated waiting time of three hours.

The news didn't bother him at all. The chairs looked comfortable, if a bit musty, and the stacked magazines were so old that he recognized some of the images on the front covers. There was no reason to have magazines—everyone read on their voip. But Benny liked the smell of the paper, if not the smell of the other people waiting.

He shuffled through the tattered, dog-eared periodicals, settling on an old copy of *Scientific American*. The cover promised to reveal everything NASA knew about the latest star-cluster map from the Rowan L5 Deep Seer telescope station. Casually flipping the pages, Stormi's comments about medical transfers being frozen kept echoing in his mind. Benny set the magazine in his lap and slipped out his voip.

"Good morning, Mr. Benny," Hannah answered. "Did you make it to Mercy OK?"

"Yeah, I'm here right now. Got a sec?"

"Sure."

"I was talking to another retiree on the shuttle and she was told that even medical transfers have been frozen. Is that right?"

The line was quiet for a long moment before Hannah answered. "Probably. There's been a lot of policy and process changes these last few days. To be honest, I've had to call Legal several times because I can't keep everything straight."

"What the hell do you mean by probably?"

She hesitated. "Probably, Mr. Benny. I'm not sure. It might be anything short of a hospice transfer will be denied. Even an emergency visit will put you back in your ward of record when you're done."

Benny squeezed his eyes shut and a single tear ran down his cheek. He wiped the tear and flicked it away in disgust. Too much crying and whining lately. Old age had made him soft, and Benny hated it. It wasn't mere grief over lost ones. He'd been endlessly pissing and moaning about everything lately.

There was a quote Eli had included in one of his papers. Benny couldn't remember who had said it, but the quote went something like, "Power doesn't corrupt, it merely reveals the existing character." Worse than the possibility that old age had made him weak, was that old age had simply revealed the weakness that had always been there.

"For Christ's sake, Hannah. You won't even go to Bile Street and I'm supposed to live there? With people running around my house at all hours? There must be something. Can I pay someone? Can I get my family to move me to another ward?"

"No, Mr. Benny. You can't. Even if someone physically moved you, they wouldn't accept the cost of your occupancy when you got to another ward."

"What the hell am I supposed to do then?"

"I don't know."

"Why don't you know? I signed my life away and you guys are supposed to fucking take care of me!" He bit off the rest of his rant and sat breathing heavily into his voip. Hannah said nothing and his anger flared again. "What do you have to say now, Hannah? You usually have lots to say when someone's misbehaving."

"I haven't been paid in a month."

"What?"

"The Department of Safety is holding our paychecks. The budget is such a wreck that people are assigned as 'working furlough' every couple of months. I can't afford to quit and there's no other jobs out there for someone like me."

The anger drained from Benny. "I'm sorry. I didn't know."

"You aren't supposed to know. And I'm not telling you so you'll feel sorry for me. I want you to know that when I say there's no money, I mean there's no money. There's really no money." Hannah sighed. "The DoS is in the red across the board. The retirement wards

are very low on the priority list. And it looks like I won't get paid this
month either."

"What about—"

"I know you have a contract." Hannah's voice was strained, but
not angry. "But that doesn't matter. It isn't going to help you. I have a
contract, too, but don't have a lawyer or any money to hire one. Can't
even wipe your ass with this contract, being digital."

Benny's shoulders sagged. "Sorry."

"I'm the one that's sorry, Mr. Benny. I don't know how to help
you. The enforcers are ignoring me. And I haven't seen Jodie in three
days. Get everything you can from the cafeteria. Stuff your pockets
with crackers if you have to."

The connection dropped.

Benny stared down at his voip until the energy-save feature powered down the screen. A familiar weight settled back on his chest.
No matter what happened here, he was going back to Bile Street. All
those years ago, Dakota had warned him not to trust the DoS, but
Eli had been all for it.

The kiosk was unable to answer if eating would interfere with
Benny's examination, and he couldn't find one of those helpful
staffers. But he knew the instant he stepped out to lunch, the doctor
would call him and he'd miss his turn and have to start all over.

And since he didn't go to lunch, it was five hours before the doctor called. Not that Benny noticed. He stared at the magazine on his
lap, occasionally trying to read snippets but quickly losing interest
each time. What Hannah told him had sucked the joy right out of
the day. The doctor could find a rabid weasel living in Benny's skull
and it wouldn't matter. There was no escaping Bile Street.

Benny stripped to his skivvies and sat in the booth as the computer took readings and blood. The doctor stood back, only seldom
looking up from his datapad. Fifteen minutes later, the exam results
appeared on a screen in the booth.

Blood pressure was high and the doctor noted signs of malnutrition. When the doctor asked about the malnutrition, his eyes glazed over as Benny tried to describe the situation on Bile Street. It could have been disbelief, disinterest, or the fear he'd have to get involved if Benny was being mistreated. It didn't matter. Even if the doctor tried to do something, he'd run into the DoS brick wall. There was no indication of a hospice transfer, so it didn't matter what the doctor thought or found.

Benny would die on Bile Street like Mack and Mastiff. If he went to hospice, he'd die like Trance.

The doctor collected Benny's thumbprint and asked if Benny had any questions. There would be no point, so Benny shook his head. He trudged to the cafeteria. There was a chance another dinner would be waiting when he got home. The possibility cheered him a little. Benny stuffed his belly with soy steak and stuffed his pockets with packets of crackers. He didn't want to go home, but there was no point in delaying it. The idea of staying at Mercy crossed his mind, but he didn't know if that would be any safer. Benny got in line for the elevator to the lobby, where he'd try to call for a shuttle.

When the elevator doors opened, Jodie was leaning back against the lobby wall, standing on one leg. The other leg was hiked up behind her, heel on the wall below her backside. Her frumpy clothes were gone. The reason Benny noticed her so quickly was her tight, low-cut red shirt and equally tight black pants. It looked like hooker wear. Benny's mother, and probably Big Mamma too, would have said Jodie was "dressing past her age."

Jodie pushed off the wall and made her way through the crowd to Benny. "I was wondering when you'd finish up. But it's not good to wolf your food. You have everything?"

"What are you doing here?"

"And hi to you too. I'm here to take you home."

Benny eyed Jodie up and down. "I hope I'm not interrupting a date or anything."

Jodie laughed and led him to the outer doors. "This is how I usually dress, you know. I only wear the schoolmarm duds to ease Hannah's delicate sensibilities. I hear she came clean with you about the DoS being broke."

Benny nodded. "Yeah. She said she hasn't seen you in a few days. So I guess you're not getting paid either."

"Nope," she said with surprising cheer. "I quit today. No pay for us after the bankers and the corps get their cuts. And all the foreign aid, and military pork barrels, and all that stuff that was supposed to change when the DoS took over."

Jodie stopped in front of a dent-covered, rust-trimmed, old Chevy pickup. It had current tags, so Benny knew it had a battery or biofuel engine. The body looked as if it might crumble away at the first bump in the road.

"Jesus, Jodie. Is this yours?"

"Fucking-A right it is." She pounded the hood with her fist.

"With tags? Some anarchist."

"Undercover anarchist, thank you. Wouldn't do me any good to get arrested on some bullshit permit violation." She opened the passenger door for Benny and helped him up, before hopping behind the wheel. The engine kicked over and hummed smoothly.

"Installed the biofuel conversion myself," she said. "I can make that stuff in my bathroom, but you've got to kiss the DoS ring to install or recharge batteries. Fuck that." Jodie gunned the engine, and the truck lurched forward and into traffic.

"Thanks for the ride, Jodie."

Jodie gave a thumbs-up. "Hannah asked if I would, even though I'd quit. She's a simpering gov-whore, afraid to laugh too loud or offend the wrong person, but she's all right mostly. She did really try to do her best for you guys, so I have to give her that."

She ran a hand up Benny's thigh. "But if you feel bad, we could work out a payment plan."

Benny reached for the door handle. "I'll walk."

"Fortunately, I don't have any feelings. But I like you, Benny. You're all right, too, for a cop. Can I give you some advice?"

"As long as it isn't about money or women."

Jodie shot Benny an expression more serious than he'd ever seen on her. "I've been on the run a long time, Benny. Believe me when I tell you that it's time to go. I watch the news outside of the BS on SafetyNet.

"I keep tabs on the corporate-wealth redistribution centers, a.k.a. Wall Street and D.C. I follow their schemes. They're tyrants, to be sure. But even they can't stop the reset that's coming. They'll come out on top as always, but we won't. You won't. Get out of Bile Street ASAP, Benny."

"That's illegal."

"They're illegal," Jodie said. "The whole DoS is illegal. And that's not including the fact that they broke their contract."

Benny scoffed. "Where would I go? I can't run away from enforcers... even the fat ones. I'm probably about six months from needing someone to hold my wiener when I pee."

"I don't have those answers. But if they don't have the money to feed you, they probably won't have the money to hunt you down. Get with your family. Maybe those people that drove you to Wichita."

"I don't want to get them in trouble."

"Even an anarchist knows no person is an island."

"Where are you going?"

Jodie winked at Benny. "I've got some friends from the good old days. Former terrorists. Maybe even future terrorists. You learn to live cheap on the lam. Part of fighting the system is being content where you're at." She shrugged. "It's up to you, but if you have family to reach out to, I'd do it soon."

"How soon?"

"Now."

Benny shook his head and stared out of the passenger window. "How can you know?"

"I know your DoS-provided voip is getting shut off. I'm not supposed to know that though."

Benny covered his voip pocket in a panic. "When?"

"Soon." Jodie offered a wry smile. "But don't worry. A replacement will be sent."

"When?"

"As soon as they get the money, I'm sure."

Benny spent the rest of the trip staring out of the window in silence. The voip in his hand felt heavy, like deadweight. It was his lifeline to his family. He could make calls and send messages from his SafetyNet terminal, but who knew when they'd get rid of that too?

As the truck approached the turn-off to Bile Street, Jodie reached a hand between Benny's legs. He pushed back into the seat and covered his crotch with his hands. A strangled "mew" escaped his mouth.

Jodie looked at him with wide, innocent eyes. "What?" Then she laughed and pulled a dark revolver from the glove box. "I'm after my tool, not yours."

The revolver was pitted and the edges worn, but Benny had no doubt it was in working order. "Jesus, Jodie."

"If you have something like this hidden somewhere, you might want to make it handy."

"It's always the apocalypse with you people."

"I'm sure the banksters will get things back in their control eventually. Never fear." Jodie tucked the revolver between her seat cushion and the center console, leaving the grip sticking out and ready to draw.

The brakes emitted a long squeal as Jodie slowed the truck to a stop in front of Benny's house. She put it in park but left the engine running. A pack of boys and young men gathered across the street, keeping their distance. For now.

Jodie wrapped her hand around the pistol's grip. "I can drop you off somewhere, Benny. I'll cover you while you get your stuff." The usual devil-may-care tone in her voice had been replaced with the icy promise of violence. "But be quick."

Benny leaned over and gave her a peck on the cheek. "Thanks, Jodie. Thanks for everything. But I'll be OK. You keep safe."

"Really, I don't mind. I'll even keep my grubby mitts to myself. I don't like the look of these little shits."

Benny gave a lopsided grin and carefully stepped out onto the street. After a long look at Jodie, he slammed the door.

"Why does everyone have to slam my door?"

"Maybe you should stop giving everyone rides, Jodie." Benny waved and turned away.

"Benny!" Jodie reached deep into her cleavage and pulled out a voip. She leaned over and handed it to Benny. "Keep that one. It'll get shut off, too, but probably not as soon as yours does. And I don't want them tracking me with it anyway. Don't worry, I deleted all my good-for-nothing contacts."

Benny took it and slipped it into one of his pockets, wincing at the sound of crushing crackers. "Thanks."

Jodie blew him a kiss and drove out of his life forever.

The squatters dispersed when the truck was out of sight and left Benny alone. Inside, he found no food left in the fridge or on the table. He emptied his pockets of crackers and cried himself to sleep.

29. And We All Fall Down

One week after Jodie drove away, Benny received a text notification from the Ward Retirement Administration Center that due to recent manning solutions, his needs would now be met by Alex Ambadujar. When Benny called Hannah to see what that meant exactly, he got a message stating that Hannah was no longer employed by the DoS, followed by a number to the national helpdesk.

Benny tried calling Alex Ambadujar, whose office was listed as being in Sacramento, and went to voicemail each time. The contact forms on Alex's SafetyNet office page either replied with a network error or an automated thank you message.

Benny didn't want to believe Jodie was right about the collapse or whatever she called it. After all, she was a sex-crazed, drug-dealing, wanted terrorist. After three days in a row of no food deliveries, and a dwindling supply of cafeteria crackers, he was definitely getting an *End of the World as We Know it* feeling.

Hunger overcame his pride and Benny finally reached out to his family. He hated begging. The request for food was couched in apologies that downplayed how fucked-up things were on Bile Street. It wasn't a collapse or anything like that, only some logistic issues.

They sent thoughts and prayers but, more importantly, a few sent care packages. And a few of the packages actually made it to his front door. With the admin office closed down, there was not the usual contraband inspection or "health quarantine" for so-called unhealthy food deliveries.

Benny was on the shitter when the mail service driver rang the bell. Without wiping, Benny rushed from the bathroom, holding his pants up with one hand. When he flung the door open, two kids were already on the porch, fighting over his package. The mail truck hadn't even driven away yet.

"That's mine!" Benny screamed.

The boys laughed at him. One let go of the package and shoved Benny back inside his house. Benny had to let go of his pants to grab the door to keep from tripping. His pants slid to the ground, revealing his bony legs.

"Ain't nothing here yours," the boy said. He pulled back as if to punch Benny. When Benny cried out and flinched, the boys laughed again and ran away.

Benny went back to the bathroom and finished. The toilet paper had run out two days ago and he was using pages from the books he'd never be able to turn back in to the office library. At least the water and power were still working, for now.

His voip chimed with a new direct message.

Hey Ben-Ben. See the food got there. Hope it helps.

Benny snorted and replied. *Yeah, thanks.*

Great! I hope the sausage is not too rich. If you need help, ask.

"Can you come bust me out of here and take care of me until I die?" Benny asked out loud. At least the very rich sausage, probably filled with country spices and accompanied by gourmet breads and crackers, wouldn't keep him on the toilet.

But he'd asked enough of his family. They'd sent food. He was the one that couldn't keep it when it got there. Desperation was gnawing at his heart and his gut. He was ready to call Eli and beg, but Eli was on vacation with Blake and Trina in the Rockies. They'd been planning the trip all year and the last text Eli sent out was they were going incommunicado for the duration.

After another sleepless night of terrifying sounds outside his window, Benny rose and ate the last of his crackers. He was going to die if someone didn't get him out of here. Someone would help. He'd come clean. He'd explain how bad things were. He'd beg and plead and throw his pride to the wind.

Benny pulled out his voip, took one look at the screen, and broke down crying.

VOIP service has been disabled.Please contact your connection management service. Have a pleasant day.

All of his contacts and conversation histories were stored in the DoS cloud and he didn't know anyone's number. He relied solely on the address book, but his voip wouldn't let him access any other screen anyway. Almost falling as he rushed to get up, Benny logged in to his terminal. He pounded his fist on the table.

Servers are down for maintenance. Please excuse our mess.

Benny laughed. The laugh turned into a cackle. It would have turned into sobbing if Benny wasn't out of breath and hope. His shoulders sagged and he deflated in his chair. According to Jodie, he was supposed to get a new voip. The neighbors would love it. When would they get it?

Soon.

The following night, Benny woke up screaming,torn from his fitful sleep by fists pounding on every window. Jeers and laughter followed, once Benny's scream played out. More pounding came from the door, and the microhome seemed to rock back and forth.

Benny's voice cracked as he screamed, "Stop it! Stop it goddamnit! Stop it, please!"

"You getting lots of fancy gifts, Pappi," called a voice from outside the nearest window. It was the same voice that had warned Benny through the window before.

Benny gripped his cane with trembling hands.

A group of children started chanting from the porch. "Old fucker, old fucker, old fucker. Get the fuck out." The chorus ended with a barrage of kicks on the door. The chant was taken up by a crowd of people surrounding the house.

"Leave me alone!" Benny's cry came out in sobs. It was met with more laughter and pounding. The jeering came to a crescendo when a brick crashed through the window closest to the bed.

Benny's scream devolved into a babbling, nonsensical bleating. He pissed himself. The cursing and laughter from outside thundered through the tiny house now that the window was smashed. Benny curled up beneath his blankets against the noise and cold air rolling in through the window. He pressed his eyes shut and covered his ears until morning.

Benny woke to strange-hued light filtering through the blinds. Crisp morning air chilled him and cleared his head. Nightmares had plagued Benny all night, but when he peeled his eyes open, the shards of glass strewn across his bed and floor reminded him it had all been real. The smell of piss from the bed made his eyes water. His stomach growled. Benny had no idea how he'd get the window replaced, the sheets laundered, or his belly filled.

Pieces of glass fell from Benny's slippers when he shook them out before putting them on. He swept up the glass as best as he could with the broom while the tea brewed. Hot tea was the one comfort he still had, even if he was down to using flowery herbals he didn't really care for. They were from one of the packages he'd managed to snatch from the mailman before the kids showed up.

There were only three teabags left. Benny glanced at the pile of used teabags he'd been collecting for reuse if needed. When his stomach growled again, Benny wondered if he could eat the tea. It was vegetable matter, right?

Once the glass was cleaned up, Benny inspected the window the colored light was coming through. He opened the blinds. The window was covered in spray paint. The sunlight filtered through the graffiti, casting a psychedelic salad of pinks, yellows, and reds through the house. Thin beams of sunlight dappled the floor from the few places on the glass not covered in paint.

Every window was the same. Benny risked poking his head through the broken window and saw that every inch of his house was covered in graffiti.

"You go, fucker," shouted a voice from Mack's porch.

Benny started and saw two older men flipping him the bird. Sitting between them was a fat white woman who jiggled her flabby breasts at him. Benny ducked back inside.

Before Benny could get to his terminal in hopes it might be up, the familiar man's voice called in through the broken window. "You better leave, Pappi. You're testing my patience." The man reached in and pulled the blinds up.

Benny met the thug's gaze and recoiled. The blade of a long knife slowly played back and forth in front of the man's sneer.

Benny hated the tremble in his own voice. "I can't go anywhere. They shut off my voip, so I can't even call. And I don't have a car. I can't even get food."

"Very sad, Pappi. Not as sad as what will happen if you don't fucking leave."

"I can't!" Benny shrieked.

"So sad for you." The thug tapped his blade against the window, dislodging a shard of broken glass. It fell to the ground and shattered with a musical tinkle.

"Go soon, Pappi. Or we make you go. There's lots of old homeless fags in the park. Go there." The man released the pull and the blinds crashed closed, causing Benny to flinch.

Benny looked around for something, for anything. An answer. An idea. There was nothing. He had Jodie's voip, but it didn't have his contacts. It didn't even have her contacts.

He did have a number. He hobbled to the closet and pulled out the chest. It almost spilled as he dug through papers inside. There it was, Dakota's and Zane's death notice. On the back was Eli's number to make arrangements, and Trina's as the backup.

Fearing Jodie's voip would shut off at any minute, Benny frantically input Eli's and Trina's numbers over and over again. He left message after message, but when Jodie's voip notified Benny that service had been discontinued, no one had returned any of his calls.

TRINA LOOKED OUT OF the window of the ski lodge and gave a long, contented sigh. Her skin still tingled from the steaming shower and her knees still trembled in postcoital bliss. Her husband, Paul, had walked in as she was peeling off her ski suit. Paul's wandering hands helped until he carried her to the bed for the perfect ending to a day of skiing.

If not for the rest of the family, Trina would wear only the red, terry cloth bathrobe downstairs. Or she'd call down for him to bring her up some food... and maybe have another romp. Large, downy snowflakes drifted from the sky outside. Her stomach growled. She sighed again and put on her loungewear before going downstairs.

A roaring fire in the fireplace cast flickering, red and orange light across the living room of the lodge. Her father must have paid a fortune for the place, but he refused to say how much or take any money from her.

Paul sat on the large couch near the fire, beer in hand. When he saw her, he patted the cushion next to him. Their two sons, who'd managed to get time off work, sat with Blake's oldest daughter. They were gobbling down the complimentary gourmet pretzels they'd just pulled from the oven. Blake and his wife were serving up cups of coffee and hot chocolate, and general good cheer.

As Trina walked towards the couch, with extra swing in her hips for Paul's sake, she felt as if she'd fallen into a Norman Rockwell painting.

This was definitely better than the last family vacation. The highlights of that trip had been finding Paul passed out in a Mexican whore's lap and everyone racing between the bathrooms of the Dallas–Fort Worth concourse to crap their brains out. Only Paul didn't get sick. He swore nothing happened with that whore though.

Trina veered away from Paul and sat with the kids instead. She stared at him until he shook his head and started reading his voip.

The board games came out, and Blake and his wife won most of them—when they actually finished the game. No one else was as interested in the games as they were, and Blake would grow red-faced when someone lost interest and wandered away. Trina only played because her father played.

Trina sat next to Paul after the second game. "Sure you don't want to play?"

Paul shook his head. He never played.

Trina whispered in his ear. "I know a fun game we can play later. Upstairs."

Paul stared at her quizzically. "You vex me, woman."

Trina laughed and rubbed his knee.

Her son Willie wiped pretzel salt from his lips. "Got any chapstick, Mom? Mine's in the car."

"In my purse there."

"Seriously?" Willie asked. "Let me rephrase. Is it anywhere I can find it?"

Tina rolled her eyes. She got up, rummaged through the purse for a second, and tossed a small tube to her son. "That was so hard."

Willie grinned and liberally coated his wind- and salt-burned lips. "Thanks, Mom. You're the best."

Trina wrinkled her face and mouthed the words back at him. Willie tossed the chapstick back to her and she shoved it into the recesses of the purse. When she adjusted the purse to make it lie flat again, Trina's voip slipped out onto the counter.

"Good grief!" she said. "I've got like forty missed calls from the same unknown number."

"Me too," Eli said. "I figured it was some autodialer that got stuck in a loop."

Trina held the voip to her ear. "Several voicemails too. Did you get any, Dad?"

Eli shrugged. "I didn't really look. Vacation plus unknown number equals 'piss off.' I just deleted everything."

Trina pressed her thumbprint to access the first voicemail. "Oh, it's from Grandpa." Her frown deepened as she listened to each message. "They're all from Grandpa. Oh my God."

Paul stood up. "What's wrong?"

"We've got to go. Now!" Trina shoved the voip back into her purse. "I hope we're not too late already."

———◉———

BENNY HUDDLED IN THE dark under his terminal's desk, eyes squeezed shut, gripping his cane so hard his knuckles throbbed.

The squatters pounded on the door and walls of Benny's house. They had shattered the rest of the windows earlier that evening. The shattered glass sparkled in the beams of light that swept through the dark house from the windows.

Benny knew he shouldn't have called the enforcers. It had been a desperation move and he realized now it would cost him his life. The one time the enforcers sent a car and they still couldn't do anything about it. The thugs scurried away like cockroaches when the patrol car came.

Benny begged to be taken to some kind of civic shelter or abused person's home. The senior officer, a burly, mannish-looking woman, told him the ones still operating were all overflowing. The enforcers managed to arrest a couple of squatters and drove away.

An hour later, the squatter gang had started to gather around Benny's house. Then the patrol car came back. The woman, Officer Manly, delivered a bag of groceries.

"I'm sorry the veggies are a bit wilted, Mr. Martin. It's the best I could do on short notice."

Benny wiped a tear from his eye. "Thank you so much. Thank you."

"I wish I could do more." Officer Manly shone her tactical light around the neighborhood and turned to her car.

Benny reached out, as if he could use some power to make her stay. "Officer?"

"Yes?"

"If, uh, I attacked you with my cane, would you arrest me? You know, put me in the lockup?"

She offered a sad smile. "Trust me, Mr. Martin. You don't want to go to lockup these days. It's a damned zoo in there."

Benny rushed inside and locked his door before the patrol car had left. He tore through the bag, stuffing himself with stale donuts and rubbery bologna until he vomited. Some of it he might be able to get back down. They smashed in the windows, while he cursed himself and tried to clean up.

The patrol car had not come back a third time and the man Benny jokingly thought of as the ambassador was back at the window. Faces leered at every window.

"I told you we come for you, Pappi. I told you no more enforcers." The ambassador threw something at Benny that bounced off the floor nearby. "You should have gone with the fags under the bridge, Pappi."

Blinding lights flooded the room from the shattered front windows. A horn sounded. It was the end for Benny. They'd brought in a car to carry his body away. He shouldn't have called. He knew it. But he was so damned hungry. So hungry. There was no running, no fighting. He didn't even have the strength to stand. Benny prayed.

Someone was kicking the door in. Each thunderous boom made Benny cry out. Calls of "Pappi! Pappi!" echoed in from outside. The door splintered and crashed to the floor. There were more angry shouts from outside.

"Oh, God," Benny whimpered. "Go away. Leave me alone."

"We're here for you, Pappi!" an intruder yelled. Dark silhouettes rushed across the house and grabbed Benny, trying to pull him from under his desk.

Benny feebly jabbed his cane at them. His war cry came out as a whisper. "Get back, you bastards. Get the fuck out!"

More lights shone in his eyes. Benny couldn't see.

"Mom! Pappi's freaking out. He won't let me get him."

Firm but gentle hands grabbed Benny's wrists. "Grandpa, it's Trina. We're getting you out of here."

Benny squinted to make out her face in the light. The voice was strained, but it sounded like her. "Trina?"

"It's me, Grandpa. And Paul, and Dad, and Willie." Her voice cracked. She stroked his gaunt cheek. "Oh, Grandpa. Oh, Grandpa. How could this happen?"

"They turned off my voip," Benny muttered.

Paul bellowed from the porch. "Get the fuck back! I said get back!"

"Hurry up in there," called another voice.

"Is that my boy?" Benny asked. "Is that Eli?"

"Yes. That's Dad."

Willie lifted Benny in his arms. "Geez, Mom. He's like a bag of sticks."

"We've got to go, Grandpa."

Benny started babbling. "I was so scared. They were going to kill me. I think they were going to kill me. I've got my cane, let's go. Oh, thank you. Thank you."

As they rushed to the door, Benny reached out with his cane. "Wait! My hat."

Trina snatched the wrinkled, old boonie hat from its hook and shoved it on Benny's head. "Let's go."

Willie turned to fit Benny through the door before stepping to the porch. Bright lights and shouts filled the night, and Willie looked around in all directions, eyes wide.

Benny wriggled around and reached back towards the house. "Tina! My chest. In the top of the closet. Please!"

Trina glared at him for a second before turning back into the house. He heard her open the closet and gag, but she was on the porch with the chest a moment later.

Paul grabbed Willie's shoulder and pushed him and Benny towards the waiting SUV that was on the front lawn. "We are leaving!"

The horn sounded again.

Willie dropped Benny unceremoniously onto the center seat and struggled to buckle him in. Trina slid in on the other side and tossed the chest into Benny's lap.

Eli glanced in the rearview mirror. "Jesus Christ, Dad!"

Trina yelled out of the window. "Paul, let's go."

"Get in!" Eli screamed.

Paul swung a baseball bat around his head as several gangers closed in. They backed off and Paul leaped into the passenger seat. When they moved closer again, he drew a pistol and waved it at them.

"Put that away," Eli hissed.

Paul pounded on the dashboard. "Get the fuck out of here. Gun it, Eli!"

The SUV's tires flung chunks of unkempt lawn into the crowd of cursing squatters and Eli spun the vehicle back onto the street. Fists, stones, and bottles slammed into the SUV. None of the windows broke and the rest of the thugs jumped out of Eli's way as he tore down Bile Street.

When they were a few blocks away, Paul clapped Eli on the back and looked over his shoulder into the back seat. "Good job, everyone. You're safe now, Benny. You're coming home with us."

Trina nodded and rested Benny's head on her shoulder. She stroked his stubbly cheek.

Eli glanced in the mirror again. "You're safe now. Dad... I'm so sorry."

———— ◈ ————

WHEN THE SUN BROKE over the horizon, Benny wept, unashamed. He was exhausted, and he could now smell his own foul stench, but he was safe. He barely recognized the skeletal face staring back at him in the window's reflection, but it looked happy for the first time in months.

Trina and Willie were softly snoring on either side of him. Eli was in the passenger seat, snoring somewhat louder than they were.His head lolled against the window as the SUV bounced or turned.

Benny exchanged a knowing look with Paul through the rearview mirror, but they saidnothing. The snack bars and water they'd given him last night at least provided him enough strength to get the chest from the floor on his own.

He shuffled through the pictures in the box, through his memories. They were still warm, but somehow not nearly so urgent. His flesh and blood surrounded him, making fresh memories every second. Dakota would never be relegated into the box as a mere memory, but Trina was right here next to him. Trance, Mack, and Mastiff were gone, but Willie, Paul, and Eli were here with him. And every-one in the SUV had faced down dangerous people to save him. They were all now technically criminals. All for worthless, old Benny Mar-tin.

But not so worthless to them, it seemed.

Benny ran a finger through Tina's, or Trina's, hair and set the chest back on the floor. He had a feeling he'd be putting more new memories in there, rather than shuffling through the old ones. It had been a mistake to hide away from his family. He didn't know how many years he had left on the good ship Earth, but he vowed never to make that mistake again.

Benny Martin tugged his old boonie hat over his eyes, put one arm around Trina, or Tina, and the other around Willie, and dreamed of the new memories he'd make with his family.

30. Benny, at Last

Trina ran her finger over the polished, biodegradable casket. It looked like wood, and was smooth and cool to the touch. Benny lay inside, wearing the grin he'd worn every day since his rescue from Bile Street. It wasn't actually that grin, but even in state she saw it on his face.

A thumb-worn stack of photos was spread on a nearby display table. They were his favorites, the ones he had revisited at the drop of his hat, or the merest hint of interest or invitation. With each showing of his prized photos, Benny explained that he liked the new photo paper well enough, but it just didn't have the feel of a "real" photo.

The top photo was only two weeks old. It showed baby Nina still in her swaddling clothes. A pair of disembodied hands steadied the writhing bundle on Benny's lap. His face was a canvas of deep wrinkles, blue veins, and dark skin spots.

In the casket, Benny's face looked much the same, though now slack and lifeless. His prized cane lay beneath his crossed arms. Small treasures from his memory box were set around him, along with more recent knickknacks given to him by his great-grandchildren.

For all of Benny's love of his pictures, he'd only ever bothered to frame one of them. Four old men in hats were lined up on the street in front of Benny's tiny home on Bile Street. They looked out grimly from behind the fingerprint-smeared glass.

As Trina considered the picture of Benny and his friends, a woman in a low-cut shirt that revealed saggy cleavage picked it up. The woman traced the four faces on the picture with a bright red fingernail.

Trina's hair was streaked with white and she'd put on some pounds since Benny's coming. At least Paul still said she was beautiful, as he was supposed to. The woman before her had obviously once had a beautiful figure, but hadn't updated her wardrobe to fit the realities of age.

"Hello, I'm Trina. Did you know my grandpa?"

The woman smiled, revealing perfect, shining teeth. "Carmen. Yes, we were very close a couple of times, if you know what I mean," she said in a lurid voice. Carmen gave Trina a knowing wink.

Trina forced a smile. Merely hearing the woman's voice made her feel dirty.

Carmen laughed as if she could read Trina's thoughts. "But we went our separate ways. I married an unlicensed dentist and got old. Life's a bitch and then you die." She blew out a long sigh.

"How did you find out about Benny's passing?"

"I keep track of my friends." Carmen set the picture down and ran her finger down Benny's cheek, to his chin, and finally the handle of his cane. A tear filled her eye and Carmen wiped it away with a crumpled tissue.

"He never let go of that thing," Carmen said. "And he'd tell anyone willing to listen all about it. Benny loved it like a child."

Trina examined the woman's face. "Do I know you?"

Carmen grinned. "No. You don't know a thing about me. But I haven't seen Benny in years." Carmen pulled out a tube of lipstick and applied a thick layer of red to her trembling lips. Ignoring the tear running down her face, Carmen planted a loud kiss on Benny's cheek. The outline of red lips left there glowed on the pallor of the skin.

Trina looked at the lipstick and back at Carmen. She wasn't sure if it was sweet or disrespectful. If it had been a sweet old lady, instead of a lewd one, Trina wouldn't have even questioned it. There was something about Carmen though.

Carmen laughed and planted a quick peck on the faces of the four old men in the framed picture. When Trina stepped forward uncertainly, Carmen reached out and enveloped her in a hug. "He loved you all so much."

Carmen started crying, and pushed past Eli and Paul as she retreated from the small church. They stood around Benny's casket and watched the strange woman go.

Paul slipped his arm around Trina's waist. "You OK?"

"Yes." She put her head on Paul's shoulder. He, of course, hadn't aged a bit in the years since Benny's rescue. He'd barely aged since their wedding. The skin on his face made him look more rugged, the silver along his temples gave him the bold look of a starship captain. Time made her look dumpy and flabby. It was a mixed blessing to be married to someone who fended off the ravages of time so well. She would always have a handsome man to please her and to show off. And his good looks would be a contrast to her fading beauty. A true gentleman would never age more gracefully than his beloved. Of course, Paul had never been a true gentleman and that was one of the things Trina loved about her husband.

At least he still told her she was pretty every day.

Eli leaned in to inspect Benny. "Did she do that?"

Trina tapped the picture frame. "Yes. And she did this too."

Eli cocked his head as he glanced from the picture back to his father's face. Trina knew he was trying to decide what to feel about it too.

"I'm not sure what to say," Eli finally said.

Paul shrugged. "How about 'way to go, Benny'?"

"But leaving these marks?" Eli picked up the picture and wiped at one of the kisses with his thumb. "I know Dad doesn't care but... I don't know. It just seems inconsiderate."

Paul gave a lopsided grin. "Don't worry. The damage is only cosmetics."

Eli groaned and Trina gave Paul a rough hip check.

"Terrible," she said. "But at least you're trying."

Eli stopped wiping the picture and set it back in place. "Well, I guess it looks like it belongs there. Way to go, Dad."

A bouncing bundle of curly, blond hair latched onto Eli's leg, nearly bowling him over. "Pappi Eli!"

"Ginevra," Eli said, kneeling down and wrapping his arms around her. Almost six now, she was about a year past Eli being able to pick the girl up. "How you doing?"

"We came to see Big Pappi." Ginevra glanced at the casket and turned away. She chewed her finger. "I'm kind of scared."

Eli squeezed the girl again. "Big Pappi will be so glad you came. He loved you so much." He put a finger beneath the girl's chin and lifted her face to his. "Would you like you say bye? I'll hold your hand."

Trina felt like melting when Ginevra's huge, brown eyes looked up at her. "Go on. It'll be OK."

Ginevra's curls bounced wildly as she nodded up at Eli. "Ok, Pappi."

Eli tousled her hair and took the girl's hand. They walked to the casket and Eli helped Ginevra climb onto a chair so she could see inside.

"Is Big Pappi going to heaven?"

"Only God knows," Eli said. "And I know Big Pappi was a good man. But wherever he is, I know he's talking about you. He always talked about his little Ginny."

"Well, I am very cute."

Eli laughed and hugged the girl. "Yes, you are. Hey, look at this." Eli picked up the stack of photos and flipped through them. He pulled a picture from the stack, flipping it so Ginevra could see. "See. A picture of you right near the top."

Ginevra reached out for the picture and Eli handed it to her. "I think he'd want you to have it."

"Sorry about your daddy, Pappi." Ginevra pointed at Benny's face and giggled. "Who kissed Big Pappi?"

"One of his friends," Trina said. "But she left already."

Ginevra's mother scooped her up and kissed Eli's cheek. The girl looked over her mother's shoulder, wiping her eyes. Colors ran together as a tear ran down the photo. She waved at Eli. "Bye, Pappi."

"Bye, sweetie."

Trina took Eli's hand. "Time for the service. If you can call it that without a preacher or ceremony. I'm glad to see so many people make it out."

"Especially with the DoS collapsing."

Trina shook her finger. "No, no. It's a restructuring, not a collapse. I know it because that's what the SafetyNet keeps telling me."

"Well, Dad won't have to worry about it anymore," Eli said. "He really liked this place."

Trina looked around at the chipped paint and gouged wood panels that served as the main décor of the 5th Street Holy Baptist Church. She'd barely missed the 1990s, but this building was definitely a product of that decade.

The visitors had no connection to the dwindling, geriatric congregation, but the deacons readily accepted the fee to bury Benny in the small church graveyard. No one had been moved to sing or tell tales of Benny's life. They simply enjoyed the company. Danial and Jayla led a single, non-denominational prayer. For all of its vagueness, it moved Trina.

Out back, the burial workers wrapped Benny in white bio-wrap and lifted him from the casket. Lifting the wrap's hood over his face, they lowered Benny into the earth. Trina sobbed as the white-wrapped body disappeared beneath the dirt. Eli started sobbing and

Trina put her arm around his shoulders. Blake came close to rub his father's back and the grave workers continued to fill the grave.

Two hours later, after the rest of the family and visitors had gone, Trina was returning the remaining photos to Benny's memory chest. Next to the box was the battered old boonie that had adorned the old man's head for decades. People had gifted him other hats over the years, but he never gave up his favorite hat.

Eli rose from the pew and picked up the hat.

Blake dumped out the dust tray and hung the broom in a tiny closet. "You know, he said you should toss that thing."

"Yeah." Eli took a deep whiff of the hat and put it on. "It smells like him. I never should have told him to sign those damned papers. We thought it was the right thing to do and he missed so much. Dakota knew better."

Trina took a final look around and closed the chest. "He sure made up for lost time though."

Eli nodded. "I'm glad he came back tous. And you two should know, you're stuck with me. I'm not making the same mistake. You're stuck with me." Eli let out a dramatically sinister laugh.

"We'll only make our own, different mistakes," Blake said.

Trina snorted. She'd definitely made her fair share.

Eli gathered his children in an embrace. He took the chest from Trina and fetched it up under his arm. "I think I'll take that too."

The old man in his father's hat left the church hand-in-hand with his children, a box of memories, and a grieving heart.

THE END

Thanks!

I hope you enjoyed this book. If you enjoyed it and would like to find out more about my other works (written as A. R. Kavli) please sign-up for my author's newsletter. You'll receive a free prologue short story to my sci-fi novel *With Our Dying Breath*.

Visit me at...

www.arkavli.com[1]